AF490891

MEAT PUPPETS, A NOVEL BY HANNAH SMART
ISBN 979-8-9996697-2-8

EDITED BY JACOB STOVALL
DESIGN & ART BY ROBERT VOYVODIC

Hannah Smart

APOCALYPSE CONFIDENTIAL

Table of Contents

0

Fidgets echoed through the darkened classroom, killing the illusion of solitude.

"Now, see, if the shooter *does* make it in here," Mr. Porter said, and then came the demonstrative creak and slam of the classroom door, "he's gonna look for movement first. You're all moving too much. None of you would stand a chance."

Sydney Morris did his best to remain still. To turn off his brain for a moment. But his brain had no power switch. His brain was a racehorse dead-set on winning its race and then continuing to plow forward once it's won, past the finish line, past the stands and the audience—a stubborn Forrest Gump of a racehorse—speeding epically and catastrophically toward destruction.

"That's better," Mr. Porter crooned. Rubber soles slapped rubber floor as he zig-zagged through the rows of desks, pretending he couldn't see what lay beneath. "Now, it might just be down to chance."

The teacher's footsteps screeched to a polished-toed halt. One moment, Syd was staring through the immediate darkness at Mr. Porter's creased, dry-cleaned trousers, and the next, he was facing a pointed, outstretched finger head-on. "Pow! You'd be dead, Syd."

"Do you want me to collapse or something?"

"No need." Mr. Porter's steps faded to an inaudible nothing. The lights came on with the type of flicker characteristic of cheap bulbs in underfunded schools. The students climbed out from their makeshift shelters, cracking joints, stretching limbs. "Great job today. Our next drill won't be for a while. One a semester—that's what they're making us do now."

After that, class proceeded hitchlessly and prototypically, with Mr. Porter lecturing the sixth graders about mixed fractions and the students staring at the clock above the whiteboard, counting down the minutes until lunchtime and willing the long hand to move faster while it seemed to slow down just to spite them. But when the bell finally rang and Syd's classmates rushed the door, pushing past each other like moviegoers at a flame-engulfed theater, Syd lagged behind.

"Lunchtime," Mr. Porter reminded him, as if he'd forgotten what the 12:30 bell signified. People often treated Syd like he was stupid—like he knew less, not more, than he let on.

"I know. I just had a question."

"Hit me."

"Why did you shoot me?"

Mr. Porter chuckled mock-sympathetically. Fingered his dyed-blond combover. "It was just a drill. I didn't *actually* shoot you."

"Yeah, but why me? Why not Bobby or Martin or Jayden—"

"It was random. Killers usually pick their targets at random. Don't place any stock in it, kid."

Syd nodded in slow motion.

"Next time, can I play the shooter?"

"It's not a game, Sydney. It's training. It's preparation—to keep you safe in case of an active threat. You know that, don't you?"

"Yeah. So next time, can I train as the shooter?"

"Why do you—"

"I mean, I wasn't going to get mad at you for shooting me. And I don't want revenge. I just thought that if I were the shooter..." He finished the sentence in his mind: *I'd have shot me too.*

Part I:
The Stockbroker

1

Mitchell Larkin stood on a Boston Common clearing in the sweltering June sun, holding a notebook gingerly in one hand, careful not to leave any oil or dirt or fingerprint traces on it, while cupping his other hand over his mouth for maximum vocal projection, apparently unaware that half an organic megaphone doesn't do much, in physics terms. He never wore sunscreen—found it itchy and slimy—but always underestimated the ease with which he'd burn.

The turnout for the auction was promising. When he'd placed the Craigslist ad, he'd been expecting merely a confused handful of people, but there were like thirty or forty here, many of them seeming to be here on purpose. Grace Reilly had evidently made quite a name for herself—and in Boston of all places. Not exactly the music capital of the world.

"I'll go for four thousand!" a woman called, chewing the final consonant for a few instants longer than was natural. Mitch weaved his gaze through the madness until he spotted her—tall, thin, and looking to be in the early throes of middle age, with the haughty air of a self-made businesswoman and a green dress that made her almost disappear among the trees.

"We had three, and now we've got four!" Mitch announced. "Anyone for five?"

"I'll do you one better—six!"

Grace Reilly was possibly the first celebrity music biographer, if such a thing existed—critics and fans alike went rabid for her. And the early notes for her latest book on Brian Jones—the crown jewel of the auction—were all contained in Mitch's hand, which he kept wiping on his Nirvana T-shirt, creating a localized and incrementally-darkening patch of sweat.

"Seven thousand!" someone said.

"Eight!"

"Ten!"

"Thirteen!"

"Fourteen!"

The attendees observed each other, awkwardly intrigued, like a classroom of freshmen being quizzed on a reading assignment none of them completed.

"Anyone for fifteen?" Mitch said. "Going once, going twice...sold! To the man with the mustache." *Cut that thing any narrower and you'll be Hitler*, he added, mentally, before shaking the guy's damp, sticky hand and trading the notebook for a check.

Mitch and his girlfriend Nell drove home from the auction in near-silence punctuated by nothing but the calming, muffled rush of outdoor airflow and some easy-listening rock song playing at minimum volume on the radio—loudly enough for Mitch to know it sounded familiar but too softly for him to identify it with any degree of certainty. He and Nell often fell into these wordless spells, but Mitch seldom felt the need to fill them. He lacked the typical human allergy to social discomfort.

"Where did you get all that Grace Reilly stuff?" Nell asked, just as the irritatingly recognizable tune faded into nothingness.

"A man can't be an enthusiast?"

"I've never heard you mention being an enthusiast of some music writer. And it was all originals. Must've cost a fortune."

Mitch paused. This topic induced the same sense of nagging inconvenience as a herpes diagnosis might, and broaching it required similar tact.

"You won't believe this," he preempted, tailgating the fucker in front of him while himself being tailgated by some other fucker, ready to slam on the breaks at a split second's notice and praying his pursuer was prepared to do the same. "We used to date." He said it the way you might say you ran into Obama at Fenway Park.

Nell didn't reply at first, but Mitch watched intently through the corner of his eye while she sent the information through her internal bullshit detector. "Were you ever planning on telling me you dated someone famous?"

"I dunno about *famous. Microcelebrity* at best."

"You just made about twenty-five thousand bucks selling her old stuff to locals." Nell tucked a couple stray brunette baby hairs behind her ears. Her giant, imposing ears were a caricature artist's dream.

Other than that, she was pretty, Mitch supposed. "Did you want to hear about every person I've dated before you?" He immediately regretted asking, because if she said yes, the pattern would become clear. "I mean, you haven't exactly talked much about *your* past relationships."

"I haven't exactly *had* many. One, in high school. He was a real dick as well. Told me I'd never make it in the art world. At least you believe in me."

And Mitch did. Nell was a painter, and she produced what she called "realist works with an abstract tinge"—scenes of bars and beachfronts and houses where everything seemed like it had been put though a subtle, hazy filter. Like reality was off kilter in some manner you couldn't quite put your finger on. Mitch appreciated that Nell recognized him for the supportive boyfriend he was but loathed the implication that, despite his belief in her talent and abilities, he too was somewhat of a "dick."

"Look, what's the big deal?" Mitch asked. "Grace and I aren't together anymore. She *gave* me all that stuff. Or left it at my house. Either way, she must not have really wanted it. And now I—actually both of us, really—get to profit. Isn't that great?"

Another silence, and then, "When I'm famous, are you going to sell the art pieces *I* made you?"

Mitch scoffed. "No—why would I—"

"Or do you not think I'll ever be famous?"

"Now you're just putting words in my mouth. Of course you'll be famous."

"Wouldn't that be crazy if you'd dated two famous people?"

Wouldn't it indeed? Mitch thought while he barreled into their apartment building's parking garage at way over the ten-mile-per-hour speed limit. He found it cute how little Nell knew—how little *anyone* knew, besides him.

One of the paintings Nell had made for Mitch depicted the two of them standing on a cliff overlooking an ocean, hand-in-hand, facing away. The background displayed more vibrance than the people, who appeared figurant-like and sketchy and first-draft-like. The waves were high and foreboding and not at all peaceful-looking, and the sky was one or two shades darker than the average beach sky, its dusky horizon promising the dim dawn of a dying tomorrow. The overall aesthetic environment strongly indicated that some strange twist of fate would soon occur. The figures in the painting didn't know what it was, and neither did the real-life Nell, but the real-life Mitch had some sort of idea.

2

Now Mitch lay alone on the bare mattress of the tenth-story Manhattan studio apartment he'd impulse-bought after selling a Nell Sullivan painting for $200,000. Twelve or so boxes sat unopened in his bedroom's corner. The floor was hard mahogany wood, solid and untarnished—you could just about see your reflection in it. Outside, antlike people reminiscent of those in Nell's paintings passed across sidewalks, appearing sped-up. If Mitch watched them for long enough, their repetitive patterns of movement made him feel trapped in one of those day-in-the-life time-lapse videos.

Four other Nell Sullivan paintings, each encased in plastic wrapping, sat in a neat stack under the bed atop which Mitch now lay. He'd sell them eventually, but he didn't know when. Or to *whom*. Or how long he'd hold off on selling them in order to increase their market value—like, how was he supposed to know when Nell was at the peak of her career and celebrity worth?

He had a financial advisor who was supposed to help him figure all this out. People could crash like stocks, he'd come to learn—some coke scandal within the past year had tanked Grace Reilly and made Mitch happy he'd already offloaded everything she'd left him. What a world it was where cops sniffed around biographers' vicinities for drugs—where *writers* could behave like singers and entertainers.

Sometimes, Mitch felt as if his existence were some fickle thing that could slip through his fingers—like someone could snap and wake him up from a dream, and he'd once again be a dumb kid with an uncanny knack for identifying future celebrities. He still *felt* like a kid, despite now being twenty-eight and no longer having any excuse for acting immaturely or unprofessionally. Once you hit twenty-five, whatever tattered remnants of the kiddy gloves people formerly used on you disappeared. Nobody believed you when you said you didn't know better.

His financial advisor, a woman named Hayley Duker, was planning to stop by the apartment for a meeting. She'd never been to

Mitch's private residence before, so this visit would be an important progression in the relationship Mitch delusionally believed to be mutually sexually tense. He'd need to do a proper setup of this place—as in like actually make the bed and organize his clothes and unpack a few boxes, maybe leaving a couple in the corner toward which he could self-disapprovingly signal and say, "Haven't finished unboxing yet. Been a hectic week"—in order to avoid the adult scorn that resulted from him being over the age of twenty-five and no longer a viable target of gentler, kiddy-glove-remnant-wielding scorn. So he shoved a couple boxes into his closet, set the other two against the wall, and strategically opened one so that it looked like he was already in the process of unpacking it.

Hayley arrived at around four, sporting a snazzy blue blazer and black slacks. She always dressed like a bit of a lesbian, which deeply unsettled Mitch; he considered it essential that Hayley be *capable* of being attracted to him, even if she wasn't right now—even if Mitch would never date her or even hook up with her on account of her near-zero chance of achieving artistic fame. Hayley was just about the least artistic person Mitch knew. But he also knew that, if being interested in men was anywhere on her radar, even as a repressed seed in the deep recesses of her mind, he could unearth it. He had a talent for making people fall in love with him. Sometimes, he did it without even trying.

"You look nice," he told her now, as she sidestepped into the apartment. The fact that she'd taken the time to dress nicely but non-provocatively told Mitch that she still saw this as a purely professional endeavor.

"Thanks."

Mitch ran her fashion choices through a mental checklist. Suit and pants: lesbian. Long, deliberately-styled hair: heterosexual. Nondescript shoes with no heels that would nonetheless still look a bit out of place on a male: the jury's still out.

"That's it?"

"Did you want me to return the compliment?" She scanned Mitch up and down, from his Guns 'n' Roses T-shirt to his knee-high basketball socks, her eyes lingering on his unkempt hair.

Mitch hastily tousled it. "Sorry about the boxes. Haven't finished unpacking yet." Signaled to the two up against the wall. "Been a hectic week."

"Right. Well, should we..." She examined the room, probably searching for a place to sit and walk Mitch through some important financial information while he tried not to gawk.

"The bed is fine," Mitch offered and then realized that the statement probably sounded suggestive, which was not actually his intention—at least not a conscious one.

Hayley paused for an infinitesimal click of time before taking a seat.

"You've got a very diversified stock profile," she said.

"And that's good?"

"Yes," with a slow grimace that stopped a couple millimeters short of a proper, polite smile. "Prevents you from ever losing too much at once."

"Or making too much."

"Well, this isn't Vegas. You definitely don't want to be gambling—not when tens of thousands are involved."

"Right. So tell me again what stocks are." Mitch knew, but whenever he desperately wished for Hayley to explain something in her soft, slightly condescending voice, this was his go-to fake blind spot.

"We've been over this."

"I forgot."

She indulged him. "Stocks are essentially tiny portions of a company." She was bouncing ever so slightly on the mattress—Mitch couldn't see it, but he could feel it, and it titillated him. "When they're issued, the company uses that money to grow the business, and if the business does well—becomes more valuable—then each individual share increases in price. If it *doesn't* do well, the opposite happens."

Mitch nodded the way you nod when a concept is just beginning to sink in. "I'm still not sure I get it."

"Think about what you do when you choose another romantic partner. You look for someone you think will be successful—"

"What do you mean?" But he knew—just didn't know how *she* knew.

She huffed in a *how-dumb-are-you-going-to-play*-type way. "You initially hired me because you sold some Nell Sullivan paintings and wanted to start investing. I asked where you got them, and you said you and Nell used to date. You've never discussed your past jobs, but you said you had a big amount come in a few years ago. Now you're dating Benji Manheim,who hasn't been cast in any films yet but looks promising. Any thinking person would be able to figure out what's going on."

Mitch was so used to being three logical steps ahead of everyone else in the room that her insight floored him. This was one of the reasons he and Hayley would never work, even if she were headed for fame or fortune or whatever the top of your league is when you're a financial advisor—she possessed not even a healthy degree of gullibility. But it was also one of the reasons he found her so intriguing— much more intriguing than any of the pseudo-partners he'd used to obtain priceless art and then discarded once they'd captured the world's attention.

"How would *I* know whether someone is going to become famous?" he asked.

"You don't, hence my analogy. You shoot your shot. It's like buying stock, but the only investment is your time."

Mitch contemplated the idea of humans having fluctuating value in a commodities market, much like companies. Then something inspired and deranged and perhaps even possible hit him. "What if that *weren't* the only investment?"

"Well, there's also money, I suppose, in the form of gifts and such, but most relationships these days are a pretty even deal—"

"No, I mean, what if I ran like...a *human* stock trade, where investors could buy shares in pre-famous people, whose value would go up as they approached fame and I became convinced they'd make me my money back? And if they didn't get famous, or if it became obvious that they wouldn't, their stock value could drop, which would mean people would be forced to sell for less than they bought for, so I'd *still* get something out of it. A *safe* investment, like you said. Either way, I'm doing all right."

Hayley didn't say anything for what felt like a good half a minute, which Mitch assumed was because she was just so blown away by his genius she'd been rendered speechless. The persistent, background clicking of his vintage analog alarm clock, one of the few things he'd bothered to unpack, seemed to slow down. "So you *do* understand how stocks work."

"Sure, I do." The clock's tick, moments ago unobtrusive, now penetrated some deep layer of his brain. The noise was lobotomizing. "I just like hearing you talk about it." He bit his lip as if attempting to prevent the next sentence from escaping. "And to be frank, I'd fuck you right now on this bare mattress were I not committed to Benji."

"And because I'd have something to say about it, presumably."

"Would you?" The word "presumably" gave him hope.

"Do you even love Benji?"

"Are you sure this is within the realm of professionalism?"

"Trust me—we abandoned professionalism a long time ago." She shifted on the bed, though Mitch couldn't tell whether toward or away from him. "Do you *actually* love him?"

"I don't know that I love *anybody*." In lieu of meeting Hayley's gaze, he stared at his own feet, noticing that the *Nike* logo on one sock was more faded than the other. "Except—"

"Don't you dare say me."

So he didn't. "Will it work? This human stock trade thing?"

"It doesn't matter whether it will work because only a complete psychopath would even attempt it."

"Right," Mitch said. "So say I'm a complete psychopath..."

"Hypothetically?"

"Sure."

She flexed her shoulders, ruffling her jacket, which she hadn't bothered to take off. She never made an effort to make herself at home with Mitch, which he assumed stemmed from an inability to acknowledge her conflictedly intimate feelings toward him but was really because he didn't own a coatrack. "Maybe. We'd have to develop metrics for measuring proximity to fame—current income, momentum, length of time in the game, general attitude toward 'the game'—all things that are quite difficult to quantify."

The fact that she was saying "we" instead of "you" told Mitch he'd won her over. "But if we *did* manage to quantify them?"

Hesitation. "It would have to be wholly underground, since it would technically qualify as amateur gambling."

"But you could help me sort all that, right?"

An uncertain sigh. "Right."

"You *want* to help me sort all that." Benji would be stopping by soon, so if they were going to sort it today, they'd have to do it fast.

"Don't get crazy."

"Come on, Hayley." Now it was Mitch's turn to adjust his position on the bed, and he moved decidedly toward her. "We're just the same, you and me. You need the extra push to be boldly psychopathic, while I need someone to guide me through the ins and outs of finance. Together, we'll be unstoppable."

She didn't respond, but if Mitch looked all the way in—past her cold exterior, through her dark, expressionless pupils, and into her head, where the soul was allegedly stored—he could see a latent excitement getting ready to bubble over.

Preface

Excuse the interruption. I realize that placing a preface three chapters into a book is a bit unconventional choice, but you'll have to bear with me—beginning-of-the-book prefaces tend to get skipped, and I didn't want you to skip this one, because what follows is pertinent and non-optional information regarding this book's background, its genesis, and the series of events that led me—an unsuspecting fiction writer and now journalist, I suppose—into the middle of a carefully-orchestrated plot.

In January of 2023, I, Hannah Smart, received the following email from a prestigious New York magazine whose name I've agreed not to mention anywhere in this "novel":

Dear Hannah,

Our editors read your short story "Imposter Syndrome," published in the February 2022 issue of *Puerto del Sol*, and found it impressive. We'd like to commission you to spend some time on the set of Peter Rankin's upcoming film *Life Imitates Art*, starring new actor Syd Morris and featuring Ola Benson, Henry Goldman, and Nathan Andrews in supporting roles. The film is Rankin's first after a long hiatus, and it is currently the subject of much critical buzz.

We recognize that your experience with nonfiction writing is minimal. However, we aren't looking for a cookie-cutter piece that follows strict journalistic conventions. We want more of a fiction writer's perspective on this whole thing, the main difference being that this will be the truth, however you see it.

We have no word limit, though we maintain editorial discretion. You will be paid a flat rate of $500, in addition to having your travel, food, and lodging expenses covered. Let us know if that sounds reasonable.

Sincerely,
Robert Ellington
Editor-in-Chief at [magazine name redacted]

My fully-funded adventures on the set of *Life Imitates Art* produced a journalistic essay entitled "Art Imitates Life," which is printed later in this "novel." The assignment also marked my first acquaintance with Syd Morris, one of the two major players in the carefully-orchestrated plot mentioned above.

"Art Imitates Life" was supposed to run in the magazine's December 2023 issue, a month before the film's premiere, but because of some legal issues that arose, it was pushed off. While I awaited its publication, I drafted a couple follow-ups or "sequels" in which I further investigated the shenanigans I witnessed on the set of Rankin's film. But then something major and game-changing happened, and my dreams of ever publishing any of these articles as nonfiction pieces with the consent of a major New York magazine met a swift end.

With the dangling carrot of journalistic prestige out of the way, I expanded my research into the book-length compendium you now hold in your hands (or on your lap, or, if you're really evil, on a posture-ruining computer screen in front of you), which includes the original journalistic piece, the two "sequels"—"Victims of Mitch Anonymous," and "Life Imitates the Life Art Is Imitating (Parts 1 and 2)"—and dozens of subsequent uncommissioned and unasked-for essays for other painstakingly-researched assignments I gave myself. For ease of reading, I numbered these latter essays and structured them like traditional novel "chapters." You've already read three.

All mentions of real people, copyrighted media products, and potentially litigious companies have been pseudonyms thus far and will be pseudonyms henceforth, which, along with publishing this "novel" on the "fiction" shelf, should be enough to protect me from legal repercussions. Any names you recognize are simply too culturally hegemonic and/or too small of players in the overall scheme of what's going on to give a shit one way or the other whether they're mentioned. Parts of this book have been dramatized for literary purposes, but I've generally made note of those places.

Everything else is one hundred percent true.

3

Benji Manheim is a tall, stringy guy with pale, weaselly features, naturally blond hair dyed gothic black, and matching, perpetually-faded black nail polish. Unfortunate fashion choices notwithstanding, he's moderately approachable and doing well for himself—at the time I'm writing this, he lives in lower Manhattan with his husband, a modestly recognizable C-list actor who's landed supporting roles on a few TV shows and done a convincingly smooth job at least two thirds of the time. You need not worry about Benji, in other words. Benji and his husband are two people who make it out of this story alive.

The first and only time I interviewed Benji one-on-one, he told me about the day he proposed to his boyfriend, Mitch Larkin. Further research has informed me that this was the same day Mitch and his financial advisor Hayley ran their ninth ever stock-trading session out of the basement of Mitch's newest property—a spacious house in upstate New York. The prior week, Benji had scored the lead role in a movie called *Gunflinger*, a kitschy art-projectish film in the vein of *Living in Oblivion* that was cancelled before it even began shooting because a big-budget studio who will remain nameless offered the director a sum of money he couldn't refuse. Had the film not been shuttered, it would have been Benji's big break.

But *Gunflinger* really *was* a big break for Mitch. Suddenly, people were lining up at his door to buy Benji Manheim stock, and he'd been forced to contract a software engineer to develop an encrypted transaction platform because Microsoft Excel was proving too shaky a system for keeping track of what was now over a hundred people with significant investments in the human stock trade.

Here's how the trade worked: people bet on subjects' future celebrity buzz. At the same time, Mitch acquired "insurance" (gifts, bootlegs, and other valuable items projected to hold future value) so as to be able to pay off investors if they sold—the insurance gained value even faster than the stock, and failed subjects made Mitch money regardless, so the idea was that Mitch always came out on top. But people were *really* betting on the celebrity buzz thing, not Mitch's ability to woo subjects into giving him gifts, so he only added people to the market if he either expected them to fail or was currently dating them. When prospective shareholders asked to purchase stock in people Mitch had never heard of, he usually did some research and got back to them, either with a fair price (when he expected subjects to remain unfamous) or a polite declination (when he expected them to become famous but doubted his ability to acquire insurance). So most of his profits came from the failures, who, much like the successes, Mitch had a Wall-Streetish eye for identifying.

Benji, an expected success, was out with his *Gunflinger* costars on the evening of the soon-to-be proposal. He showed them the wedding band he'd bought, allowing it to gleam from every conceivable angle in the low light of the restaurant, which was an upscale Italian place called either Giovanni's or Georgiani's. His and Mitch's names had been engraved in microscopic cursive on the inner side. Priscilla Tremont asked to hold the ring, made the motion of weighing it as if her palm were a scale, and then guessed the price within a couple hundred dollars. Isaac Henson kept saying, "That's great. That's *so* great" in increasingly laudatory tones until the proclamations sounded facetious and self-parodic.

Benji told his costars that he and Mitch were happy, and though Mitch had never brought up marriage and Benji'd occasionally felt threatened by Mitch's bisexuality, especially as it pertained to his financial advisor Hayley, and though this sort of thing was always a bit of a delicate dancing act with gay guys because how were you supposed to know who should propose to whom, Benji knew marriage was the right decision. And besides, Benji had always been the one to get things moving when it came to entering untreaded intimacy territory—like, for example, it had been Benji who'd urged Mitch to sleep with him for the first time and then later to live with him, so Benji naturally assumed Mitch probably expected him to request Mitch's hand in marriage too, what with Mitch being (in the most endearing terms possible—Benji retains a weird fondness for Mitch to this day that can only be considered cultlike in its logic) "sort of an adult baby" and all.

Benji had told Mitch that he wouldn't be home until later, but after talking the proposal through with his costars, he realized it couldn't wait. He wanted to really surprise Mitch—catch him properly off-guard. Mitch was "super anal" when it came to times and scheduling, always asking Benji for precise estimates of when he'd arrive home and demanding that he be out of the house for hyper-specific intervals, and as I listened to Benji tell me all this, I couldn't help but wonder whether he'd at any point considered a much more garden-variety explanation for Mitch's secrecy than the real reason, which was admittedly ludicrous and would have been nearly impossible to guess, but it was becoming clear to me that Benji was an "adult baby" in a much more benign sense than Mitch—namely, that he was naïve and marked by a stubborn refusal to see anything but the best in others.

How I've pieced this all together is that in the meantime, Mitch was playing the role of sweaty back-alley stock-dealer in his basement, which was a bit dingy and unfurnished compared to the rest of his house. At some point during this trading session, a young man approached Mitch and asked to bet on someone new.

"Syd Morris."

"Who's that?"

The kid making the request couldn't have been older than seventeen—Mitch would need to do some serious ID cross-checking before he'd even consider selling to him—and had acne all over his face and neck and even his *arms*, and the rest of his body had seemingly aged and filled out before his head had even reached puberty, so he looked like a grown-up torso with an infant's head on top of it.

"Some weirdo who spoke at my high school about how he quit drugs and found Jesus."

"No. Go away."

"I'm serious though. I think this guy has something. Hard to say just what, but..."

Mitch couldn't quite gauge the kid's sincerity—wasn't accustomed to examining the facial expressions of infants for signs of facetiousness. "I don't know enough about this guy. Come back later."

"You mean once he's already famous and expensive? Because you're not gonna learn anything about him online."

"Sure. Just get out of my hair, kid."

Soon after this exchange—anywhere from a few seconds to a few minutes later—Benji burst through the upstairs front door, gripping the wedding band tightly in his palm, trying to decide how to do this thing—like, if he were to get down on one knee and do it the straight way, would Mitch be offended?

Mitch froze at the sound of Benji's arrival.

Benji carefully descended the staircase, following the sound of the ruckus—a sound that had abruptly quieted when Mitch had held out one hand and put the other up to his mouth in a shushing motion and shushed the hell out of the basement's occupants, which he figured in hindsight must have made everything seem even *more* suspicious when Benji arrived downstairs to see a bunch of strangers standing around nervously in artificial silence while Mitch bent scoliotically over a card table with three computers in front of him, crunching numbers, looking like a sports announcer for online chess.

Based on Benji's description of the scene, he didn't quite grasp the intricacies involved—just thought Mitch was perhaps just running a private college football betting business or something.

"I got home early, and I, uh..." Benji's eyes wandered. "What's going on?"

"Party," Mitch answered, having anticipated just that question.

"Weird party."

"I'm a weird guy." He attempted a charming grin.

"Right, well, I just wanted to, uh..." He fumbled with the ring, his hands twitching. "Not quite sure how to do this. If you want me to get down on one knee, I can."

Mitch took a second to fully apprehend what was happening.

"Or, uh, two knees?" Benji crouched down in his skinny jeans, uncertainly tucking one leg behind him, followed by the other, and as Mitch watched him grovel, he thought not about how honored he felt or how endearing he found the proposal but how unapologetically pathetic his boyfriend was. Mitch figured whoever *did* end up with Benji would have to endure this obsequiousness for decades: always waking up to having his coffee pre-made and being forced to watch Benji watch him drink it while Benji repeatedly asks, "Is it okay?" and "Are you sure?", the poor imagined future husband unable to even answer the questions because it's impossible to focus on the damn coffee; Benji cooking dinner and burning himself on the gas stove and becoming distraught by the reality that he'll never be good enough for the faceless imaginary husband (what good is a lover who can't even cook a proper meal for the one he loves?) and Benji rearing his kids to believe that he believes his sole purpose in life is to love the kids and the husband unconditionally, Benji telling the kids regularly that they should be thankful that the husband is such a wonderful father, "but don't you worry about old Benji—he's not taking your praise," referring to himself in the third person in that insufferable way he often did and telling his son, "Benji should have known better" while cleaning the drool and vomit off the toddler's chin after his son had begged for and then eaten a "Gotta Have It"-sized ice cream bowl from Cold Stone, complete with three different gustatorily-dissonant toppings, and then thrown up in a totally understandable and predictable turn of events for which future hypothetical Benji takes full responsibility—and at this conception of the horrors that awaited Benji's eventual husband, Mitch felt not pity but some twisted brand of detached, humorous longing.

Now Mitch had the attention of the room. He knew the shareholders expected him to accept the ring and basically had dollar signs in their eyes at that prospect: it would mean an increase in their hypothetical wealth, plus the capacity for future gifts, which meant more people would purchase stock.

But Mitch also knew they were expecting him to leave Benji, because that's how this thing worked, and an agreement to marry might make some buyers waver in their commitment and begin to doubt that this was even a ploy—like, what if Mitch had fallen in love with Benji *for real*? they might wonder, in which case the ring wouldn't be perceived as an auctionable item, and they'd worry their stock's price had peaked. Essentially, Mitch's agreement to marry could cause stock owners to panic and sell *en masse*, leading to a small-scale Great-Depression scenario.

Mitch took the ring in his hand. Examined it with one eye closed, and then the other. The engravings on the inside would make it even more valuable. "Thank you."

"Well?" Benji tentatively extended one of his legs so that he was down on one knee again—he still appeared utterly convinced that his choice of posture was the thing that would make or break the proposal.

"You didn't ask me anything."

"The question was implied, I thought."

"Thank you for the gift," Mitch reiterated. Benji's excruciating passivity, usually a pitiful annoyance, had given Mitch an easy out. "You want me to have this, correct?"

"If you want it."

"Of course I want it."

At that declaration, Benji's face lit up. He assumed Mitch's acceptance of the ring constituted an acceptance of the proposal he'd never made, but Mitch and the shareholders knew better. Mitch exchanged knowing glances with a few of the still-silent, gaping guests to reassure them that his primary commitment was to *them*, not to the products they invested in.

He'd dump Benji later—pretend he thought the ring was a breakup present and tell Benji that they'd both known this was coming to an end for a long time now, had they not? And that Mitch wished he had gotten Benji a gift in exchange, but he hadn't been aware that breakup gifts were customary in gay relationships—none of his girlfriends had ever gotten him one.

So this day marked, for Mitch, a sharp and pivotal increase in Benji's stock price; for Benji, it marked the end of a relationship he'd wrongly assumed would end in marriage.

For Mitch, this day also marked the first time he heard the name "Syd Morris," a name that would hang around him like a wet stink for years to come.

Hayley said nothing throughout the exchange. Mitch had looked at her just once during Benji's proposal, and, unable to read her face, declined to look again.

4

Mitch's future-celebrity turnover rate had always been high, the transition between subjects emotionless and calculated—he usually went as far as to pick out his next prospect before closing on his current one. This time was different, however. It had been six months since he'd let Benji down in a manner he'd thought gentle and pretty much as smooth as a thing like that could go over but that Benji had perceived as a rude and thoughtless awakening.

But the true thoughtless act hadn't been *leaving* Benji, Mitch knew—it had been getting with him in the first place. Mitch was beginning to suspect that there may be some ethical issues to take into account when it came to his financially-motivated dating habits—though, if you got right down to it, all relationships were "transactional" in the loosest sense of the word, so the question of whether his particular brand of transactional relationship was any less moral than the average romantic entanglement or simply less socially acceptable could probably withstand rigorous subjective debate among entire generations of ethicists without a solid conclusion ever being reached, and Mitch was no ethicist, so he didn't get very far in terms of philosophically dissecting the whole thing. However, the idea's existence in the back of his mind may have contributed, subconsciously, to his reluctance to make another opportune investment.

Unfortunately, there was still the pressing issue of all the people who owned shares of various promising budding artists on whose shareholders' investments said shareholders anxiously anticipated return.

The whole thing gave him a headache and felt rather like trying to diagram a complex, preposition-laden sentence from way back in his Catholic schoolboy days while an angry nun stood ominously over his shoulder, making him feel like he was headed Hindenburgishly straight to Hell for putting the word "on" in the wrong place.

He had bedded his financial advisor Hayley three times over the past two years, which, they say after the third sexual encounter there's a good chance of a date, so he was trying to sort through the complex network of conflicting desires that arose from her potential desire to enter this next stage of their relationship. He was meeting with her today to go over his tax returns for the past fiscal year and ideally find out not just what exactly a fiscal year *was* but also how he might transfer some of his money into foreign investment funds to avoid being taxed into oblivion.

In order to stave off any impending audits, Mitch and Hayley had set up a foolproof money-laundering scheme: a bookstore, which they'd bought from an old retired couple who'd expressed excitement at the prospect of selling it to another husband and wife—this way, it would continue to be a family-owned business, they'd explained, their faces hideously wrinkled in abject glee. Neither Mitch nor Hayley had had the heart to correct them.

After sprucing the place up and deciding that changing the name from Nelson's to either Larkin's or Duker's would involve tearing down and then re-designing and re-building the light-up sign outside the store, which would essentially amount to throwing wads of good money straight into a strong gust of wind (plus, Hayley was a staunch independent feminist-type and would never go with Larkin's—that would be tantamount, in her mind, to taking Mitch's surname in a traditional religious marriage ceremony), they'd done some elementary furnishing—changing out the flooring, redecorating the walls, and replacing books that had been sitting there for decades and touched by dozens if not hundreds of greasy fingers and no longer looked to be in the mint condition people expected when they set out to buy a new book. They had a brief spat over whether the old books should be donated to the library (Hayley) or moved to the "used" section of the store and discounted slightly (Mitch), a spat Hayley won on account of Mitch not wishing to forfeit his once-per-eight-months sex privileges.

But now Mitch had all this added emotional junk to factor into his increasingly complex financial situation, which he couldn't fathom sorting through on his own and thought too boring to try, and he'd virtually become the helpless baby he used to pretend to be whenever Hayley was around. He relied on her not just sexually but legally as well, which put him in a difficult position—he did not enjoy relying on people, especially people with sufficient evidence to send him to jail.

Today, the two met at the bookstore and sat on opposite sides of the checkout desk. He listened to her explain in detail how his tax write-offs would work, not absorbing much but confident that she knew what she was talking about and that he was safe in her delicate and meticulously groomed hands.

"In short," she said, right as he felt his eyes starting to glaze over, "you're running out of money."

He didn't immediately accept the gravity of the statement—it felt so fundamentally and mathematically wrong—but then again, he *had* zoned out for the mathematical portion of Hayley's lecture. "What do you mean?"

"You can't afford to keep spending like this. You'll go bankrupt."

In an instant, he went from trusting her fully to being confident she didn't know what she was on about. "Nah. I'm rich."

"You're upper-class," she agreed, swiveling back and forth in the cashier's chair. "Or you were. But you're spending like a celebrity actor. What are you on, your second house? And you *still* haven't sold the apartment?"

"I was gonna rent it out."

"Which is great, if you actually *do* that. The problem is that you don't actually *do* things, Mitch. You wait for someone else to tell you how to do them. When are you planning on learning to take care of yourself? You're thirty years old, but you act like a child."

His predicament was not helped by the fact that Hayley *treating* him like a child turned him on. "Have you ever wanted to have sex in a bookstore?"

"Nope."

"Worth a try."

"You know we're technically open right now, right?"

"Yeah, yeah."

"Like, we should probably attempt to maintain a thin veneer of being a legitimate business, right?"

"Right."

"Speaking of fucking, who's your latest proto-celebrity lover?"

"That's the problem—don't have one."

"Rare form. Well, I hate to recommend this behavior because I think it's despicable, as you know, but in terms of your financial situation, you might want to think about getting one."

"I've been looking." It was neither a complete truth nor a complete lie. The way in which he'd been "looking" was purely theoretical, like the way you might look at Harrison Ford while watching *Star Wars: The Empire Strikes Back* as an adolescent and be unable to keep from imagining having sex with him whenever he's onscreen, and how the sex of your imaginings might go smoothly and without a hiccup, but you nonetheless know you're only excited by the hypothetical nature of it—like, if you were actually confronted with the reality of sleeping with Harrison Ford, you'd likely be unable to do anything but gape and back away slowly, so it's the kind of thing best appreciated in a fully detached, implicationless way. At least, that's how *I* interpret Mitch's attendant feelings about the whole thing.

"In the meantime, have you thought about maybe you and I...?"

And now she'd dredged up the exact topic Mitch had been afraid of. "What are your plans for becoming famous?"

"If I became famous, that would be bad news for both of us."

"Well, there's your answer."

"You've never wanted to try going out with someone you were actually interested in?"

"Who said I was interested in you?" But he was, and the way her expression slackened after his blunt refusal lent him an involuntary surge of guilt. Fortunately, he'd trained himself not to experience guilt on any kind of subjective level—he let the waves wash over him but didn't judge them as good or bad.

"You'd have to be okay with me fucking other people," he added.

She lifted her gaze to a place beyond Mitch's face, somehow looking *through* him rather than *at* him.

"I mean, we could always just fuck in a friends-with-benefits way while I court whichever future celebrity I'm working on," he continued, "but that's not much different from how it is now."

"Except there's no future celebrity right now," she mumbled and then cleared her throat, nodding dispassionately, like she was nodding at some aspirational essence of who she wanted Mitch to be rather than his authentic bona fide self.

"Like I said, I'm happy to fuck you here if you'd like, though," he went on as if nothing was amiss. "No strings attached. Just two people going at it in an empty bookstore."

"Speaking of which—"

"What's your problem?" he demanded, fearing that his conceptualization of Hayley was every bit as theoretical as his current dating prospects. He loved the idea of them together insofar as it remained an idea. But now, as he watched her stare past him as if he were just some obstacle between her and her true affections, he recognized that it was only an idea to her too, and he found himself unable to neutralize the accompanying emptiness and unignorable loneliness.

"Excuse me," Hayley said, gently pushing Mitch aside. "Sorry. I can assist you." So Mitch spun around to see a high school-aged girl holding a paperback copy of *Of Mice and Men*, turning the book over methodically in one hand while her other hand squeezed a twenty-dollar bill with the committed intensity of someone wringing a small animal's neck.

Part II:
The Kid

1

The C.S. Lewis Christian High School auditorium was a blank sheet of white—blindingly white walls, repainted twice yearly, light-bulbs that seared white-hot in a thirty-foot-high ceiling, and white faces (in more than one sense). If Syd thought of himself as preaching to an empty white sheet as opposed to a bunch of individuals—students with parents who were paying a pretty penny for them to sit in an over-air-conditioned assembly hall and be lectured at by some nobody, plus a handful of overworked, God-fearing teachers—the whole thing felt easier.

He said, "This is my story."

Nobody laughed or chortled. They were already accepting his every word as Gospel truth.

"When I was in the eighth grade, I got hooked on CNO.[1] My friends were ne'er-do-wells. Atheists," he added, and to no surprise, a bunch of teachers and white-faced students nodded as if they knew exactly what it was like to get offered a rare DIY drug by your thirteen-year-old atheist friends. "I thought, you know, what's the harm? My best buddy Grant showed me how to snort." Syd gave a sniff that could have been either a choking back of overwhelming emotion or a demonstration of the kind of snorting involved. He took a brief read of the silent, white room. A couple teachers in the front row wiped their eyes.

"Before long, I fell into the grips of addiction. It's hard to say how much of this came down to circumstance and how much was the result of my personal failings as a human being. In any case, I take full responsibility now. My debt with God has been squared."

---

1   CNO, I'm informed, is a lesser-known stimulant that typically comes in powder form and is made up of a small amount of cocaine and a lot of filler drugs, including prescription uppers, acetaminophen, and sometimes prescription opioids(!). Occasionally, the cocaine is foregone altogether. The manufacturing process is intense, chemistry-wise, and I'm required for legal reasons to recommend that you not attempt it at home.

Devout Christians lapped this born-again stuff right up. And news spread fast in the private school network—one good presentation often meant dozens of emails flooding Syd's inbox, offering him ludicrous sums to come speak at their districts.

"This is the story of how I quit drugs and found Jesus."

＊　　＊　　＊

Syd had become a pretty seasoned speaker at Christian schools as of late, and upon his scheduled arrivals, administrative higher-ups all but held his hand and led him into some dubious location to wait, like a dangerous criminal about to testify against another dangerous criminal. Today had been no exception. The cramped classroom they'd brought him to had been occupied by C.S. Lewis's student body presidents—seniors Jake Ackles and Laurel Wise, whose joint job it was to debrief him on how the assembly would go. Syd had sat around what appeared to be an oversized card table while the presidents explained that he wasn't to deviate from his regular script—the one he'd used at St. Mary's and Luther High and Aquinas Institute and the half dozen other schools he'd already told his story at—one iota.

"But it's *your* testimony, of course," Jake added. He had both the broad shoulders of a football player and the horn-rimmed glasses of a mathlete. Syd wasn't sure whether he'd spent his high school career shoving people into lockers or being shoved into them. "Just be honest, and you'll be fine."

"Can I be honest with you now?" Syd asked, repressing a smile in a fashion he hoped seemed involuntary.

Both Jake and Laurel nodded. Laurel pulled a couple stray hairs out of the overtight knot of her tie. Her head just slightly eclipsed her facial features in proportionality, Syd noticed—it was as if her eyes, nose, and mouth had been cut and pasted into a Microsoft Word document, scaled down a few decimal points at the corner, and then re-pasted onto her face.

Syd slipped a small plastic bag of CNO out of his jacket pocket, pinched it open, poured out a neat line, and snorted it with practiced ease. They both gaped with the guarded awe of those who have never seen a drug before.

"Want some?" Syd signaled to the baggie of remaining CNO. If he could get a student body president to try it—if he could establish a kind of blackmail stalemate with them—then nobody would blab.

Laurel made a face of vehement refusal, but Jake hesitated.

Syd jiggled the bag enticingly. "Might be the only chance you get."

"Might be the only chance I get," Jake repeated to Laurel, speaking in the mindless, servile tone of the Jedi-mind-tricked. Syd often got the sense he could talk people into walking off a cliff if he wanted.

Jake leaned cautiously forward, took an overzealous huff, and then immediately drew back his head with the force of someone who's just been shot in the temple. "Ow." He pinched his nose. Laurel glared at him with a wifely *I-told-you-so* expression. Syd couldn't discern whether she and Jake were an item.

"So they're just paying you to lie to people?" Laurel asked, her back now completely turned in a see-no-evil-type way.

Syd debated pouring out more CNO but wasn't sure he wanted to endure the whole outrage act again. "They're paying me to tell people stories that make them feel good."

✳   ✳   ✳

The part of the story he was telling now tended to get emotionally heavy. "Grant overdosed when we were sixteen," he said. Syd actually wasn't totally sure CNO-overdose was possible—had felt no impulse to research it, given that people at these preppy Christian schools generally thought you could overdose on a single puff of weed. Convincing them that a drug as hard and scary-sounding as CNO was capable of physically wielding a weapon and stabbing you to death in your sleep was probably within the realm of possibility as long as God was invoked at some point. "I hadn't heard from him all day and thought I'd go over to his house to check on him. The front door was locked, and he didn't answer no matter how many times I rang or knocked.

I knocked until my knuckles bled. I felt a strange catharsis looking down at my own bleeding hand and feeling no pain. Numb in both body and spirit."

Syd bit his lip, which he couldn't feel—his mouth felt numb now for the same reason his hand had supposedly felt numb then. It wasn't due to any kind of spiritual destitution but the crude physical effects of a hard drug.

"I punched out the window and felt nothing more than a dampened ache. Opened it from the inside and crawled in. He was on his back on the floor."

The memories currently flooding Syd's mind pertained not to the imaginary Grant but to his own adopted father—for, in spite of the callous front he'd put up for the student body presidents, Syd hadn't lived a life completely devoid of loss. He *was* capable of thinking about real stuff that made his eyes water so that he could make a show of drying his tears. The tears were real, even if the story wasn't. Everything was about everything, if you really thought about it.

"I grew restless. I didn't sleep that night, or the next. But what I thought was the delirium of CNO-withdrawal was actually God enjoining me."

If Syd were an impressionable youth in the audience watching someone give the speech he himself was currently giving, he'd probably bop the guy in the nose for having the gall to be so cheesy and uninspiring. "I've been four years sober as of today, and every waking moment since has been a kind of prayer."

A prayer for money, perhaps, and one that had repeatedly and miraculously come true. God, if He existed, had dropped a niche and prodigal career path straight into Syd's blessed lap.

"Thank You, God," he said now. "I'll be thanking You until I take my last [likely between vomit-logged chokes, if he continued at this rate] breath."

2

Another morally questionable avenue Syd had recently been experimenting with for income-supplementation was selling art. His avant-garde works used only common office staples, which he punched into canvases in sparse crosshatchings to form abstract clumps and indeterminately humanoid shapes and general textural distortions he thought looked "quite rad," and the four or five people who'd bought his pieces thus far must have thought so too. Syd had always derived an odd sense of relief from punching deliberate and measured holes in things, so creating staple-art didn't really feel like work. The few pieces I've seen are compelling in a novelty-type way but nothing to write home about artistically.

Times Square was prime selling turf—the area was lousy with tourists who congratulated themselves on being open-minded and understanding unconventional forms of expression. Today, however, Syd hadn't had much luck—a couple interested glances from some promising-looking white guys with dreads but nothing much else.

Now one stout, older lady with cat-eye glasses and a messy bun stopped, took a long look, stroked an invisible beard. "What exactly are these supposed to be?"

Syd couldn't tell whether she was about to buy a canvas or draft a strongly-worded *New York Times* opinion piece about how the sanctity of art as a concept is being destroyed by Generation Z.

"Metaphysical representations," Syd replied. That was always his go-to line because it sounded distinguished and transcendent. If he could trick people into thinking his genius was beyond the comprehension of even the artistically inclined, he could often strike triple-digit quantities of USD.

"Representations of what?"

"I like to think of them as psychological horror." Complete bullshit, but he was an eternal fount when it came to bullshitting. "Like a modern Rorschach test that reflects the violence and chaos of creation."

"I see," with the long, overconfident pronunciation that characterizes people who don't really see but desperately want you to think they do. "So what I notice in here is..."

"What *do* you notice in here?"

She lifted the canvas delicately using only her fingertips. Turned it on its side and then upside-down and then righted it once more, squinting the whole time. "War," she said at last.

"That's a common one."

"Yes, see. There's a hill here, and soldiers are firing from the top of it," pointing to the upper right-hand corner of the canvas, "and then if you look down here," dragging her finger slowly, diagonally to the bottom left, "there's absolute carnage."

Syd nodded. "That's definitely one interpretation I had in mind." It wasn't.

"What does it mean?"

"In terms of your subconscious diagnosis of the human condition, you mean?"

She nodded, looking him in the eye with uncomfortable vigor.

"It's sort of, you know...an elucidation of the fragmentary nature of social causes and what people fight for."

Nodded again, clearly expecting more.

Syd cleared his throat in two nervous grunts. "As in a, like...you know how the staples are all really small?" This was truly top-of-his-head nonsense. "Well, they sort of make a bigger whole, but not really. There are always things that don't fit. During the old wars, there was such a united, grand narrative—two sides against each other, the entire world embroiled in the conflict." He grabbed the piece gently out of her hand and held it so they could both see it, and she leaned in closely so her cheek was almost touching his neck. She smelled like some strange, novel perfume. "Now everything is fragmented—wars popping up left and right, people not really sure what causes they believe in. No more grand narratives. We're so divided that none of us even knows *what* side we're on."

She continued gazing at the canvas with the lopsided squint art voyeurs employ when they're deep in abstract thought.

"Anyway, that seems to be your diagnosis of the, uh, modern human condition."

Still nothing. For a moment, Syd suspected that she had sniffed out his fakery. But then, after what felt like an endless stretch of her breathing in his ear, she said, "You know, I think that's really profound. I *have* felt that way about the human condition lately."

Syd smiled knowingly, but deep down he couldn't believe he'd pulled it off. One of his clumsier performances, as far as pseudointellectual artistic monologues went.

"How much?" she asked, holding the piece at shoulder height.

"Three-fifty."

"Do you take checks?"

Etc.

However, not all his interactions proved fruitful. Within ten minutes of selling the first piece, he was approached by what appeared to be another prospective buyer—an average-height, average-build white man, prototypical in every conceivable way except for the fact that his hair was a kind of sandy red and his complexion was ruddy and he wore Vans shoes and a shirt advertising some obscure indie band and essentially dressed like someone who intended to come off as chic and relatable to the youths despite likely having a wife and one or two kids at home and wearing boring, nondescript office garb from nine to five on Monday through Friday and hating every minute of it.

"What's all this?" the man said, gesturing expansively toward the two remaining canvases.

"Staple art."

"Interesting." The guy furrowed his barely-visible blond brows. Syd couldn't shake the image of him stepping into his modestly-sized suburban condo after work and yelling, "Honey, I'm home!" without even bothering to close the door behind him or take his keys out of the lock, all the while dropping his trousers and doing that kind of wretched, unbalanced hop on one foot that characterizes someone who wants to remove his shoes but doesn't want to bend over for some reason, and then ungratefully discarding his blazer, which his wife gets dry-cleaned on a biweekly basis, onto the ground behind him while simultaneously unbuttoning his dress shirt and throwing on an Arcade Fire T-shirt, his red-haired seven-year-old son watching him the whole time, feeling secondhand shame.

"It's a commentary on modern life," Syd went on, figuring that if he talked long enough, he could hook this guy the way he had the woman.

The man stared dumbly for a few more seconds before finally saying, "It's shit."

"Not everyone gets it," Syd replied, which was usually enough to shake these sorts. Not this guy, though. This guy was different, as I'm sure you've gleaned.

"I didn't say I don't *get* it; I said it's shit."

"Well perhaps if you allowed me to explain. The staples symbolize the—"

He raised a finger. "You're about to make something up, and I'm not interested."

"Well then piss off, why don't you?"

The man's face assumed an expression that struck Syd as vaguely French. "How much do these go for?"

"I thought you said you weren't interested."

"I might change my mind. How much?"

"Three-fifty."

"Hopefully that's three dollars and fifty cents."

"Nope."

"Nobody will pay that much for one of these."

"The several people who have already made purchases would beg to differ."

At that, the guy's facial expression tightened. He moved his eyes from the canvases to Syd. His eyes were the other non-prototypical thing about him—they were piercing green and looked like they could almost burn a hole through your face if you let them. His gaze felt *hot*, somehow, in the most fundamental, non-sexual sense. "You're telling me you've actually *sold* some of these?"

"Hell yes." Syd wondered whether this guy would buy one if he deemed them "trendy" enough. Based on the way he dressed, the probability was high.

"At *that price*?"

"Did I stutter?"

Now he was observing Syd like a bacterial subject of an intensive lab-study, which made Syd want to remove his own skin and wriggle away all damp and fleshy. "I don't believe you," the man decided, after one of those pretentious, contemplative pauses designed to make one seem aged and wise. "I can sniff out a liar a mile away. It's basically my profession."

"Then you should probably be fired."

The man's nostrils twitched. "What's your name?"

"Syd."

"Short for Sydney?"

"Yeah."

"Isn't that a girl's name?"

"I don't..."

"D'you spell it with or without the Y?"

"There's a way to spell Sydney without a Y?"

"One or two Ys? Smartass."

"Two."

"Yeah, that's a girl's name."

"Are we done here?"

The man alternately lifted his surprisingly dainty feet and massaged them in obvious discomfort. It was probably the Vans, Syd figured. They weren't renowned for their arch support. "You're odd. What's your surname?"

"I'm not giving you that. You're probably IRS or something."

"Is it Morris, by any chance?"

Syd took a spooked step backward.

"Is it?"

All Syd could figure was that the man was somehow involved in the Christian school network, though he looked better suited for the concert of some indie band whose brief window of cultural cool had already closed. "No."

"Ha! Liar. I got you."

"What do you want?" Syd felt his voice growing thick and hoarse with exhaustion. At first, it had been fun to shoot the shit with this guy, but Syd should have trusted his instincts. He had a real gut instinct for base, character-level unpleasantness.

"Would you like to go out with me?"

Now Syd's interest had been piqued again. He knew a few gay people, but he'd never seen one so poorly dressed. "You're like, forty."

"Thirty-one."

"Your hairline says otherwise. Besides, I'm straight."

"How do you know that? Ever fucked a man?"

"No."

Truthfully, Syd hadn't fucked *anybody* and was a bit terrified of sex as a concept, but he'd never admit that publicly.

"Then you don't know, do you?"

At this, Syd fell silent—there was really no reasoning with these new-agey, the-spiritual-is-the-sexual, everything-is-fluid-and-subjective people.

"So you really put three hundred and fifty dollars' worth of love and care into these artworks, is that it?" The man picked one up with flippant irreverence.

Syd tried to grab it back, but the man, who I'm sure you've deduced is Mitch Larkin, yanked it out of reach.

"I'm sure you'd be *really upset*, then, if I—"

What happened next happened instantaneously and wasn't premeditated, unless you count minutes of seething hatred as premeditation. Undirected premeditation at most. It was at the very least not *calculated*—a split-second, uncontrollable whirl of pent-up aggression. Syd didn't even understand what had occurred until he was shaking out his fist, his knuckles burning, and Mitch was clutching his bleeding nose with both hands, and the canvas was clattering around the pavement below them.

"The fuck you do that for?" Mitch spluttered. His words came out congested. A small crowd had gathered. Someone asked sheepishly whether she should call the cops.

"I'm sorry," Syd said, but he didn't feel it. "I'm sorry," he tried again, choking back what he wanted to pass off as tears of remorse but what were really tears of unadulterated terror. In all his years of hard drug use, Syd had never had a run-in with the police—even his many school fights had been dealt with at the sub-judicial level. But this wasn't some asshole on the football team—this was a grown man who knew his full name and had the power and probably the competence to take him to court. "I didn't mean it. I'm a pacifist. I would never—"

"*I'll* call the cops," someone else volunteered.

"Don't," Mitch told her, and Syd felt a surprising surge of gratitude toward him. "Seriously, hold off."

Mitch tilted his head slightly back, his nose still trickling blood and badly bruised but ideally not broken. Syd's mind conjured an unshakeable vision of Mitch receiving unwelcome X-Ray results and making a post-haste trip from the hospital to the station.

"I'm a talent acquisition manager," Mitch said. He pronounced "manager" like *madager*, on account of the nasal trouble. "I'd like to take you on as a client. For free."

Syd gaped. The man's motives seemed to clash almost as much as his dumb outfit. "But you think I suck."

"I think you have great potential. A possible genius."

"Sorry," Syd replied, struggling to keep his ego from succumbing to the inflationary powers of the word "genius." Everyone else who'd ever called him a genius had also been dumb enough to fall for his tricks, so he'd never placed much stock in their assertions. "I work alone."

"Very well." Mitch turned to the snitchy lady in the crowd, who held her cell phone out expectantly. "Give the cops a dial."

"Wait," Syd said, remembering again why he'd punched the guy. He feared he might take a second swing. "I'll do it."

"Never mind," Mitch told the woman, who scoffed audibly this time. Mitch smiled. He kept smiling for far longer than Syd thought necessary.

3

Syd rode in Mitch's backseat on the passenger side, leaning as far away as he could conceivably get from Mitch without falling out. Attempting to murder Syd from Mitch's kitty-corner driver's position would present some difficulties, Syd hoped, but Mitch drove a Prius, which was the car of a pussy, so Syd didn't think he'd try anything. This guy definitely wasn't involved in any street gangs—at most, he did some mild embezzling from time to time.

"Okay back there?" Mitch asked, his eyes glued to the road. He was a very bad driver. He didn't hit anyone or run red lights or break any common traffic laws, but Syd could always tell when somebody was comfortable and confident behind the wheel as opposed to not knowing what he was doing and just hoping everyone around him was skilled enough to compensate. Mitch was the latter. His nervous spontaneity put Syd on edge.

"Is this a kidnapping?" Syd asked. "Because if it is, I know Taekwondo. I'm also friends with some powerful people." Neither of those statements was true.

"Relax. It's nothing of the sort." He used the exact tone a kidnapper might.

"Because I don't know much about talent acquisitions or any of that shit," Syd continued, "but this seems more like a kidnapping than a talent acquisition. If we were to just, like, create lists of the defining characteristics of each and then list the characteristics of this situation and compare that list to the talent acquisition and kidnapping lists and develop another list of all the overlapping qualities for both—"

"You talk a lot," Mitch observed. He hadn't looked Syd in the eye since the two had left Times Square together; with how he had his mirror positioned, his face wasn't even visible, and Syd very much doubted he could even see through his dirt-caked rearview.

"Just trying to determine the depth of shit I'm in." The New York City skyline was now well behind them. The outside air smelled like cow dung, and the scent somehow permeated the car even with the windows rolled up. As if reading Syd's mind and hellbent on annoying him, Mitch cracked his.

"Don't let more dung in."

"What dung? It's nice out."

Syd wondered whether living in upstate New York had made Mitch completely immune to the smell of poop. He briefly considered testing his theory but decided against it.

"So are we headed to the warehouse where you keep all your other talent acquisitions?" Syd asked.

"Very funny."

"Just, like, store them all in cages somewhere until they need to go to an audition."

"I'm actually fairly new to this, if you want to know the truth."

That much had been immediately obvious to Syd. He wouldn't trust this guy to acquire talent of even the most menial sort—not with the whole unfashionable getup he had going on, and the red Prius, and the legal blackmailing and whatnot. "So what did you do for the first thirty years of your life? Just bum around pretending to be an art critic?"

"That's an interesting question and one I've been meaning to ask *you.*"

"You first."

After a brief delay: "Oh, a whole host of things. Mostly miscellaneous office jobs. Clerking and such."

Syd drummed his fingers skeptically against the hard rubber of the car door.

"You next," Mitch prompted.

Given that Mitch had known his full name and probably knew about the Christian school stuff, Syd wondered whether to even bother inventing something. He decided on a partial truth—those were sometimes just as convincing as the full ones. "I'm only twenty-one, so I'm still looking for something long-term."

"Yeah? Did you go to college?"

"No. I was a drug addict." Shifted restlessly in the seat, hit by a surprising and substance-unrelated jolt of energy. The seatbelt rode his neck, not quite painful but uncomfortable—a grating, repetitive micro-motion that might start to leave a mark after an hour or so. He never wore seatbelts, but Mitch had insisted, right before proceeding to drive like a madman. "Not anymore, though," he continued, figuring the cop-calling thing might still be on the table. "The statute of limitations has expired," he added, just in case.

"You use a lot of big words for someone without a college degree." His tone was that of someone congratulating a toddler for making it to the toilet in time, but the condescension seemed inadvertent.

"Yeah, well. I read a lot. Anyway, now I mostly give speeches at schools and stuff."

The back of Mitch's head moved up and down in recognition. "Like Christian schools?"

"Yeah. About quitting drugs. Hey, how d'you know about that?"

Mitch shrugged. "Word gets around."

Their car was one of several in line to enter a wealthy, gated community. When they got to the front, Mitch gave a half-assed wave—the kind that doesn't involve any movement past the wrist—and nodded at the gate operator, who wore what looked like a boating captain's hat and an expression of corporate exhaustion that abruptly changed to one of worried concern, and it took Syd, who hadn't seen Mitch's face for the entire ride, a few seconds to remember that his nose must still look pretty ghastly.

"Yardwork mishap," Mitch said. The complete change in his social demeanor unnerved Syd—for a few seconds, he seemed like a real person one might encounter on the street rather than an off-putting parody of a person.

"Yikes" was all the gate operator had to say in response.

The subdivision roads sloped steeply up and down, as was typical for upscale neighborhoods where gas mileage wasn't a consideration. Mitch drove past a park with a degree of tree coverage Syd had never seen before, its vast field packed with assorted dogs fetching Frisbees and bougies talking animatedly to each other while waiting for said dogs to return. Kids played in their backyards completely unsupervised. It was becoming increasingly apparent to Syd that Mitch had some serious cash lying around.

As soon as Syd stepped through the front door of Mitch's house, which door had one of those almost stained-glassish semicircular windows in it, a few more realities about Mitch presented themselves. The most obvious was that he lived alone. Syd had initially expected Mitch to have a wife and maybe even a kid or two, and then, after Mitch had asked him out, he'd thought maybe a husband who he cheated on with early-twenties burnouts to stave off midlife dread, but the place seemed wholly untouched by additional human presences. It was a pigsty of the sort married men can't get away with—not without a swift serving of divorce papers, anyway. The living room and kitchen, though spacious and grand and full of high-class potential, were littered with empty beer bottles, smelly clothes, magazines, junk mail that hadn't yet been sifted through, dirty dishes, and empty bags of chips. Syd thought about informing Mitch that there's this really cool futuristic technology nowadays called a "trash can," which you can throw stuff into and have it magically whisked away once weekly, but he didn't feel like testing his luck, mainly because this seemed to be the home of a serial killer, and Syd wouldn't have been one bit surprised to open the refrigerator and see disembodied human organs Saran-wrapped with the same nonchalant care a Midwestern housewife might give to leftover tuna hot dish.

"Let's find your talents," Mitch suggested, not even drawing attention to the elephant (no, more like *blue whale*) in the room (no, more like *entire house*). Even during Syd's most fervid weeklong benders, his apartment never reached such dire shape, and that was saying something considering he owned pretty much the shittiest property you could find in the entire New York metropolitan area and was too lazy to clean most weeks. This wasn't a couple weeks' mess though; it was years'. "What can you do?"

"I can make staple art."

"You can't." Mitch tossed his keys onto the closer of the two living room couches, where they disappeared into a pile of junk. "But what you seem to be *very* good at is *convincing* people to buy your staple art, if you know what I'm getting at."

"Well, when there's a high demand for bullshit, let me know." Syd waited uneasily for Mitch to sit, mainly with the intent of sussing out just how one might make oneself at home in a place like this and what etiquette and hygiene issues to take into consideration before moving somebody's trash to make room for oneself. He eyed the upright wooden piano against the back wall of the living room. One empty cardboard box covered the left half of its bench.

"So you admit it's bullshit. Is that the first true thing you've told me today?"

"One of them."

"And are you telling the truth now? If we're going to work together, you've gotta learn to be honest with me."

Syd rocked back and forth on his heels, which was something he often did during uncomfortable speeches at private Christian schools. His current discomfort derived from the fact that he didn't even want to "work" with Mitch, whatever that entailed. A voice in his head, growing ever-louder, was telling him to leave without a word—run, hitchhike, whatever, just get the fuck out of the immediate vicinity of this guy before it was too late. "Yes."

"Good."

"I also play the piano," he volunteered, and it was true—he used to accompany his adopted dad at jazz recitals.

Mitch had cleared a spot for himself on the arm of a couch. "Hit me."

Syd took a cautious seat on the empty portion of the piano bench, his fingers shaking. He hadn't played in years. He couldn't summon any jazz riffs to the forefront of his memory, and the fact that this was an absolutely unrecoverable loss of something he'd once cared about deeply made something inside him feel tightly wrung. "What do you want?"

Mitch shrugged. "Know any Radiohead?"

Syd racked his brain, hoping his recall was correct and that the song he had in mind was actually by Radiohead, a hope Mitch confirmed by saying, "Nice, 'Karma Police.'"

Syd played the verse and chorus, occasionally falling a split second behind the beat while he searched for the next chord but not completely derailing until he reached the outro and forgot what came next. "That's all I remember."

"Not bad, but nothing too impressive," Mitch commented, and Syd wanted to drag him by the nonexistent collar and put *him* in front of the piano and ask *him* to play a song he'd never played before but had heard on a Spotify station entitled "'90s Depression" maybe five or so years ago. "How long have you played that one?"

"Just now."

"No, like, how long have you *known* it?"

"I mean, I heard it sometime in the past. Not sure when. That was my first attempt at playing it." He tried to sound calm and collected, but he'd performed in enough settings to know he was kind of a freak in this department.

"Do you have perfect pitch?" Mitch asked.

"What's that?"

"When you can identify a pitch just by hearing it."

"Oh. Then yeah. Kind of a weird designation. You don't say people who aren't colorblind have 'perfect color.'" This was his go-to line for feigning coolness when it came to his perfect pitch. It gave off the impression that he'd never so much as wondered whether the way he learned songs might be atypical.

"That's not going to work, then," Mitch replied, somehow acting even cooler about it than Syd. "I've d—worked with a few perfect-pitched musicians before; they never get off the ground. It's a crutch, not an asset."

Syd frowned, suddenly feeling more empty than scared. After all, if Mitch were going to serial-kill him, he would have done it by now. Syd having his back turned for long enough to play two thirds of a song on the piano would have given Mitch ample time to plunge a knife into his heart.

"Well, then I'm out of ideas." Syd stood up, the universal indicator of getting ready to head out because you have somewhere else important to be. He had nowhere to be, and Mitch probably knew this, but every minute spent with the guy was one more minute that could be spent on more pleasurable pursuits, like creating staple art or gouging his eyes out with a rusty sewing needle. Besides, his body ached for a hit, and the longer he went without one, the more evident his sniffing and irritability became. "Sorry. I tried. Hope you won't get me arrested." Affected a pleading, innocent expression. "I have my whole life ahead of me."

"You know what *I* think you should be? It's what you are every time you talk about finding Jesus."

"A motivational speaker?"

Mitch looked emphatically at Syd, who quickly averted his eyes. Eye contact always made him uncomfortable, but something about the way Mitch initiated it—like he was a robot programmed to carry out certain human gestures at discrete intervals of time—made it worse. "An actor."

4

If you've read the non-optional preface, you already know the acting thing worked out for Syd, but his success wasn't immediate. He bombed his first audition so hard Mitch didn't talk to him for a few weeks in late July and early August—seemingly more out of panic than malice. After four more failed attempts, he began feeling personally slighted, even with Mitch assuring him that rejection was the default in this tough business. Though Syd liked to delude himself otherwise, he still shamefully believed, deep down, that he was somehow uniquely special and/or transcendent and that any right-minded person would recognize him as such. Therefore, when others didn't notice the one in a million genius-level talent he thought he'd made immediately evident, he perceived the resultant rejection as either a dumb and stubborn refusal to admit the obvious, a failure on his part to *convey* the obvious, some gruesome combination of the two, or (worst of all) a failure to accurately judge his own prodigiousness.

Today, Syd was trying out for a low-budget TV show that probably ended up hitting a smaller streaming network, entitled *Twelve Kids, Four Adults, and a Weird-Looking Dog*, which featured twelve kids, four adults, and a weird-looking dog living in some kind of extended-family condo arrangement. Two of the four adults were brother and sister, which meant the kids were all some flavor of siblings or cousins. Syd was going to read for Alec, the oldest of the kids, a seventeen-year-old moody Holden Caulfield type who was slated to develop a drug dependency about halfway through Season 1. Mitch considered this an ideal role for Syd because it would allow him to "just be [himself]." In accordance with that theme, Mitch had permitted Syd to pick his own audition outfit, so he was sporting some low-waisted jeans and a skull-and-crossbones T-shirt he'd refashioned into a tank top.

Speaking of drug addictions, Syd had not made even a peep about his own dependency to Mitch, nor had he acquiesced to any of Mitch's requests to come over to his (Syd's) place, because he knew that any thinking person, even a person as hygienically deficient as Mitch, would immediately identify his apartment as a drug addict's—the uneven cleanliness, the trash can next to the couch, the dishes stacked on the coffee table, the mysterious dusting of white on a few selected surfaces, etc.

"You a'ight?" Mitch asked, his car idling at a stoplight. Traffic was thick enough that the next green light didn't guarantee successful intersection-crossing. The car in front of them had a bumper sticker featuring the phrase DICK TATER next to a phallic potato wearing the signature star cap of Maoist China. Syd wondered what concordance of life experiences and psychological traits might compel someone to not just purchase such a sticker but proudly display it.

"I guess." Syd possessed a weird mix of Stockholm Syndrome and genuine care, with regard to Mitch. Part of this feeling derived from the fact that, though Syd hadn't fully decocted the finer points of Mitch's personality, *Mitch* seemed to genuinely care about *him*—to want him to succeed independent of any external considerations.

"So what *aren't* we going to say to the casting directors?" Mitch prompted him now.

"No cursing. No criticizing the way they're doing their job. No insulting them in any way."

"Right. You can say that type of stuff to me, because I *know* you, Syd."

The traffic light had turned green, and Mitch was alternately pumping the accelerator and the brakes as the cars ahead of him eased into a comfortable coast.

"Hardly." But secretly, he felt an inexplicable purgative rush. "You know, you don't get very good mileage that way."

"*Don't* I, Sydney? You're gonna lecture me about *gas mileage* when you don't even own a fucking *car*?"

"You just kind of..." Syd bit his lip. He liked to start sentences he knew would be deemed offensive and make the other person goad him into seeing them through to completion.

"I kind of what, huh?"

"Never mind."

"No, I want to hear it."

Syd clicked his tongue performatively. "You just kind of strike me as someone with, like, poor money management skills. I don't know.

Maybe a snap judgment."

"Definitely a snap judgment."

"Okay."

"Okay."

"So we're done then?"

Nearly a minute's silence followed, during which Mitch maintained a stern gaze and occasionally raised his eyebrows or huffed emphatically as if reacting to something Syd had not even said. Or reacting to something Syd had said earlier that he was just now making full sense of. They squeezed through the green light this time around.

"You strike me as someone who is still on drugs," Mitch opined with vindictive finality.

"I'm not."

"Okay. I've just seen many lives ruined by drugs. One day you're on top; the next, your value tanks."

"My *value?*"

"Cultural value," Mitch amended. "Like, your relevancy in the cultural sphere."

"That's a bit farther ahead than I'm willing to look."

The parking lot of the building could have been the parking lot of a hospital, or a warehouse. The construction was drab, symmetrical, and soulless. The waiting room didn't do much to quell the hospitalish atmosphere of the whole thing—sitting around him were various thin, strung-out-looking, brunet young men, their eyes scanning their scripts, their mouths moving silently.

Mitch had informed Syd that his physical appearance would play a major role in the casting process. And TV execs didn't judge looks the way common folks did, so movie ugly and real-life ugly were not the same thing. In order to be movie hot, you basically needed to be in the top 0.1 percent of attractiveness for the general population—a ten out of ten on the hotness scale, Mitch had said. Actors cast as movie average tended to be real-life hot—anywhere from a seven to a nine. To be movie ugly, you needed to be average or slightly below average—they don't want any eyesores, which is why anyone with more than a few minutes' screentime is at least a four. Mitch had told Syd that this put him in a tricky quandary, because by Mitch's estimation, Syd was a six out of ten, and notice how none of the above categories are looking for sixes. Sixes might as well be the black sheep of the act-ing world. If you want to get a role as a six, you've either gotta settle for being an unassuming background character or "really blow people's socks off" acting-wise.

Needless to say, all this statistical shit had given Syd a bit of a com-plex, and now he found himself aesthetically sizing up his competi-tion, trying to quantify their physical flaws. This one looked more like a cannibal than a drug addict, that one had a bit of a belly, this one had a disproportionate nose and a weird haircut—

"Ignore them," Mitch said, seeming to read Syd's thoughts. "Study your script." The script sat nearly untouched in his lap.

"Got it memorized."

"You haven't even looked at it."

"I took a peek."

Mitch grabbed the script out of Syd's hand. "'Alec, you're not go-ing to *believe* what Darryl and I found in your bathroom,'" he read.

"'Not a crack pipe, surely,'" Syd mumbled.

"Say it like you mean it."

"It's called deadpan."

"I'm not believing the character."

"Well, luckily, your opinion doesn't mean shit."

One of Syd's clones shot them a flinty glance just as the door of the audition room swung open. "Sydney Morris," a petite young woman said.

"That's my cue." Syd stood up, and Mitch followed suit.

"Who are you, sir?" the lady asked Mitch. She couldn't have been much older than Syd, and in platform heels, she came up to about his chin level. She had a pencil tucked behind her ear and a certain librarianish appeal.

"His manager. I'm coming in with him."

"Does he *want* you to come in with him?"

"Nope," Syd chirped, partially to the lady and partially to Mitch. "He makes me uncomfortable," he added, this time more to the lady, though with the perverse bonus hope that Mitch would still take it to heart.

"Sit down, sir," the woman told Mitch, grimacing politely.

The inside of the studio resembled a classroom, and Syd half expected to see a pious, preppily-uniformed student body president waiting to give him a rundown. Instead, a panel of two men and a single woman sat in an evenly spaced row at a long table.

"I'm reading for Alec," Syd said.

"Right, well, I'll be Mrs. Green [Alec's mother]," the woman said. She had blonde hair and spoke with a smoker's hoarseness.

"I'll read for Marvin [Alec's younger brother]," the man on her left added. He resembled a stock photo of the CEO at a midrange office supply chain.

"And I'll be Darryl [Alec's father]," the other man said. He resembled a stock photo of someone working directly under the CEO of a midrange office supply chain.

"Ready when you are," Syd told them, feigning courtesy.

"'Alec, you're not going to *believe* what Darryl and I found in your bathroom.'"

"'Not a crackpipe, surely,'" Syd deadpanned.

"Cut!" the CEO-looking man said. "More passion. More energy."

"Really?" the working-directly-under-the-CEO-looking man put in. "I thought that was in character."

"Try it another way," the woman suggested. Hacked up something nasty. "'Alec, you're not going to *believe* what Darryl and I found in your bathroom.'"

"'Not a *crack*pipe, *sure*ly!'" With every time Syd uttered the phrase, its connotation harshened. By now, jittery and fatigued and desperate for a fix, he felt as if the script were mocking him.

CEO: Cut.

CFO (that's one example of someone who might work directly under a CEO): See, I liked it better the other way.

Woman: Me too.

CEO: Same. Let's go back to the other way.

Syd: Wouldn't want to be *rude* or anything like that. I was just wondering, since you folks are responsible for determining whether I find work and all that, whether you might want to get your fucking heads together and develop some kind of consensus on which end of the chipper-to-deadpan continuum you'd like for me to play this. You know, so it doesn't come off like you don't know what you're doing or like the show I'm auditioning for has no real vision or artistic merit or anything like that.

[*Syd looks down at the ground. Is feeling apprehensive, having just broken every one of Mitch's no-rudeness rules in a single catastrophic breath. Wants to look bashful to play it off as an innocuous social boner.*]

CFO: See, that's exactly the kind of energy we need for this Alec character. [*His expression betrays uncertainty as to whether Syd's invective was genuine or some kind of method-act and even more uncertainty as to whether he cares.*]

Woman: Yeah, play it smug and dickish. Let's try again. "Alec, you're not going to *believe* what Darryl and I found in your bathroom."

Etc.

When Syd returned to the waiting room, Mitch bombarded him with incessant questions. "Did they look pleased?" "Did they ask you to read more than once? Always a good sign if they ask for another read." "Did they say anything like, 'We'll be in touch'?"

Syd, who had already depleted his social battery for the day and possibly the week, said he didn't remember. He went home and got high and locked himself in his room with the lights out and lay very still on his back on his twin-size bed.

Though Syd had set his expectations ego-deflatedly low, his impatience and defiance had apparently impressed the casting directors enough to prompt a callback offer. He responded to the newest of his sixteen unread messages from Mitch, all of which were some iteration of has he heard anything, telling him the good news. On the day of the callbacks, Mitch picked him up in his Prius at 7 AM sharp, and Syd squinted in the glare of the sunlight on his windshield.

"Remember to be nice," Mitch nagged. "It seems to have worked last time."

"I wasn't even nice. They didn't become interested in me until I sassed them."

In lieu of a reply, Mitch clicked his windshield wipers a few times, attempting to clean off a patch of bird poop, but the poop had already dried.

"Ever thought about giving me one of those staple arts you do?" Mitch asked with an affected casualty. His voice sounded tinny to Syd, who wasn't used to getting high this early—wasn't used to getting *up* this early—but had no desire to be both awake *and* sober.

"The ones you hated?"

"I've thought about them more and grown to love them."

"Bullshit." But despite knowing it was bullshit, Syd couldn't for the life of him figure out what Mitch's real motivations might be.

"How about as a gift? Since I got you an acting callback?"

"You didn't do shit. You gave me advice that would have sabotaged me. Luckily, I trusted my gut."

More silence.

"What if I bought one?" Mitch offered.

"How much are you willing to pay?"

"A hundred?"

"Insulting."

"Two?"

"Four hundred or no deal."

"That's more than you were selling them for in Times Square."

"You *annoy* me more than the people I sold them to in Times Square."

Silence again. "Fine."

In the waiting room, Mitch sat on Syd's right. "You're tweaking," he pointed out, gesturing to Syd's jostling leg.

"No," Syd said. "Nervous."

The room's population was sparser this time—only four others, two of them sevens on the hotness scale, one eight, and one five.

Another six arrived and took a seat at Syd's side. "You here for Alec?" he asked.

Syd nodded just once.

"I've never been called back before." The guy spoke in a squeaky, enunciated whisper. "Exciting, isn't it?"

Syd could tell he was one of those sprightly, optimistic types who instantly dragged down the whole mood of a place and induced despair.

"What about you?" he went on. "First callback?"

"Uh, yeah." Looked down at his sneakers in a show of disinterest.

"If I land this role, this will be *big* for me, and I mean *huge*," he continued, obstinately refusing to take a hint. He could pass for Syd's age, but the filled-out nature of his core told Syd he was a few years older. "I mean—" He lowered his whisper to an even quieter whisper, his breath hot in Syd's ear. "—I'm a *clown*, for Chrissake. Like, I put on the big red nose and blow up balloons at kids' birthday parties."

At this, Syd chortled. He exchanged a brief, knowing glance with Mitch, who was also visibly amused, and this felt like a real and rare instance of camaraderie between them.

"Big upgrade," Syd commented. He was suddenly more interested. "What's your name?".

"Blake." Blake offered up a handshake. "Blake Aaron Olsen, Krazy Klown Entertainment, incorporated. That's Krazy with a *K*. Same with Klown."

"Two K's in a row. Bold."

He didn't react. "And I use my middle name so I'm easier to search."

"Like a mass shooter," Syd put in. "Or assassin."

Mitch turned away, fist to his mouth.

"What's *your* name?" Blake asked, hand still extended.

"Harold M. Flurn, Esquire," Syd answered without hesitation.

Blake didn't even smile. "Nice. Easy to remember."

The door to the audition room opened a crack, and the librarian-esque woman whose name Syd had never bothered to learn poked her head out. "Blake?"

The clown stood up. "Guess I'm up. Best of luck to you, Harold."

Syd turned around in fleeting confusion before remembering that Harold was the name he'd just given as his own. "Yup."

As the door closed behind Blake, Mitch and Syd let loose their repressed laughter. They laughed so long that Syd forgot what was even funny. It felt good.

"Man, I couldn't crack that guy," Syd spluttered.

"He was impossible."

"I couldn't tell whether he was in on it or not."

Syd's right hand sat limply on his still-jiggling knee. He hadn't moved it an inch since arriving.

5

Near-successes hurt worse than outright rejections. This was something nobody had bothered to tell Syd, who, when his phone rang at 10:36 PM the week after his callback, fumbled to answer it from bed in a nearly-sober trance with the servile tone of a person willing to jump any requested height.

"Is this Syd Morris?"

"Uh-huh."

"This is Anna Harding from the *Twelve Kids* casting team. I've got your callback results."

"Thanks. It's not the kind of role I'd always dreamed of, but I accept."

"Accept what?"

"The role."

"You didn't get the role."

Syd straightened out. "What? Who did?"

"We can't tell you that."

"Was it that clown? Blake with the three names?"

"We can't tell you."

"Blake is my friend. I'm just going to call him and ask."

"Please don't harass him over it."

"Knew it. Fucking hell, *Blake*."

"Have a nice night, sir."

The next morning, Syd began researching Blake Aaron Olsen and Krazy Klown Entertainment. It wasn't difficult; Blake wore, as Syd suspected, his heart on his sleeve, and on his website, apparently—the homepage featured a colorful and eye-soreish list of upcoming birthday party tour dates, most of them residential addresses. This coming Saturday, Blake would be pimping himself out at 51 Greer Road, a location conveniently accessible via public transit. You'd have to be insanely rich to own real estate this close to downtown New York, Syd thought—rich enough to afford higher-class entertainment than a travelling circus clown, at least.

Syd had no intention of telling Mitch about his materializing scheme. Mitch, in his fatherly wisdom, would likely urge Syd not to crash some eight-year-old's party and accost its resident clown. Plus, Syd had just duped Mitch into buying an overpriced piece of staple art and didn't want to risk being unable to sucker him out of more money down the line. No, this would be a Syd solo endeavor.

October had brought higher winds and cooler temperatures and those annoying scattered blips of rain that passed as soon as they came and came again twenty minutes later. Syd often found himself leaving his house in a trench coat, which, despite the unfortunate Columbine associations, he believed he could still pull off, and today was no exception. But besides some strange and furtive looks on the subway, Syd's coat didn't elicit much reaction, which I get the sense vaguely disappointed him.

51 Greer Road was a cute little brick home on the outskirts of Brooklyn. Pink banners reading "HAPPY BIRTHDAY KAYLA" draped the property's entire perimeter, but the real action was happening in the backyard—a fenced-in, shaded area with a slightly overgrown lawn. A Disneyfied, radio-friendly pop tune Syd identified as being in the key of D blared over a tinny speaker sitting on one of those webbed, outdoor metal tables and buzzing with friction every time the bass hit. Segregated clumps of parents and children populated the area. Most parent conversations seemed to revolve around their kids.

To Syd, having children seemed a bleak endeavor—a consignment to a lifetime of servitude. Once you had kids, you lost your individual identity and became a faceless projection of and mouthpiece for said kids. Every now and then, an identityless mom (because let's be honest, the dads were few and far between and appeared storklike and out of place, as if they'd been randomly dropped here like RollerCoaster Tycoon 2 NPCs and were trying to get their bearings) pointed to a child—most of whom were batting around mouth-inflated balloons and/or sitting on multicolored chairs at a short, plastic table, molding Play-Doh, though a few of the grimier boys were digging a hole and pouring diet soda into it—to show the other moms that that one was hers, and she was sure proud of it. Of him or her. The whole situation was pretty sad, but Syd nonetheless longed to be pointed out in a crowd and identified as special or important. To be more than an afterthought.

With the exception of one occasion he was trying to block out, he'd never had a birthday party. When he was young, his then-step-dad Glen would sometimes bring home a cupcake from Pfeffer's, the only bakery in Village of Walton, upstate NY, where he grew up. The cake was always smooshed and lopsided, and most of its frosting stuck to the folded-over tabs of the packaging and needed to be licked off, so Syd would take a lick followed by an immediate bite of the naked cupcake to simulate eating it in its intended form. His stepdad would sit next to him at the table, silently reading *The Wall Street Journal* on his iPad, until Syd finished. Then Glen would club him on the shoulder and say, "Happy birthday, kid," and Syd would tiptoe word-lessly to his room, careful not to wake his unconscious mother, and cry himself to sleep.

Syd had always been an afterthought, but now, with Mitch breathing down his neck so closely Syd could smell his morning cof-fee, he was at least one person's reason for getting up in the morning. Sure, Mitch was a lamentable creature, but there was a certain degree of lamentability required to see Syd as a beacon of hope.

Still no sign of any clown nor even of Blake dressed in a normal outfit carrying what Syd imagined as one of those over-the-shoulder burlap sacks filled with laundered clown clothes. Syd had been sur-prised by the utter prototypicality of Blake's outfit when he'd met him at the callback—a button-down shirt with pockets and some slacks—as well as struck by the disconcerting reality that clowns walked among us, disguised as normal people going about their daily business, blending seamlessly and sinisterly into the amorphous, os-tensibly-clownless human social mass.

Syd took a seat at one of the adult tables, where he slumped for-ward and rested his chin on his palms. Kids frolicked in the field. A blonde girl with a pink cardboard birthday hat and overalls, who Syd assumed was Kayla, sat huddled with a couple other girls in a circle on the ground, the three of them ripping grass out of the dirt and sprinkling it on each other's heads in some pseudo-religious ritual. The moms at Syd's table bragged about how creative their kids were and took turns giving Syd suspicious glances of upper-class judgment.

"She's always coming up with games like that," one mom mused, referring to the grass ceremony. She was shorter and plumper than the other two and had an unnatural-looking brunette dye-job.

"Mine too; she has these tiny drawings she cuts out for us—for her father and me—and a little shop," said another mom, who was tall and thin and blonde.

"Mine is always building things out of her brother's Legos. Takes apart his sets and makes totally novel designs," said a third mom, who looked like if you combined the first two moms via a free face-blender app, and who giggled falsely before adding, "He gets so mad about it, but the stuff she comes up with is sometimes better than what the instruction manuals teach you to make. Just last week, she built a Barbie Dreamhouse out of her brother's Death Star."

Syd noted with mild bemusement the passive-aggressive power-plays involved in loving motherhood. These moms weren't just making conversation—they were one-upping. Each needed her kid to be the superior kid, because in the world of mom politics, that would somehow reflect back on *her*. After every comment, the mom who'd uttered it indiscreetly sized up the table as if hoping the other two would respond with, "Wow. I can't top that. You win" instead of anecdotes of their own. The conversation exhausted even Syd, who was just a spectator, so he couldn't imagine how these loving mothers felt.

"She charges anywhere from one to seven dollars for each, and she makes a killing from her dad and me," the second mom continued, as if the third hadn't spoken. The absurdity of the statement made Syd wonder whether he'd misheard.

"Some of the games mine makes up are really complicated. The grass game they're playing right now is one of the simpler ones."

"Her Lego creations are so well-designed. I always tell her she should submit one to Lego Ideas."

So far, the Lego girl was winning, by Syd's measure, assuming the third mother wasn't grossly exaggerating her daughter's abilities.

"She's made about a hundred bucks total. She just leaves her earnings there in the closet next to her drawings. I'll have to teach her about financial security someday if she's going to run a business, but this is fine for now."

"Sorry," Syd cut in, having held his tongue so long it was beginning to lose metaphorical blood supply. "Did you just say you pay your daughter *real* USD for cut-out paper crap?"

All three mothers' mouths expanded into lopsided O's, as if each of their daughters had been personally insulted. Seconds ago embroiled in fierce competition, they now formed a united front.

In an instant, the second mom's lips went from loosely agape to prudishly puckered. "Yes. Have a problem with that?"

"It's just not realistic—you're not *doing* anything with them. You're only buying them to make her feel better. Why not just throw free money at her if you have all that lying around."

"To encourage *creativity*," the first mom put in.

"Excuse me, who are you?" the second mom added.

"Older brother," Syd said quickly. After a lifetime of freelance lying, he'd learned to always divulge as little information as possible and let the lyees fill in the rest.

"Whose older brother?"

Syd pointed indistinctly toward a couple boys playing tag.

"Carlos's?" the third mom cut in. "Or Brayden's?"

"Mmhm."

"I've never heard Brayden's mom talk about having another kid."

"And Carlos is an only child—his mom and I play bridge together."

"I thought Brayden was too."

"I'm on break from college," Syd added. "Gonna go grab some refreshments."

The refreshments were depressingly non-alcoholic. He fingered the CNO-filled baggie in his trench coat pocket, debating the ethics of doing a line in the presence of second graders. It's not like they'd know what he was doing, but it still seemed inexplicably depraved.

So Syd stood on the sidelines, sipping a Capri-Sun juice box, wondering where the fuck Blake was and what the fuck he (Syd) was even doing here. He'd somehow planned out every minute of the trip without giving himself any real objective.

One of the out-of-place dads tottered Roller-Coaster-Tycoon-2ishly over to him. He had graying hair and a pointed nose and the physique of someone who works out about twice a month. "Which one's yours?" he asked.

Syd searched the field for the two kids he'd pointed to earlier but couldn't find them, nor could he remember what they even looked like. He was terribly face blind, especially when it came to kids, who looked like if you pasted custom hairstyles onto about three or four different available default templates. "I'm an older brother."

"I assumed. Which is yours?"

Syd picked a little boy at random, praying that it wasn't the man's son. "That one's mine."

"I meant that other one," Syd amended, pointing to an adjacent kid, who had just put the first kid in a headlock and was now noogie-ing him while the first kid stumbled around blindly, trying to free himself.

"Nah, I'm just messing with you. That's not my kid. Should've seen the look on your face though."

Which told Syd the man knew Syd didn't belong here, but the man didn't appear particularly bothered by his not belonging here—seemed to believe tourism of random children's birthday parties was a common pastime for early-twenties drug addicts.

"I'm Peter." The man outstretched his hand. What Syd didn't know, while he took it cautiously, half-expecting a whoopee-cushion-like prank or something even more nefarious, was that this was Peter *Rankin*, the indie film director.

"Syd."

Suddenly, the yard erupted in a collective high-pitched cheer, and Syd turned to see the First Mom from earlier escorting a clown through the house's back door, the clown walking with the familiar, demeaning waddle of clowns everywhere, a few long, uninflated, twistable balloons hanging out of the pockets of his ridiculous outfit. Syd slouched behind Peter and covered his face, though the trench coat made him more conspicuous than he would have liked.

He felt depressingly sober. He was soberer than he ever wanted to be again.

"You all right, kid?" Peter asked him.

"Shhh."

"I'm a *Krazy Klown*, and I'm here to *entertain you*!" Blake ex-claimed, wiggling his arms as if they were made of jelly.

The kids cheered again.

"Afraid of clowns?" Peter asked now. Syd couldn't decide whether he wanted to deck the clown or Peter first.

"Where's our Kayla, huh?"

The blonde, birthday-hatted girl's hand shot immediately skyward. More cheers.

"You're a *special girl*, Kayla. Your name starts with the same letter as *klown*. Did you know that?"

"There's a word for that fear," Peter went on, speaking out of the corner of his mouth, his head half-turned. "They call it *coulrophobia*. Did you know that?"

Syd nodded in a bare-minimum acknowledgement of Peter's existence.

"For Kayla, we have a *special* surprise today, but first—"

The klown's heavily made-up eyes met Syd's. For as long as Syd could stand to look at Blake's garish visage, he detected excitement, then realization, then suspicion, then fear, then murderous intent or possibly some rare combination of all five.

"Is that Harold M. Flurn, Esquire I spy?" Pointed to Syd.

Syd felt his body melting into the floor. He considered it a miracle he wasn't an embarrassed puddle of corporeal glue.

"Who wants to hear a funny story about Harold?"

Cheers.

"Once upon a time, Harold and I were trying out to be in a TV show. Who here likes TV shows?"

Most of the kids raised their hands, captivated. A couple of the more attention-challenged ones fiddled with grass, as if the klown's presence or lack thereof were a matter of utter indifference to them.

"I'm not kidding. We both wanted to be on TV. Isn't that right, Harold? Wanna come finish the story for me, Harold?"

For someone who thought he was about to be attacked, Blake's provocations were unusually forward.

Syd now felt not two but about thirty eyes on him, including those of Peter, who looked to be in the process of deciding whether amusement was too inappropriate a reaction to the fracas.

Syd cleared his throat. "Sure." The word came out raspy.

"Come on; come up in front of the class," Blake invited, motioning with a white-gloved hand.

Syd approached slowly.

"It looks like Harold and I are both dressed silly today!" Blake spoke to his audience in the patronizing voice intellectually insecure adults reserve for children. Syd remembered being spoken to like that as a child and hating it. He wondered whether *any* kid enjoyed it—perhaps they just weren't game enough to speak up.

The kids all laughed.

"We tried out for a lame TV show for sellouts," Syd told the crowd flatly.

"He's a bit of a sad klown," Blake added, holding his fists to his eyes and twisting them back and forth in a mock gesture of krying.

"This guy," Syd went on, nudging Blake's ribcage with a force he hoped was gentle enough to look playful but aggressive enough to actually hurt, "came in there looking totally wigged out, like...on drugs or something."

A few confused-looking parents sprang from their seats to object and then sat halfway back down, hovering in liminal squats.

"Harold's klownsults have gotten a bit squeaky. He might need to go back to Klown Kollege." More laughs. Syd was losing this fight—he could tell, much like he could tell which moms were losing the kid-off earlier. Despite his deprecatory prolificity at the callbacks, he now felt surprisingly unequipped to deliver damaging blows. Blake had become a completely different person when he'd put the clown costume on. Now *he* was in on the joke, and *Syd* was the outsider.

"Do you kids want to hear why Klown Harold is so *sad*?" Syd asked, referring to himself in the third person as was klown kustom.

The kids cheered.

"Birthday parties make Klown Harold *sad* because Klown Harold's daddy was *killed* during one. Do you kids know what *killed* means?"

They nodded, noticeably subdued.

"Whose daddies are here today?" Syd went on.

A few tiny hands went up.

"This klown over here—" He nudged Blake again. "—told me he's going to *kill* one of them today. He said it's because the word *kill* starts with the same letter as *klown*. He's not a very nice *klown*, is he?"

Some of the more mentally deranged kids whooped, while others began sobbing, and the rest just looked mortified. The parents exchanged affronted expressions that wordlessly asked whether the others were going to do something about this or what.

"Okay, okay," Blake said, his klown persona faltering. Then to Syd, mouthed through gritted teeth, *What the fuck, man?*

"Klown Blake said a *bad word*," Syd proclaimed loudly. "Say it again, so they can hear you better."

"Okay, dude, what's your deal, huh?"

Syd barely heard him through the sound of his own brain's static. His earlier aimlessness had transmuted into a singular, visceral purpose: impair the klown in some mental or physical way. It took active, concerted effort not to further damage the reputation of trench coats.

"He said *fuck*," Syd informed them. "Who's an angry klown?"

At that, a few parents stood up. "Where'd you find these guys?" one of the dads yelled across the field to Kayla's mom.

"Yo, do you wanna *go*?" Blake shoved Syd's left shoulder. After not even a moment's pause, Syd roundhoused him in the stomach, and he crumpled. A few kids cheered and klapped. Nobody seemed totally sure what was part of the fictional klown performance and what was real.

Syd lifted his arms into the air like a terrorist giving himself up for arrest. "I'm done. But let's vote: who thinks Klown Blake won that klown kompetition?"

A few scattered affirmations from the kids, with an undercurrent of worried, buzzing chatter from the parents, one of whom (a dad) had Syd by the wrists and was pulling his arms behind his back as if to handcuff him.

"Who thinks Klown Sy—Klown Harold won?"

Whoops and applause. Syd wished he didn't derive satisfaction from such a paltry state of affairs.

And the last image Syd saw of the party before he was strongarmed off the premises was of Blake squirming around on his ass, trying to get to his knees, resembling a spun coin on its final few rotations.

Syd took a worn-out seat on Kayla's neighbors' curb, lit a cigarette, and cried. A thick, unnatural mucus developed in the back of his throat.

"You mind if I join you?"

He turned in the direction of the voice. Peter was squatting down on his left with a creaky, middle-aged difficulty.

"Sorry I ruined the party," Syd said quietly.

"*Ruined*? That's all anyone will be talking about for *weeks*. My son is gonna be impossible to shut up."

Syd shook his head, simpering.

Peter pinched his fingers in a mute request for a cigarette.

"You're a terrible father."

"You're a terrible clown." The cig bobbed in Peter's mouth as he struggled to ignite it. Syd offered him his own lighter just as he got a good one. "But one hell of a performer."

"What do you mean?"

"That thing you guys just did. You stole the show."

Did Peter perhaps think the outburst was a planned ordeal the way some of those other parents had? He seemed smarter than those other parents, so Syd doubted it.

"You're sick."

"I'm serious. I'm a filmmaker, you know."

"No way..."

"I am. And I know talent when I see it."

"I'm an actor." It seemed almost divinely prearranged.

"How'd you like to audition for my upcoming film?"

At this, Syd was thinking that either Peter was clinically insane or Syd was being messed with.

"Come on..."

"I'm serious. I'll give you my card. Come to my studio at nine AM Friday. I'll have the script ready."

✳   ✳   ✳

The rest of that day, Syd debated whether to tell Mitch what had happened. As a manager, Mitch had been just slightly more useless than a damp rag, but as a friend, he'd been somewhere between useless and mediocre, so Syd felt he owed it to him. When he did finally ring him up, it was in the middle of a CNO'ed-out midnight daze, and Mitch's voice was groggy on the other end.

"Syd, it's nearly one in the morning."

"I know. But I got an audition for a movie."

"You're kidding."

"Who's that?" a sleepy female voice asked.

"Syd. Shh, go back to sleep."

"Are you with a woman?" Syd wondered whether she knew that Mitch had asked to be his boyfriend before his manager.

"Yes."

Syd waited for him to elaborate, but he didn't. "Heard of Peter Rankin?"

"Hell, yes. Are you saying you got an audition for a Peter Rankin movie? Syd, that's insane. That's *prestige*. You're a skinny Philip Seymour Hoffman."

"All I had to do was beat up a birthday clown." He wasn't sure why he was telling Mitch the truth, but now that he'd started, he couldn't stop. "And I'm on drugs. Have been for years."

"I already knew that, and that's not important."

"You're not mad that I beat up a clown?"

"*Mad*? You could've *killed* someone and I'd be thrilled. Just don't make a habit of it. Bad for your image."

"Are you *serious*, Mitch?" the muffled female voice asked.

"Get off the drugs," Mitch went on. "Do whatever connection-granting violent acts you can get away with and none more." Syd hadn't seen this side of Mitch before—Mitch, who at Syd's last audition had given him itemized instructions for how not to breathe on anyone the wrong way. "You're going far, Syd Morris."

Then the line went silent. Syd lit another cigarette and cried again. He watched the smoke trickle out the window and drift away.

Art Imitates Life[2]

Most people go their whole lives without ever stepping foot onto a movie set, and there are a couple reasons for this. The first is that nearly every actor is the son or cousin or niece or sibling of some other actor or director or producer, so your average Joe is pretty insulated from the industry. The second is that entering a warehouse filled with expensive equipment and dozens of constructed environments that look like blown-up dollhouses permanently kills some of the big-screen magic. In any case, that's what I feel when I first lay eyes on the set of Peter Rankin's *Life Imitates Art*: a death of some kind of magic.

1. GETTING MY BEARINGS

When I arrive at PsychoNaut Studios on Wednesday, May 15, 2023, filming is slated to take seventy-seven days. This is day 12. A shaggy young man named Freddy greets me outside the main building, which looks like a sardine can scaled up by a factor of a billion, and introduces himself as my "volunteer tour guide"; it's unclear whether this is an official title or one he's given himself. He's an intern, about to begin his third year at NYU's Cinema Studies program, and he's very adamant that I'm in good hands.

The main building turns out to be the largest warehouse I've ever seen—so large that the mere fact of being indoors feels like an afterthought. Few people know that big enough warehouses get drafty from time to time. Freddy claims that there's a rocket factory at the Kennedy Space Center where it occasionally even *rains*. Since he's thus far demonstrated an impressive recall of useless informational bits, I ask him whether he knows how I might go about interviewing the director of *Life Imitates Art*, to which he has this to say:

---

2   Reproduced here is the journalistic piece that launched this entire project. Besides the pseudonymization and a few new editorial footnotes (henceforth designated "NEF") that I added during the editing process of this "novel," "Art Imitates Life" appears exactly as I sent it to the magazine.

"Oh, I don't think he'll want an interview. [Peter] is pretty private. I mean, he's not so much private as just really busy right now. He doesn't have much time for journalists, really."

2. WHAT THE ACTORS ARE LIKE

They are, for the most part, curt and snobbish in the particular way that being at the top of your craft makes you curt and snobbish. During my first day here, I accidentally brush by one Herman Floop, who asks me who the fuck I think I am. I nearly ask him the same—*would* ask him the same if I had a slightly larger set of figurative balls. According to Freddy, Floop[3] plays a reasonably small role in the film—only has about six lines total—and then he'll be back to his unglamorous day job of teaching acting classes in Delaware. I take a bit of pride in this knowledge.

3. WHAT *LIFE IMITATES ART* IS ABOUT

Based on what I've gathered from my time here, the general plot of the upcoming movie is as follows: a struggling Philadelphia visual artist, played by relatively unknown actor Syd Morris[4], paints and sculpts for a living. Only not a very good one—his stuff hardly ever sells, and in his stubborn refusal to invest in an MBA or get a job at a local grocery store, Morris is left working for scraps. Literally—several heartbreaking and mildly comedic scenes feature the fat-suit-less and teenage-bodied Morris crouched down in his studio eating what looks like chewy dog food off the floor. A few delightfully cringeworthy sequences show him pleading with museum curators, disgrun-

---

3   NEF: And in the interest of answering the obvious question, yes—his treatment of me *did* influence my decision to pseudonymize him in this way.

4   And he really looked the part. It's amazing what the right costuming can do. When I first spotted Syd Morris, he wore a blue tuxedo and had his hair combed back neatly and was clean-shaven enough to be mistakeable for someone who cannot yet grow facial hair. He also, at barely twenty-two, still had the wiry frame of a teenager, plus was portraying a character about eight or nine years older than himself, so he wore a modest fat suit and had some light crows' feet drawn around his eyes with makeup.

tledly setting up stations at local art shows, and even attempting to sell pieces off the side of the road at the Pennsylvania State Fair.

At the end of the state fair scene, after making exactly zero dollars in twelve hours, Morris is approached by a strange man dressed a bit like an oversized leprechaun, played by Herman Floop. Morris asks Floop whether he'd like to buy a piece, and Floop says that's not why he's there; instead, in the stereotypical mystical seer voice that tends to filmically signify magical properties of some sort, he proposes a deal: Morris will start selling art at a tremendous rate, provided he follows a couple rules: he must not fall in love with his artwork, and he must not sell his most valuable piece. The exchange takes place in the evening, and only about half of Floop's face is visible, illuminated by the dim lights of the creaky state fair rides, which illumination gives him a symbolically unsubtle yin/yang cast, and creaky-ride-induced screams echo in the background, so the scene possesses a palpably sinister vibe. We're led to believe Morris is skeptical of the offer, which he's (and likely you've) noticed bears an uncanny resemblance to those clichéd "man sells soul to devil at crossroads" tales, but he's too desperate to refuse.

In a pleasantly surprising turn of events, Morris sees an immediate influx of artistic success. For a while, he's doing well. He gains a fat suit and buys a nice blue tux. Art dealers wait outside his house in hours-long lines that seem to stretch out into infinite oblivion. He begins eating at lavishly expensive restaurants. Women take a newfound interest in him, and he courts so many he loses track—in one humorously awkward scene, he accidentally calls his expensive dinner date another woman's name, so she dumps champagne onto his head and storms out in a manner that both alludes to and parodies the pivotal pre-climactic clichés of traditional rom-coms. This segment foretells his downward spiral.

His doom is further forecasted when he paints a piece that threatens to sell for a million dollars—a life-sized portrait of a beautiful woman in a puffy lavender dress with flowing dirty-blonde hair prancing through a field of tall grass, holding an umbrella. Morris thinks back to the deal he made with the leprechaun and decides that since he (Morris) received the success he was promised, he kind of owes it to Floop to hold up his own side of the agreement. So he repeatedly rebuffs potential buyers, insisting that the lady is not for sale. He continues to paint and sculpt, and his lesser art continues to sell like hotcakes, and all the while, the million-dollar painting hangs, watching him, maybe even tormenting him a bit.

But then something a bit *Pygmalion*esque goes down. Morris's persistent refusal to sell the portrait means he's been spending quite a bit of time with it, and he soon finds himself falling in love with the lady he created. He skips out on art shows to consort with the inanimate painting. Women he priorly had on speed dial get left on read. Long compilations of short segments show Morris sitting in front of the painting and gazing into the woman's acrylic eyes, totally lovesick. At first, Morris doesn't know what to make of his feelings, and he spends a lot of time rationalizing them in schizoid sequences wherein he paces his studio erratically and mutters to himself while looking like he hasn't slept in days. He doesn't want to admit that he's broken one of the two sole stipulations of the deal he made with the garishly dressed devil. But the feelings persist. He becomes reclusive. He takes great pains to avoid letting the painting out of his sight, fearing what might happen to it while he's away.

Then the movie takes an Ovidianly predictable surrealist turn: the woman in the painting comes to life in the form of actress Ola Benson—as in, Benson steps out of the frame and begins strolling casually around Morris's workspace. It's not initially clear whether this is a literal coming-to-life or Morris is simply off his rocker, because whenever any third party enters the room—a potential buyer, generally—Benson tucks herself comfortably back into her painting dreamscape, thus becoming a living woman imitating a mere painting: Life imitating Art.

At first, Benson's literalization is a literal dream come true to Morris, who can now exchange lovesick niceties with her and ideally receive niceties back, but we (and Morris) soon learn that Benson does not share her creator's romantic feelings. Morris makes a number of attempts to court her, all of which she turns down. In one overly dramatic sequence, he brings a dozen roses up to his studio, and she rips the flowers off their stems one by one with her teeth, spitting confetti of red in Morris's general direction while he clasps his face in horror and cries. Morris grows increasingly distraught, and eventually, sleep-deprived and at the end of his psychological rope, he offers Benson an ultimatum: take him as her lover, or he will sell her. He's already broken one stipulation of the deal, he figures, and he's already forfeited his dignity, his sanity, and many other -ities too numerous to even attempt to count, so what more does he have to lose? Benson turns him down once again, and Morris says All right then—you'll be sold first thing tomorrow.

Tomorrow comes, and it looks like everything might work out okay for Morris after all. In just a few short hours, he'll finally be free of his anguish and can resume his former life as an unsuccessful, starving artist who eats dog food off his studio floor. The movie's final scene opens to show the woman back inside her painting, the sunrise's rays adorning her with an allegorically obvious halo, while Morris snores peacefully in the bed he moved to his studio with the intent of spending every waking and sleeping moment with the painting. Morris sits up, stretches, and rubs his eyes, a soon-to-be dramatically ironic grin plastered across his smug face. He taunts Benson, who remains inanimate. He dares her to make some sort of move before he enacts his final will upon her. It's your last chance, he says. Now or never. The doorbell rings. Morris announces to the two-dimensional painting that oh look, here's the buyer now; time to let him in.

His back is only turned for a second, but that's all the time Benson needs. In a seeming thematic nod to Wilde's *Dorian Gray* (this film is absolutely replete with literary reference), Benson steps out of the frame and impales Morris in the back of the head with the tip of her umbrella, which Morris apparently painted sharply enough for it to function as a lethal weapon. Morris falls to the ground, dead, and the film's final shot is of his cold, lifeless eyes staring back at us as the camera slowly zooms out and invites us to ponder the fact that now *Morris* is an inanimate object upon whom someone else has enacted her will, and isn't that a neat and ironic little reversal?

4. MEAT PUPPETS

During Thursday's lunch break, while I eat my room-temperature turkey sandwich, provided gratis by [magazine name redacted] staff, I lurk at the camera crew's table with the intent of learning a few things about the actual filming process. And I do, but my main reve-lations pertain to actors, or more accurately, how actors are perceived by those who spend their days watching them. The three cameramen and one camerawoman at my table were gracious enough to let me re-cord their conversation so that I could include it word-for-word here. I've transcribed the relevant portion below:

Greg: So what are we thinkin'? Meat puppet or no?
Kyle: Who? The kid?
Greg: [nods, shovels some mashed potatoes into his mouth]
Raya: Too soon to tell.
Greg: Really? I think he's got it. I think he might be a real meat puppet.
Me: Sorry to interrupt. "Meat puppet"?
Scott: Like a good actor, man. A full-on actor. [turns to Greg] It's your term; how would you describe it?
Greg: [swallows another bite of potatoes, his Adam's Apple bob-bing buoyishly] So you know how there are some actors who get type-cast? You know what typecast is, right?
Me [starting to suspect that they think I'm dumber than I actual-ly am]: Yeah, of course.
Raya: It's like the opposite of that.
Kyle: Well, not the *opposite*, but usually, typecast actors just play some variation of their actual selves. Like, when I worked with Har-rison Ford, he just plays [sic] different variations of Harrison Ford, you know?
Me: You worked with Harrison Ford?
Kyle [not acknowledging the question, making it unclear whether he heard me or is even still talking to me]: He's great, but he's not a meat puppet.
Greg: His approach to acting is just: what if I played myself and modified whichever traits are specific to this character?
Raya: Yeah, but see, is that not what *everyone* does?
Greg: [shakes head vociferously, his bangs flying all over the place] Meat puppets *don't*. They start from scratch. You take a non-meat-puppet: first thing he does is ask, "How do I behave like this person?" Assumes a baseline and copy-pastes ninety-nine percent of his man-

nerisms onto the character. The first thing a meat puppet does is ask, "How do I act *human*?" He builds a whole person from scratch. His body becomes a vessel for the character. Hence, meat puppet. He allows the character to use his mortal, flesh body like a puppet.

Kyle: It's kind of unsettling to interact with meat puppets off set though. Impossible to know who they really are—whether they have a soul or a personality of their own. Extremely rare type of actor.

Me: And you're wondering whether [Syd Morris]...?

Greg: Really rare to see genuine meat puppets this young. That's the only thing that's giving me pause. He'd have to be like an actual genius.

Raya: He did sort of come out of nowhere.

Scott: Hey, can you turn that off a second?

Me: The tape recorder?

Scott: Yeah. Can you turn it off?

So by this point, I'm intrigued, and my overall goal/*raison* has shifted from "find out what the filmmaking process is like" to "find out whether Syd Morris is a meat puppet."

5. WHAT PETER RANKIN IS LIKE

Rankin is a famously erratic director, but those who work with him admire that about him. He often writes scenes the night before they're scheduled to be filmed and makes his actors learn their lines the day of, which gives his movies a deer-in-headlights quality. Before shooting sessions begin, the nervous echo of flipping script pages fills the air. Rehearsals for scenes that will shoot later can be viewed in little gray studio rooms, and while these sessions are worth attending if only for novelty reasons, you likely won't stay long—they're infuriatingly dull and repetitive and make you want to pull your hair out.

I watch Rankin on set between takes, and he's got a manic energy—he's flying all over the place, barking orders without caring who gets caught in the salivary crossfire, occasionally stopping to rub his nose or sniff suspiciously. He's animated and perpetually in the zone. He and Syd Morris seem tight even though they're several decades apart in age and this is Morris's first film. They behave like old chums, and I suspect that they will work together in the future.[5] Morris, despite acting doucheily around his costars and the film crew, is frankly charming and gracious toward Rankin—comes across as the sort of person you'd love to take out for coffee and pick the brains of. Which brings me to...

6. WHAT SYD MORRIS IS LIKE

I think this one can be distilled down to a few concrete examples:

1. When Peter Rankin asks him whether he'd like to reshoot a short portion of the "devil-holds-up-his-side-of-the-deal-and-artist-starts-making-bank" montage, Morris asks in return whether this will mean showing up for another day of filming and being "forced" to accept more money. He says it in a tongue-and-cheek tone that cleverly implies both 1) that his answer to Peter's question is dependent on financial considerations and 2) that he realizes it's a bit assholeish for his answer to be dependent on financial considerations. Everyone around him begrudgingly laughs.

2. When I approach him between shooting sessions in the hopes of interviewing him and learning a bit more about his acting "process," he points to my notepad and says, "Sorry. I only autograph body parts." He leaves the "body parts" in question to the imagination.

3. On day three of filming, Syd slips outside for a smoke break, and I join him. When he offers me a cigarette, I tell him I'm trying to quit.[6] He scoffs, blows out a long stream of smoke while squinting directly at the sun, and says, "Can't imagine that's working out well for you if you're constantly taking smoke breaks with smokers." "I'm microdosing," I reply, quick on my feet as any reporter must be. "Detoxing. I'm inhaling secondhand smoke the way some people apply

---

5   NEF: This prediction turned out to be wrong.

6   Which is true.

nicotine patches."[7] He raises an eyebrow as if seriously weighing the merits of that idea. I ask how long he's been acting. "I'm not talking to the press," he says flatly. "I'm not the press, really," I tell him, "and I'm just making conversation." He takes another puff. "Whatever the fuck you are," gesturing contemptuously with the hand that isn't holding the cigarette. The hand that *is* holding the cigarette holds it loosely between his first and middle fingers—a telltale sign of an expert smoker. Another telltale sign is the way he French-inhales each puff a few times before blowing it out, leaving very little secondhand smoke for me to "detox" with, which I secretly appreciate. I ask, "Man of few words, huh?" "I can neither confirm nor deny without a lawyer present." "I get that. As a writer, I feel like people are always trying to legally corner me for technicalities." My tape recorder has been on this whole time. "Right?" he exclaims, his eyes lighting up. I say, "Yep. If you have any sort of commitment to the truth—to presenting your art the way you want to—you're bound to get sued from time to time." "*Tell* me about it." Shakes his head tiredly while he sighs/exhales smoke. "Like, I sometimes worry some reporter will find out how I—" He falls silent. "Oh, okay," he says, pointing at me vehemently with the cigarette stub. A few sparks nearly hit my chest and then fall invisibly to the ground. "*I* see what you're doing. Very tricky." "What?" "Reporting," he answers. Takes another drag. "You know, you're not half-bad, for a reporter. Most just wanna shove cameras in my face. You're sneaky about it. I'll have to keep my eyes peeled."

7. THINGS TAKE A WILD TURN, OR, THE PORTION OF THE ESSAY MY EDITORS WILL PROBABLY CUT FOR LEGAL REASONS[8]

The odd escapade that follows commences on day two, immediately after cameraman Scott asked me to shut off my recording device. When I did, he gave me a dubious invitation, which I started taking

---

7   Which is less true, but he proved annoyingly difficult to corner, mainly because he kept a brooding redheaded man within nine or ten feet of him at all times; seriously, this guy shadowed him like a body double.

8   NEF: Unsurprisingly, they did cut it. Since the essay was never published, I'm reinserting it.

notes on before I was swiftly encouraged to stop doing that as well. But in my frustration at having my journalistic integrity compromised (the first of several frustrations, the others soon to come), I later wrote out a paraphrased version of the conversation, which, because I transcribed it from memory, is probably not one hundred percent accurate, but I do pride myself on having a pretty stellar memory:

Scott: Do you wanna go to poker night tomorrow at this guy Mitch's house?
Me: Sure.

So when I arrive home after my second day on set, I embark on some research. I view about twenty different YouTube crash courses on how to play poker and observe the identical affectless drawl with which every instructor speaks. I take detailed notes spanning four pages and contemplate including them in here but then figure I don't want to piss off my editors even more than I inevitably already will when I turn this thing in. I imagine a variety of hypothetical poker hands and decide whether I'll bet, raise, or fold in each scenario. I stay up so late studying that the entirety of day three is a blur because I'm constantly dozing off, even while watching my new cameraman/woman friends film the movie's pivotal climactic scene. Every time I close my eyes, I hallucinate images of Bicycle playing cards floating across the insides of my lids. I practice what I'm going to say if the other players try to peer-pressure me into betting real money ("I'm a starving artist. Just like Morris in the film, come to think of it. Life really does imitate art, huh?").

I arrive at the house, which is fairly large and makes me wonder again what this Mitch guy's job is, and knock on the front door. I wait. After probably half a minute or so, Scott comes around through the back gate, sporting a purple Hawaiian shirt, an unlit cigarette dangling from his thin lips, and leads me to Mitch's basement's backyard entrance with the trademark gangly saunter of the disproportionately tall and skinny. "He doesn't like guests snooping around other parts of the house," Scott explains.

When I enter the basement, a couple things immediately stand out. The first is that the place looks wholly uninhabited. There are no couches, no family photos, nothing. A complete blank slate minus the dark-beige carpet, which has some scattered stains on it. The second is that nobody is playing poker. People drink, smoke, consort, and wait in line at a single card table, where Mitch sits poker-faced collecting what seems to be cash while a couple men and one woman type furiously on outdated Dell computers.

"[Scott], my man," says one mildly hammered guy who looks like he belongs to a frat for midlife crisis-sufferers. He slaps Scott's hand testosteronically. Then he scans me up and down. "Who's she?"

"Potential buyer," Scott replies. "Hannah, are you taking notes again?" He snatches the notebook out of my hand, spends a few seconds reading my near-illegible first page, and then rips it out. "None of this, okay?" He waves the mildly crumpled sheet in my face like someone scolding a dog for pissing on the hardwood floor.

"What's going on?" I ask.

"Yo, are you recording?" The guy points to the microphone clipped to my collar.

"She's a reporter," Scott mutters.

"You brought a *reporter* to—"

"Shh." Scott holds up a hand. Points at me. "Turn it off."

I pretend to click the tape recorder's power switch, which is admittedly not my most journalistically integrous moment, but I have an overwhelming intuitive sense that I'm not going to want to miss what follows. However, I'm not a meat puppet, so Scott subsequently grabs it and turns it off for real.

"Can you do *anything* without taping or writing it down?" he asks angrily (paraphrased, off the record).

"It's kind of my job."

"Not now, it's not. You're not on the job right now, okay? Cut it out."

"Why'd you bring her here?" the other guy complains.

"I thought she'd wanna make an investment."

"When does the poker start?" I pipe up, though I've already pretty much discerned that this isn't a casual poker night.

He sighs. "This is all off the record, yeah?"

I nod.

"This isn't a casual poker night."

8. SECOND SECTION THAT WILL PROBABLY GET THE AXE: MY REVELATION

"You're all meat puppets," is what I now say something along the lines of. "It's not just the actors. You've spent so much time *watching* the actors that you've absorbed their entire ethos. You all live lies.

"You lured me here under false pretenses. You made me waste my time viewing instructional poker videos. And for what?"[9]

9. THIRD SECTION THAT WILL ALMOST CERTAINLY BE PRONOUNCED D.O.A.: THE ANSWER TO THE RHETORICAL QUESTION RAISED AT THE END OF SECTION 8

It turns out that there's some kind of hush-hush illegal stock-trading operation going on involving real people, many of whom are actors in the very film that is the subject of this essay. Ola Benson is one. Syd Morris is another. Syd and his potential meat-puppet status are the talk of the warehouse, and owners of Syd shares are trying to get more people to invest in him because it will mean an increase in his value.

10. WRAPPING UP

On Saturday afternoon, the cast, director, crew, and I all go out for friendly drinks at Winston's Brew. I observe the ways in which the cast, director, and crew behave just like one big family might. Positive sentiments abound.

CONCLUSION

I don't know whether Syd Morris is a meat puppet. To be honest, I'm not convinced that his meat puppet status will ultimately affect his career prospects. After all, actors are *more* than their onscreen

---

9   Okay, so what I really said wasn't quite this grand or dramatic and involved significantly more stuttering. Without my trusty tape recorder or notepad, creative liberties had to be taken.

jobs—they have entire manufactured "personas" or "essences" that they purport to embody in real life, off camera. And because they've already proven that they can live lies convincingly, we have no way of knowing whether these personas are any more "real" than the movie characters they play. In Morris's case, it's this *offscreen* persona, not his acting skills, that I anticipate may someday sink him.

But who knows. Perhaps, when the predictable results of his occasionally-charming assholery come to fruition, he'll simply shapeshift into something else, leaving the public to wonder, much as I've wondered these past few days, who the *true* Syd Morris is—whether he even exists as an independent entity or is merely a hollowed-out shell that takes on the personality of whoever he needs to be in any given moment. And maybe he's not unique in that sense.

So I guess the real question is whether this matters.

6

The whirlwind year that followed Syd's birthday party appearance was possibly the most exhilarating of his life. Celebrity buzz around him increased, even with *Life Imitates Art* still in post-production. With a Rankin project on his resume, he scored a single-episode bit part on Season 7 of a popular, mid-shark-jump comedy show. Fans liked him so much that his character was written into four additional episodes. He landed supporting roles in *Sgt. Nebula* (a shlocky sci-fi series with a cultlike fanbase) and *MusicaLaw* (an art film starring Ned Wesham and directed by Shannon Marshall—both pretty big names in the indie scene). At Our Lady of Intense and Perpetual Suffering High School, while he warmed up for what would be the last motivational speech of his life, a nun asked for his autograph.

And Mitch was absolutely glowing with youthful delight and prosperous warmth. He delivered groceries biweekly to Syd's apartment and drove him to and from rehearsals. Syd still wasn't nearly famous enough to be recognized regularly, but he'd been wary about showing his face ever since a harrowing accostation at a Trader Joe's involving a Sharpie and an unsheathed penis. He now seldom left his house and even seldomer got visitors besides Mitch, who by this point more or less just walked right in through the back door, never bothering to knock or even take his shoes off, so you can probably imagine Syd's surprise when his doorbell—a doorbell he confesses to not being aware he even *had*, before this precise instant—made its presence known.

Syd didn't have a peephole, so he placed a steak knife into his back pocket for self-defense reasons, not wanting to find himself in a John Lennon scenario. While he warily cracked his apartment door, which opened motel-like to the great outdoors and somehow both squeaked and rattled, he tried to give off the impression that his hand was just casually resting on his ass.

The man standing outside looked oddly familiar. He had round glasses and a bowtie and a slim-fit tweed jacket and basically looked as if he'd forgotten his cane and top hat in his car. Syd considered telling him this last part but didn't want to risk a wrong-footed start.

"Sydney Morris?" the man tried.

Syd flicked his forehead with his free hand, trying to scramble his brain enough to identify the man. "Yep."

"I'm Stanley Morris." Extended his right hand, straight and firm. "Your father."

Syd's own right hand's fingers were still wrapped loosely around the handle of the knife, and he had a brief and intrusive vision of plunging it hilt-deep into the visitor's chest—a scarily tantalizing prospect—but then settled for just not shaking the guy's hand. "No, you're not." But he'd known the instant Stanley had opened his mouth that he was, much the way a word that was just on the tip of your tongue seems obvious the moment someone says it.

"I am. May I come in?"

Syd didn't answer, but Stanley entered nonetheless. "A bit of a mess."

"You don't get to decide to finally start parenting me *now*."

"I know, I know." Stanley rubbed his pointer finger along the arm of Syd's couch, sniffed it as if checking for radioactive waste, and took a posh seat.

"How did you find me?" Syd hadn't seen or spoken to his father since he was of single digit age. When his parents had split, his mom had gotten sole custody, and his dad had left the country. *Syd* would have had difficulty finding *him*.

"Came upon your website. Contacted your manager. He gave me the details. What was his name...?"

"Mitch?"

"Yeah, that was it." Stanley affected a pseudo-Transatlantic accent, which, along with the bowtie and jacket, seemed scrupulously engineered to give him an air of class, but Syd knew better.

"*Mitch* told you where I lived?" Syd had been under the impression that Mitch respected his privacy, but he apparently respected his celebrity a lot more.

"Mm. Take a seat, son." For Syd was still standing, about equidistant from the door and the couch, alternating his weight back and forth between his two feet, trying to decide whether to sit next to the man who had sired him or evacuate the apartment in his socks and immediately find a new place to live and then not give Mitch or his father or anyone the new address. Become an unlisted shadow-person living in an elaborate mansion in the middle of a huge field in Wyoming or somewhere—it's not like he was hurting for money anymore.

"Why are you here?" Syd asked, his voice reverberating backward through his ears in that particular way that always preceded a CNO comedown.

Stanley then began a long and convoluted rant about how he'd been driving a product shipment truck cross-country (see? Syd had known the wealth thing was a put-on; he imagined Stanley taking his week's pay and asking the sales associate at Kohl's to make him look like Cary Grant), listening to the radio broadcast of a well-known talk show host I'm not at legal liberty to identify here, and sure enough, Syd's name had been mentioned in connection with some art film, and at first, Stanley had thought it must be a different Syd Morris, but then the talk show host and his guest had further elaborated on Syd's appearance, while dropping more expletives than Stanley could count—what was the need for so many fucking expletives these days? (expletive mine)—and anyway, yes, the host had gone back and forth with the celebrity guest, who had mentioned that Syd was twenty-one, and the talk show host had said to wait while he pulled something up on his phone and then confirmed that actually, Syd had turned twenty-*two* this year—birthday on April 5, 2001, according to his *Wikipedia* page (here, Stanley took a brief verbal detour to elaborate on the utter unbelievability of Syd possessing an actual Wikipedia page)—and Stanley said that by this point, evidence of this Syd Morris being his own offspring was mounting because how many Syd Morrises had been born on that day of that month of that year? So he'd contacted Syd's manager, and (the Transatlantic accent really slipping now) here he was.

Syd gave him a few slow nods. "So that's it, then? You came to cash in on my fame...or whatever?"

"I determined I could actually *find* you," Stanley replied. "Before then, I had no clue where you were. And your mother was obviously of no help."

"My mother doesn't know where I am either."

"Right."

A stilted distance separated them—an invisible barrier like the energy that stops two negatively charged magnets from connecting. Syd had played with magnets a lot as a kid, always trying to force together the ones that wanted nothing more than to stay apart.

"Did you ever think of reaching out back when you *did* know where I was, Stanley?"

"You can call me Dad."

"Like, sometime during the fifteen years I lived at the house you ditched, for example?"

"I didn't *ditch*; your mother kicked me out."

"Ever think of calling me up on my birthday or sending me a note in the mail or giving me some indication that you're still alive and still think about me more than once every decade?"

"Your mother wouldn't have let me talk to you on the phone. And if I'd written, she would have just thrown it out."

"How do you *know* that if you didn't even *try*? You're a poor excuse for a human being and an even worse excuse for a father."

Stanley's eyes looked genuinely sad—the brand of sadness you can't fake unless you're a really good actor. Syd liked to think that his own acting had reached the level where *he* could fake that kind of sadness, if he wanted to. But right now, he was faking callous indifference.

"I'm sorry," Stanley said. "Does that help? Is that what you wanted to hear? Do you want money?"

"I *have* money. It's *you* who should be asking for money from *me*."

"Can I have some money?" Stanley said weakly, and Syd couldn't be sure whether he was attempting to play off a genuine request as a joke or truly joking.

"No. Get out."

"Can't we have a relationship now?"

"Why? Hoping I put you in my will for when I fucking OD? Bold of you to assume *you* won't OD first. Which of us is it gonna be, *Dad*?" He tried to make the word sound even harsher than "Stanley." "Huh? Who's gonna overdose first?"

Stanley cleared his throat and made eye contact with an empty Pepsi can on the floor. "I'll have you know I've been clean for two years now."

"*Great.* I've been clean for—" Syd used his free hand to check his phone, whose lockscreen's background was a selfie he'd taken with Mitch in the break room on *Life Imitates Art*'s first day of filming. "—thirty-nine minutes. And it's already been far too long. Get the fuck out so I can relapse, already."

"It's, uh...*disappointing* to hear that you've picked up substances," Stanley said with not even the remotest semblance of a Transatlantic accent.

"Yeah, well. Maybe if I'd had a father to tell me not to, things would have turned out differently. Unfortunately, at around the time I was picking up substances, my dad was likely off smoking deluxe meth somewhere in Aruba."

Stanley loosened his bowtie. "I can help you get clean, if you want. I can—"

"I don't need your fucking help. I've made it twenty-two years without even a lick of assistance from you, and I don't see that changing now." Stanley now sat hunched over in a near-fetal position, and Syd felt a bit bad for him. For the first time in his life, he experienced *pity* toward the man who, up until this point, had been the recipient of only some abstract, theoretical, objectless hate. Now that the hate had a form, it didn't stick. He didn't hate this guy. Couldn't. "I hate you, man."

"You don't mean that. You're acting. You're an actor."

"I've never been more serious in my life."

"Still acting." He began laughing, but it wasn't a laugh of hilarity—it was the haunting cackle of a clown, with a deep and volatile sadness lingering just below the surface. "You're tricky. Almost got me."

"Get out."

So Stanley did as he was told. While he headed out to his car, Syd called, "You forgot your top hat and cane!"

✳   ✳   ✳

The next time Mitch stopped by to drive Syd to rehearsal, he entered Syd's apartment through the back door and waltzed casually over to his couch. Syd, embroiled in his fourth binge-viewing of *Breaking Bad*, didn't greet him.

Mitch said, "Ready to rock and roll?" with the affect of a WASPy father who's just finished using a restaurant bathroom while his three kids waited in the "How many for tonight? Four? Come with me" area.

Syd clicked the volume up a few notches, wishing Mitch would take a hint. "*You got me riding shotgun to every dark anal recess of this state,*" Jesse Pinkman complained. "*Be nice if you clued me in a little.*"

"Everything okay, man?" Mitch asked.

Syd looked up at him with an annoyed reluctance. "Why did you sic my father on me?"

"Your...oh, Stanley?"

"Don't play dumb. Who else?"

Mitch sighed and sat down next to Syd, who immediately moved away. "He called me and said he wanted to reconnect with you. He seemed genuine. And I assumed you'd feel the same."

"You don't think his 'wanting to reconnect' has *anything* to do with me being a shit-tier celebrity now?"

"Maybe. A bit. Why does it matter?"

But Mitch knew all about Syd's dad—knew the entire sordid saga of Syd's childhood, in fact. Sure, it was an uneven arrangement—Syd still didn't know whether Mitch had siblings, or whether he talked to his parents, or whether those parents were even still alive, and Syd had never pressed him on it—but Syd had told Mitch things he'd never told anybody else, and Mitch had looked him in the eye and nodded at all the right times, and when Mitch had said he felt sorry, Syd had believed him.

"I've been unusually gracious toward you," Syd reminded him. "I gave you staple art."

"You *sold* me staple art," he replied, eyeing the selection of pieces currently stacked against the wall as if sizing them up for how well they'd do on the black market. Mitch looked at Syd that way too, sometimes.

"Look, if we're going to go on...like this. Having a relationship and all that." He didn't elaborate on what he meant by "relation-ship"—didn't fully know himself. "I need to know you're on my side.

Like, that you're working for *me*. I don't know much about management, but everyone I've talked to has said that's the way it's supposed to function."

"Of course," Mitch replied. "I've always been on your side."

Syd wasn't convinced. But no matter how many peculiarities he noted—like the fact that Mitch had propositioned Syd but now seemed by all accounts to have a girlfriend or maybe a whole slew of girlfriends, or that he was wealthier than the management of one microcelebrity could really account for, or that he hated Syd's staple art but had paid him $400 for a single piece—Syd still couldn't cohere it into a picture that made any sense. He was missing a dimension. He knew he was being used, somehow, but he enjoyed the use—had gotten addicted to being treated like a human being with merits the way he'd gotten addicted to CNO and cigarettes and a whole bunch of other things he knew were bad for him in the long run.

"But the thing with my dad..."

"I wouldn't have done it if I hadn't thought it was in your best interests. I still maintain that it probably was. But I should have asked you first. Boner on my part. I'm truly sorry."

And Syd believed it—or at least, he could trick himself into thinking he did if he unfocused the part of the brain that controls logical thinking, like how you can blur your vision by unfocusing your eyes. His thoughts were blurry, and nothing made sense, and everything felt both wrong and right at the same time.

"Now get your shoes on, and let's book it," Mitch said.

Syd obeyed, turning briefly away from Mitch, but he glanced back just in time to see his manager slip something into his tote.

Syd froze. "What's that?"

"What's what?"

"In your bag."

Mitch furrowed his brow in insincere confusion.

Syd snatched the tote and pulled out a staple-punctured canvas. "*Stealing* from me, *Dad*?" He hadn't intended to say that last word.

"I was going to pay," Mitch said with the cadence of an experienced liar. He didn't comment on the slip.

"It's not for *sale*," Syd exclaimed, setting it down by the others and vowing then and there to never again let Mitch out of his sight.

"*We having second thoughts?*" Walter and Skyler White's mortgage broker asked..
"*Every second of every day.*"

7

On the surface, Syd continued to prosper. He shot his scenes for *MusicaLaw* in late 2023. *Sgt. Nebula* entered the final stages of production, and the cast planned to promote it at the 2024 World Science Fiction Convention in Seattle. With Mitch's help, he moved out of his old, dingy apartment and into a swanky Manhattan suite. Mitch brought his girlfriend Hayley along, and there was an odd secrecy to the whole episode, with Mitch and Hayley constantly exchanging mute expressions but not really saying much. Their chemistry was not that of intimate partners but of actors who'd been cast as intimate partners in a low-budget porno flick and were trying to navigate how to interact offscreen and fully clothed. She would grab something, and Mitch would step aside as if dodging a laser in a low-budget spy movie. They'd ask Syd logistical questions that were clearly intended for each other. They'd make accidental eye contact and then break it. While Mitch carried Syd's CNO-dusted coffee table to the moving van, Syd asked Hayley how long the two of them had been together, but she seemed unable to answer even *that*, let alone inquiries about Mitch's other clients, his net worth, etc.

Though *Life Imitates Art* had premiered months ago, Syd still spent much of his recreational time getting high with Peter Rankin, whose drug of choice was cocaine. Peter often stopped by Syd's new apartment uninvited, where the two would proceed to snort various substances and put on some dumb TV show and laugh until they couldn't breathe. Syd now split his time more or less evenly between Mitch and Peter, and Mitch had begun to give off the whiny and jealous impression of someone who feels he's being edged out. He was, in a way. Peter had an openness Mitch lacked.

"My wife is divorcing me," Peter told Syd during one coke-fueled session at Syd's place.

Syd spluttered, choking on nothing. He began to chuckle but then thought better of it. "Not a surprise."

"You can laugh; you can laugh."

But now that Peter had made the formal invitation, Syd wasn't quite sure what he found funny.

"She wants to know why I'm spending more time with you than my own kids," he went on, emanating still-inexplicable hilarity.

"Oh, God. That's a *good* one."

His voice levelled out to a deadly serious flatness. "So I thought you could enlighten me."

Syd shrugged. "If you don't enjoy it, then stop."

"I enjoy it," Peter replied, though Syd himself had to admit that pushing fifty and kicking back with someone barely old enough to be out of college was an unconventional choice. Pathetic, almost, though Syd didn't personally think so—it's more just that he could see how someone *might*. "I'm just trying to figure out what it is about *you*."

Syd, who'd received less than the healthy recommended dosage of attention in childhood and hadn't expected adulthood to be any different, couldn't provide much insight. The Christian school thing had felt like his first real big break—totally surprising but intoxicating in some perverse way. Finally—suddenly—his specific brand of charisma filled a niche. But of course, it wasn't real. Some part of him always knew the "him" those Christian teachers loved was an unreal, fictional incarnation. And now, people loved him for precisely his ability to convincingly portray unreality. The unreality had become more transparent, perhaps, but it hadn't become any realer. Nobody except for Mitch had ever shown any interest in his true self.

"Do your Marlon Brando impression," Peter said now. "It might cheer me up."

* * *

If Syd had been paying more attention to the signs, he would have foreseen the dreaded phone call that changed everything. But despite his suspicions and confusions, Mitch was the one person he'd expected to remain a constant. The fans were fleeting—here one day, replaced by others the next. Syd assumed Peter would someday outgrow the midlife crisis his friendship with Syd was a sure sign of. But

Mitch wouldn't let him down. Syd had never so much as considered the *possibility* of Mitch letting him down.

The call came late on the night of Syd's twenty-third birthday. Whether Mitch knew it was Syd's birthday or had simply lost track of time due to his own multitude of issues is still not clear to me. Syd's phone's buzz jolted him from that transient not-quite-asleep state where you're sure you're falling to death one second and then thankful to be alive the next. Episodes like those were the only real times he felt thankful to be alive.

"Mitch?"

"I quit."

Syd moved the phone to the other ear, its blue light leaving a blinding tracer in his otherwise black field of vision.

"What do you mean?"

"Being your manager. I'm done."

Syd waited for him to elaborate on what was surely a practical joke. "Why?"

"You *really* don't know why?"

Syd shook his head, forgetting Mitch couldn't see him.

"Come on...take a look at all that's happened this past year. I can't keep doing you favors. You're a ticking time bomb."

"Do you want me to pay you?" Things still wouldn't ever be the same between them, but Syd could mentally block out the transactions and pretend nothing had changed.

"No amount of money could make me keep working for you. So get that through your thick skull, huh?" The way he said it felt artificial and borderline rehearsed.

Syd opened his mouth, waiting for an objection to materialize, but his now-ex manager had already hung up.

So he sat dumbstruck for a few minutes, passing his phone back and forth between his hands, feeling mercilessly and inconsolably alone. He poured out a line of CNO but lacked the resolve necessary to consume it. Finally, without much conscious deliberation, he platonically booty-called Peter, who picked up immediately. "Syd?"

"You're awake!"

"Syd, are you okay?"

"My manager dumped me."

"Ah, well. Who needs him?" Peter's voice sounded chipmunked and overcharged. Syd never noticed his intoxication when he himself was tweaked out, but right now, it was painfully apparent.

"Are you high?"

"As usual, baby."

"I wanna talk to you for *real*, Peter."

Peter let out what sounded like a sharp exhale. "What do you mean, for real?"

"Man-to-man."

"Lay it on me."

"Do you ever wish you could live your life over again? See where you went wrong?"

"I dunno, man."

"Seriously. You understand, I would think. Your marriage is falling apart—"

"Oh, and is *your* marriage falling apart, Sydney?" He guffawed again. Syd wished he could punch him through the phone. "Boy, that's a good one. A real knee-slapper. Don't develop personal feelings for your employees. Get a new manager."

"I don't want a new manager—I want Mitch."

"Managers with ten times Mitch's expertise must be busting down your door with requests by now, I would think. Hell, just a couple months ago...at the premiere. God, what was her name?" A few finger-snaps sounded through the phone speaker. "You've got options, is what I'm saying."

And Peter was right, but Syd had turned everyone else down. He didn't see the point in taking on a business relationship with someone who only believed in him because things were already going well. He needed someone who'd been there from the start.

"I'm telling you, man, this is a total non-issue," Peter reassured him. "You're being a little diva about it."

"Can you just like...tell me you're sorry or something?"

"Look, it's late, I'm wired, and I'm not sorry—why would I be sorry? This is all part of the game. You'll forget about it within a week."

And then he was gone. All things considered, this was only Syd's second worst birthday.

Victims of Mitch Anonymous[10]

Today's date is March 12, 2024, and I'm attending a support group meeting—not for addicts or cancer patients or grieving loved ones of the tragically deceased but for "victims" of one "Mitchell Larkin." Mitch's existence was made known to me last year on the set of *Life Imitates Art*, and at the time, he struck me as an innocuous figurant in the grand scheme of things, but he's apparently got quite a few skeletons in his closet.

Seven, to be exact. For skeletons, they look pretty good—a few of them are a bit on the skinny side, but overall, they appear normal and well-adjusted. I recognize two: Paul Anger, a leather-clad pop-punk singer whose music was foisted on me once during an eight-hour car ride and made me contemplate highway suicide, and Chrissy Might, an actress who, if I remember correctly, played the wife of Jason Segel in some film or TV show. Upon learning Nell Sullivan's name, I recognize her too—I saw her art at a museum in D.C. once. The others don't ring any bells. There's Benji Manheim, a goth actor who has appeared in some low-budget art films; Grace Reilly, a washed-up music biographer who looks like a spitting image of my not-so-distant future; Lisa Price, a fitness "influencer" whose actual day-to-day occupation eludes me; and Henry Friendly, a YouTuber with 1.7 million subscribers[11] and the most uneven haircut I've ever seen—seriously, his barber deserves jail time.

But being moderately famous isn't the only thing these people have in common—they've also all dated Mitch Larkin. They also all began dating him before they became famous, during which time they gave him some then-trivial but later-valuable gifts. They're also all no longer dating him. You probably get the gist.

---

10   The first sequel to "Art Imitates Life," as promised in the preface.

11   He really wants us to know the exact number, too. Whenever he discusses his audience, it's never his "subscribers" but his "1.7 million subscribers." Example: "Last week, when I was developing a promotionary [sic] contest for my 1.7 million subscribers…"

Henry, the session facilitator, has allowed me to sit in on the meeting because he's under the impression that I'm writing a hit-piece on Mitch. I am permitted to take notes but not to record. I'm also permitted to ask questions, but support group members reserve the right to not answer them.[12] I've agreed not to use anyone's real name.

Though I've never taken part in any sort of recovery group, Victims of Mitch Anonymous (VMA) seems to follow the format of a typical twelve-step meeting for alcoholics or drug addicts. It's actually a very distant offshoot of those organizations—Henry had a "pretty wicked coke addiction" in his mid-twenties, and participants in his local Narcotics Anonymous chapter selflessly and compassionately motivated him to make some tough but necessary changes in his life. That was where he met Grace—NA—and after learning that they'd both been wronged by the same exact Mitch, they spent some time mutually pondering how many others Mitch had screwed over, and an idea dawned on Henry—an idea brilliant enough to broadcast to his entire then-1.3-million-person audience of YouTube subscribers, which was how the other five regular VMA members caught wind of the Program.[13]

Much like all drug addicts' stories follow the same trajectory (begin recreationally ingesting drug, begin compulsively ingesting drug, realize drug is necessary for daily functioning, make some unsuccessful half-assed attempts to quit drug, join a twelve-step program), so do all of Mitch's exes' stories (get wooed by Mitch, date him, enjoy dating him, give him gifts of priceless art the way any good partner would, begin gaining public recognition for said art, dump or be dumped by him, learn that he sold the aforementioned priceless gifts for copious sums, feel alone and violated, join VMA, discover that the same thing happened to a handful of others, feel less alone but somehow even more violated, begin working toward recovery).

The exes now sit in a perfect circle in a Raleigh, NC[14] Church of Christ basement, ready to discuss their shared trauma. A portion of

---

12   Duh?

13   Members' colloquial moniker for VMA is simply "the Program."

14   Headquartered here because it's where Henry and Grace live. The others flew/limo'ed in.

this discussion is paraphrased in direct quotations below.

"I'm Benji," Benji says, quaintly adhering to the AA method of introduction despite everyone here already knowing his name.

"Hi Benji," the others reply.

"Hi Benji," I reply after a slight delay, which earns me stern glares from the in-group.

"I feel kind of awkward being the newest member of the Program, what with Mitch and me only splitting up a couple years ago. I keep waiting for another member to show up." Looks behind him as if expecting one to come sauntering in right this instant. "It's embarrassing, in a way. Like, you're telling me six other people went through this before me and I somehow wasn't clued in?"

Everyone nods, blinking far less frequently than is typical and appearing perpetually on the verge of tears. Paul Anger mutters, "Maybe more."

"Maybe more," Benji repeats indignantly. "I think the worst part is that I'm confused. I don't know how to feel. Like, should I be upset that he left me because I miss him? But *should* I even miss him when the 'him' I'm missing isn't the real him but a fake incarnation he opportunistically embodies whenever he wants something? And shouldn't the fact that I'm engaged to someone else now prevent me from missing him at *all*? And if I don't miss him, or *can't*, do I even have the right to be mad? Shouldn't I be flattered that he saw my talent before anyone else did?"

"He'd make a mad talent scout," Grace agrees.

"I want to circle back to what you said about being unsure whether to feel flattered, Benji," Paul says. "I'm Paul, by the way."

"Hi, Paul." I don't join the chorus this time.

"Hi. I think I'd feel *more* flattered if he'd taken an actual interest in my music, you know? He seemed *very* interested in how my music was *doing* but never the music itself." Paul folds his knuckle-tattooed hands in his lap. I can't quite make out what the tattoos spell. "So that hurt a bit, I think. And then he sold the demo—the one I'd recorded for him and *only* him because I wanted it to be special—to my record label."

I tell him I'm not familiar with that particular tune and invite him to perform a few lines for us now, pen at the ready for direct-quotation purposes.

"I suppose." He affects a bashful demeanor and then begins singing a cappella in the aggressive, dynamically-stagnant pop-punk style. "I told you that I love you/Oh, but what am I to you?[15]/I told you that I need you, baby/But what am I to you?/Wanna be with you forever/But I need to know the truth/Oh, what the fucking shitting balls am I to fucking you?"[16]

The circle erupts in a shitstorm of applause. I finish jotting down the lyrics verbatim and then give a few perfunctory claps.

"I love the double meaning of 'fucking you,'" Nell tells Paul. "Like, it could be an intensifier, but it could also be a verb. You know, like, he's your boyfriend, so you're fucking him."

"Except I wasn't, is the thing. We never fucked. Unless you count him fucking me over."

"How long did you date for?" I ask, tightening my lips to avoid another inappropriate outburst, still recovering from the "Hi Benji" fiasco.

"About six months."

"Wow. And you never *once* slept together?"

Paul shakes his head.

"By a show of hands, how many of you had sex with Mitch?" I follow up, half-expecting them not to indulge me.

Grace raises her hand. Chrissy raises her hand. Nell raises her hand. Lisa raises her hand. I begin to sense a pattern. Benji raises his hand.

"Wait a second..." Henry says slowly, his expression showing the telltale signs of dawning revelation. "Is Mitch straight?"

"What am I, burnt toast?" Benji shoots back, arm still in the air.

"Maybe he was never attracted to *any* of us," Lisa says glumly. Adjusts the sleeves of her white, dry-fit shirt so that her biceps are fully visible (and they *are* impressive—good for her). "And maybe you guys lucked out not having sex with him. It wasn't great sex. And it sucks

---

15   Rhyming "you" with "you"—a staple of the pop-punk genre.

16   I feel uncomfortable poking fun at Paul's overemployment of curse words since I do it in my own writing.

to be used." Shakes her head sadly. "He really had me convinced he loved me for my body."

"He's a hell of a liar," Grace concurs.

"Would he make a good actor, do you think?" I ask.

A few vociferous nods.

"Mitch is an empath," Chrissy says. "He can read people."

"I don't think that's what empath means."

"A *telepath*," Grace corrects her.

"You think he can literally read minds?"

Six of them hesitate, but Lisa answers, "Oh, absolutely. It's not like mindreading is some super rare thing. Why do you think psychics become psychics?"

I don't want to open that metaphorical worm-can, so I don't respond.

"*My* psychic always says she picks up energies," Paul puts in. "And I think that's sort of what Mitch does. There's a certain mystic energy he looks for in partners."

"Talent?" I suggest. "Creative drive?"

"Whatever it is that psychics have, he's got it," Chrissy says.

"Where do you think Mitch is now?" I inquire, mainly because part of me wants to interview him but I'm not journalistically or personally bold enough to just show up to the place he lived a year ago and ask whether he still lives there and then, if he does, whether I can ask him a few on-the-record questions about his secret illegal stock trading business.

"Same place he's always been, just dating some other poor soul," Chrissy opines. "I wish I could warn whoever's currently having their head messed with, but I don't know who they are, or even where he lives."

"Jail, probably," Nell says.

"Why jail?" I ask, wondering whether they know about the stock thing.

She shrugs obliviously. "He's always doing skeevy stuff."

"Like what?"

"Like what he did to all of us," Henry says. "If I hadn't broken a million YouTube subscribers, I wonder whether we'd still be together. It all happened so fast. And then he sold my unused video essay scripts to another creator after I left them at his apartment."

"That's skeevy, but it's not *illegal*," I say. "What makes you think he'd do *illegal* stuff?"

"No morals," Nell mutters. So they seem not to know. And perhaps *I'm* a bit skeevy for not telling them.

"I don't think he would," Grace says with the psychic foresight of a prediction that's already been foiled by dramatic irony.

"Why's that?"

"He knows how to follow rules. If one thing is true of Mitch, it's that he's a rule-follower. He doesn't step on any toes."

"Do we really know that, though?" Benji asks. "Did we even know him at all?"[17]

---

17   Okay, so this last rhetorical question is not from Benji—it's my own editorialized addition, and I'd be as dishonest as Mitch if I didn't admit that upfront. It seemed to be implied by the whole environment, though, and putting it in someone else's voice and footnoting it feels more poetic than just attributing it to myself—audiences hate to feel like an author is telling them what to think. And nobody reads footnotes anyway.

Part III:
The End of Something...

1

The Hayley Duker I know is stern and well-put-together and has the kind of head on her shoulders that, were it on mine, might threaten to crush me under its weight. She has long, straight, blonde hair and a gentle crease to her brows and dresses like someone who thinks even mundane events are important and formal affairs.

I have difficulty imagining what she was like when she was with Mitch—if she bore any resemblance to her current self, I can't picture her doing all the things she apparently did. But love is blind (and deaf and head-mass-decreasing, apparently).

Today, Hayley and I sit across from each other at my kitchen table, my nearly spotless living room in proud view. I spent over an hour cleaning the place today, anticipating that Hayley would be the type to silently judge people for clutter. I tell her this as a sort of icebreaker, and she laughs and says to trust her that whatever this place looked like before, she's seen way worse. I believe her.

The story she relays now pertains to the first time she and Mitch had sex. For her, the encounter was unexpected, but for Mitch, it signified a heavenly, cosmic unification of reality and fate—Hayley had been the primary object of his carnal desires for years, and he never missed an opportunity to tell her. Thus, her persistent refusal to sleep with him ("I'm not going to help you cheat on Benji," "I don't want to be responsible for ruining your [scam] relationship," and other such ridiculous excuses) essentially amounted to an old, decrepit dam's bulging floodgate.

But on this particular afternoon, Hayley let her raw human drives get the best of her. Even the most principled among us have our rare moments of weakness, I suppose, although she admits to no longer being able to consider herself principled. She believes Mitch corrupted her. I'll let you decide how true that is.

So, yes, anyway, their "first sex," as Hayley calls it. It occurred after a consult at Mitch's home regarding Mitch's progress with the Benji stocks and the best path forward re Benji more generally, especially with the COVID pandemic showing no signs of slowing down and many people being too afraid to leave their houses, much less visit some sketchy basement and engage in an underground stock trade that consisted of owning portions of living people, and after about forty-five tedious minutes of Benji-related discussion, complete with little financial charts Hayley had created on Excel and then printed out, which Mitch found inexplicably cute and sexually arousing, Mitch and Hayley noticed that hardly any physical space separated them—so little space, in fact, that kissing was basically a technicality, and after that, the whole levee broke.

Hayley, who at this point still had *some* principle about her, insisted that they use a condom, and Mitch embitteredly agreed, albeit after complaining that condoms "killed the mood." They kind of did, Hayley concedes, but the bigger mood-killer was Mitch's incessant whining, and the biggest mood killer of all would have been an unwanted pregnancy.

It's funny—Hayley retains a sort of weary pragmatism now. She discusses her former self—the self who dated Mitch—with a detached alienation, as if the Hayley of the past is someone this Hayley never knew well but met once at a potluck and refused to consume the potato salad of, on principle.

"That was even better than I thought it would be," Mitch said after they finished (after *he* finished, Hayley addends). But he didn't yet understand that the primary source of its goodness was its forbiddenness. Their first sex had the titillating and pornographic air of a roleplay—"Useless, Baby-Brained Man Goes to Absolute Town on His Wise and Principled Financial Advisor." Later sexes would be less good, at least for Mitch, because they'd be kosher; "Cohabitating Boyfriend and Girlfriend Get Hot and Nasty Before Bed" doesn't have quite the same ring to it.

"This can't happen again," she said firmly. It would happen one more time before Mitch and Benji even broke up and many hundreds of times after that.

"Of course not."

"I mean it. You're in a relationship."

"A money relationship. I'm a gold-digger, when you think about it," Mitch replied, in a rare moment of self-awareness.

Hayley groaned and covered her face with her hands, an action that couldn't have been sanitary given what had just transpired. "God, what am I *doing*? I don't even *like* you."

"You don't? Weird way of showing it."

"I mean, like, no offense—you're fine—but have my sexual standards gone to absolute shit or what?"

Mitch didn't have a dignified answer. He could feel his heartrate slowing, and the incessant ticking of his ever-annoying nightstand clock seemed to slow with it, dragging out the silence.

"Should I break up with Benji?"

"Do you want my financial advice or my personal advice?"

"Either? Both."

"They're in conflict now." She sounded wearily perturbed. "You've created a conflict of interest."

"So have you."

"I'm aware, thanks."

More silence. Paralyzing silence. Mitch felt something within him shift. A minute ago, he'd experienced an elation more powerful than that of the strongest stimulant drugs (Mitch had never done any stimulant drugs besides caffeine). Now he just felt empty and broken, like someone who had just come down from stimulant drugs.

"It definitely feels like the end of *something*," Mitch went on, goading her. "I don't really know how else to describe it." Mitch and Benji would continue to date for another year. "Benji is cheap. I don't think he'll ever give me anything worth much. He's a believer in *sentimental* gifts."

"That's cute," Hayley muttered, unable to help herself.

"You know what's even cuter?"

"Don't say me."

So he didn't.

"What kind of gifts *does* he give you?" She kept her tone measured, embarrassed that she lacked enough dignity to not just wonder but actually *ask*.

Mitch let out a dehydrated titter. "He made me this." Held up his left wrist, from which a weaved and faded purple-and-white friendship bracelet dangled. "He hasn't been cast in a movie yet, so money is tight."

Hayley flicked the bracelet a couple times. "And you're wearing it now."

"Kind of a pain to take on and off."

"Right."

"Anyway, I figure this won't sell for more than a couple hundred, even if he hits the big screen. So I'm trying to determine how worth it this whole relationship is." And he was. But he was also trying to gauge Hayley's interest in him. Her words said one thing, but her behavior said something completely different, and Mitch didn't know which to trust. Hayley now tells me she was a mixed-up mess of cognitively dissonant emotions and would rather not talk about it.

"Do you sleep together?" Hayley asked.

"Sometimes. Why?"

"Never mind." She now felt a jealousy so complex and multifaceted that it "can't really be described in words."

"I mean, it's kind of what you do when you're with someone."

"So it doesn't mean anything to you?"

"What doesn't?"

Hayley gestured to her still-naked body and then immediately felt ashamed of her nudity. She'd made herself vulnerable to a morally incompetent and emotionally stunted man two years her junior only for *him* to use *her* in exactly the way she'd tried to use him. Both parties felt (and had been) used. She stood up and pulled her slacks back on, one leg at a time.

"What are you doing?"

Glanced at Mitch's clock, its tick-pace a settled and consistent largo. "Our appointment is finished. If you want another hour, it'll cost extra."

"Hayley, don't do this," Mitch begged, sitting up so fast he bumped his forehead on the bedpost. "Come on," he said, clutching his skull, his temples searing with pain. "It's not like that with us."

But she'd already slipped back into her blouse and blazer and pulled up her pants, and Mitch watched helplessly through his impact-dazed eyes as the blurry outline of her figure made a conclusive exit, and his final words got lost in the gunshot-sharp slam of his apartment's front door.

2

The month was July, and the air was thick with Atlantic humidity, and Mitch and Hayley, who had not yet professed their reluctant undying love for each other, sat on the bench outside Nelson's bookstore, taking a rare break from their otherwise packed schedule of checking out about one customer every couple hours. Mitch stirred his coffee with a disposable wooden stick he'd found in the storage room that housed spare copies of books. The coffee had come from there too—the place was full of surprises.

"Isn't it a little late for coffee?" Hayley asked, shielding her forehead with her hand. The noon's very air seemed to glow with brightness.

Mitch checked his Movado wristwatch. He'd never been the watch-wearing type, but now that he could afford semi-expensive ones, he rarely left his house bare-armed. "Eleven fifty-four. Still technically the morning."

"A little hot, then?"

Mitch shrugged, but the coffee's steam in conjunction with the weather made his armpits feel like two mini saunas. "How long does coffee take to go bad?"

"Probably four or five months. Why? How old is that coffee?"

He stared at his warped reflection in the mug. "Dunno. Older than four or five months, I'd guess." Took a sip, nearly gagged, and then ejected the stuff onto the pavement.

"That bad, huh?"

"Yeah." Mitch coughed a couple times. Some of the coffee had dripped out through his nose, and it smelled about as good as it tasted. "But we should totally ransack that storage room sometime—might be some promising canned foods or military rations."

For a few seconds, they both smiled, but then their expressions softened back into the sexually-tense, business-partner default.

"I forgot to tell you," Mitch said, though he hadn't, really—had more just hoarded the information, much the way he hoarded everything, to be tactfully deployed when Hayley was in a good mood. "I got another client."

"Another significant other, you mean?"

Mitch set the coffee mug onto the bench next to him, its contents rippling. "No, not this time."

"Straight dude?"

"Yep."

"Don't even bother."

He frowned. "Why not?"

"In order for someone to trust you enough to give you stuff, there needs to be a romantic commitment. It won't work otherwise."

"I dunno." Mitch kicked a small rock across the cement, where it skipped a few times. "This is kind of a special case."

"How so?"

"Kid has emotional dependency problems out the wazoo. Daddy issues like you wouldn't believe. Seems to be a druggie too, though I haven't gotten any solid proof of that yet."

Hayley nodded slowly, taking it all in. "So you're exploiting a mentally ill man—or did you say...*kid*?"

"He's twenty-one."

"Okay, so basically a kid. You're preying on a mentally ill, drug addict kid." It sounded worse when she phrased it like that. "That's kind of a new low, even for you."

"Oh, don't act all innocent yourself."

"I don't choose the victims—that's on you. If it were me, I'd choose differently." She repositioned herself on the bench, which was composed of two slabbish rectangular logs that pinched your ass between them. "What do you even see in this kid anyway? Sounds like a complete trainwreck."

"He is, which means he's also desperate. And he's gotta be like the greatest bullshitter known to man. Would make a talented actor—I'm sure of it."

"So you're posing as, what, his acting coach?"

"Manager. He's already tried out for one role—some animated movie with sharks in it. Not important. He didn't get it, but it's only a matter of time."

Hayley raised a disapproving eyebrow.

"What?"

"It's just...*I'm* wrapped up in this whole scheme too. Shouldn't I get a say in who the conquests are?"

"I thought we agreed—you handle the money side; I handle the interpersonal side. We play to our strengths."

Hayley's mouth assumed several indeterminate sequential shapes. "Okay, well then can I give you a bit of *money* advice?" Mitch started to answer, but she plowed ahead before he got a word in. "I think this is a bad investment all around. Firstly, I don't think someone like this will be profitable in the stock market. I think he's only headed downhill from here. Keeping that in mind, I think it's unwise for you to be complicit in his downfall—both financially and just, like, morally. If he has some kind of fatal overdose, do you really want to spend the rest of your life wondering whether it's your fault?"

"I'll try to get him off the drugs, then."

Hayley ignored him. "Secondly, let's say, by some miracle, he has some success as an actor and makes the shareholders some money. Let's also say he gives you some artifacts—which would be what, in this case?"

"He has these dumb little art pieces he makes using staples."

"Like, office staples?"

Mitch nodded.

"Right, so let's say he gives you one of those. Let's say that somehow, by yet another miracle, it becomes valuable."

"I'm with you."

"It's only a matter of time before someone like him burns out. His value will go up, people will make back their money and more, and then his price will plummet—could *always* plummet unexpectedly, is what you have to remember—and suddenly you won't be able to sell the art for *nearly* enough money to break *even*, much less *profit*."

"He won't plummet."

"And *then*," Hayley said, with a kind of breathless finality, "you'll have to worry about the setup of the whole thing. I really doubt this guy..."

"Syd."

"...this guy Syd is a normal, well-adjusted adult capable of breaking off a relationship and respecting boundaries. If he's got attachment issues, he's going to follow you around like an annoying little buzzing fruit fly for the rest of your mortal life, regardless of what happens to him fame-wise. Do you really want that?"

This last portion of Hayley's prediction scared Mitch more than any of the stock stuff, ironically enough—his delusional bubble of financial invincibility had not yet burst.

Hayley decisively repositioned a few strands of her hair. Mitch liked the way the gentle wind kept mussing it, thwarting all her efforts to keep it looking professional. The blouse she wore today was more feminine than her typical lesbianic blazers, so she looked positively and erotically heterosexual.

"I am telling you, as your advisor and your friend," she added tiredly after a few beats of nothing, "that this is a futile and moronic venture."

"You're really beautiful, you know." He meant it, too.

"Irrelevant."

"No, it *is* relevant, Hayley. Because this means we can finally be together. I've found a way to acquire a subject without dating him. I am available and no longer looking. I want you and only you."

Hayley stared deliberately at the sidewalk in front of them, her gaze alternately fixed on the pebble Mitch had kicked and the coffee he'd spat out. "So you think that, what, now that you want me, I'll just be right here waiting for you with open arms?"

"Basically," Mitch admitted. "Is that wrong? Besides, I've *always* wanted you. You know that."

"I guess I was just hoping you'd grow up a bit before we got together, but it's become *astonishingly* clear that that isn't going to happen."

"So we're on the same page, then."

"Spending any amount of time with you feels like babysitting a child, but I *am* attracted to you."

Mitch grinned again, his head tilted slightly forward. Hayley describes Mitch's idiosyncratic smirk as winsome but irksome in its persistent subversion of all attempts at serious conversation. Mitch knew this and deployed it regularly as a disarming tactic.

"Stop looking at me like that," but now she was smiling too.

"Could a child do this?" He leaned in and kissed her. Though it wasn't the first time, it felt realer than the others.

"Evidently," Hayley replied when they broke apart, but then *she* kissed *him.*

In a moment of temporary biochemical telepathy, they both stood up, lips still locked, and shouldered their way through the front door of the empty bookstore. "We're violating, like, a million business regulations," she informed him, breathless between smooches.

Mitch undid the single button of her blouse, and it burst open in a kind of sigh of relief.

"Do you really want to do this *here*?" she asked.

"Do what? Sex number four?"

Hayley's lips went limp, and she pulled back. "Huh?"

"Our fourth sex," Mitch repeated, as if it should be obvious.

"You're *counting*?"

"Our fourth sex is supposed to happen someplace scandalous."

"Says who?"

"The sex rules."

She laughed, unbuttoning his trousers, and with their removal came a release of uncomfortable tightness—a seeming restoration of nature. "You're just making this up."

"No, it's real," Mitch insisted, performatively repressing his own laughter. "The same rules that say the third date should be the first time you fuck."

"Then what date would this make this?"

Mitch closed his eyes, his brain a gibberish matrix of overlapping integers. Felt her kiss him again, which only scrambled his mind's wires more. "This is why you handle the money side."

3

The final real good experience Syd and Mitch had together happened the week before Thanksgiving of 2023, a few months after Syd received a small speaking role in Shannon Marshall's movie *MusicaLaw*. On the day in question, the two sat across from each other at Syd's coffee table, playing chess, while New York's first snowfall's snow fell. Syd looked totally wigged out, which Mitch tried to ignore.

"You never want to do anything," Mitch commented, capturing one of Syd's black pawns while the ceiling fan went around and around and around. "You just sit around all day."

"What's there to do?"

"I dunno. Wanna go out for ice cream or something?"

"*No* ice cream."

"Right. Almost forgot." Syd had a big traumatic backstory thing involving ice cream.

A few silent moves, broken by Syd asking, "Why don't you ever want to tell me about *your* family?"

Shrugged slightly, advancing a knight. "Not much to tell, really."

"Really?"

"Pretty traditional upper-class Irish Catholic upbringing."

"Traditional in what way?"

"Make your move."

Syd scanned the board, and then his face lit up. "Check," moving his queen. "Traditional in what way?"

When Mitch was in the first grade, a nun made him stay inside during lunchtime and write "I am Mitch Larkin" on the whiteboard hundreds of times because he forgot to put his name on a homework assignment. By the end of it, his name didn't look real anymore—just a meaningless pattern of squiggly lines. His name hadn't really looked real to him since.

"We went to Mass. Celebrated holidays and feast days. My mom made us Easter baskets and hid them."

To teach Mitch the true value of sacrifice, his mom observed a yearly tradition of forcing Mitch to watch her rip his basket to shreds and flush it down the toilet, one piece of candy at a time. He should have come to expect it, he supposed, but every time, she'd tell him that *this* year, he'd get to redeem the basket's goodies. However, whenever he found it—usually in the dryer or behind someone's bedroom door or in the drawer under the TV—and brought it out proudly, his disposition one of momentary optimism and cheer, his mom snatched it away, at which point he'd chase her to the bathroom, heart pounding and eyes already welling with tears, knowing what came next but feeling powerless to stop it.

"I wish *my* parents had done something like that," Syd said. "Make *your* move."

"Were you religious?", taking Syd's undefended queen.

"Nah. In name, maybe. I can't even remember, to be honest." Syd shifted from a squat to a kneel, leaning in closer but appearing unfazed by the capture. A strange heat emanated from his hair. He smelled like cigarettes and cologne, neither scent masking the other. "What's it like being Catholic?"

"I did all the sacraments. Went to confession a lot."

In the weeks leading up to his First Reconciliation, Mitch had learned that confession was the only way to reverse mortal sins—otherwise, they remained on your conscience and sent you straight to Hell when you died. And mortal sins weren't just the obvious things like killing people or consuming illegal drugs or using God's name in vain; they could also be mundane things like lying or missing Sunday Mass or disrespecting your parents. Pretty much any misdeed that in any way related to one of the Commandments might be mortal, and one could never know the true severity status of a given sin—God had full discretion on that, and He pretty much made up the rules as He went. This is how Mitch remembered it.

Anyway, soon after Mitch's First Reconciliation, he became acutely aware of all the mortal sins he was committing every day, and since his teachers always emphasized that you could die at any point—like, for example, you could get in a gnarly car crash on your way home from school, or your house could burn down, or a rogue assassin could pop you off while you're outside playing with sidewalk chalk, or the Rapture (of biblical fame) could happen right while you're in the middle of a timed math quiz—and that dying in a state of mortal sin meant eternal and unceasing and unfathomable torture, Mitch's only logical means of recourse was attending confession every day, which he did, for a few weeks, until the same parents who believed Jesus' sacrifice was so important it necessitated flushing a kid's candy down the toilet each Easter decided that daily drives to church weren't cost-efficient, fuel-wise, and told Mitch to just suck it up, basically.

Syd laughed. "Aw, man. Catholics, man. You're not still Catholic, right?"

"No."

"But is it true what they say about the guilt? That it never goes away?"

Mitch liked to think he'd completely transformed his whole mental framing of guilt so that, if it wasn't gone, it at least didn't feel like it used to. "Dunno."

A few moments of silence whirled by. Syd clicked his shoeless heels together like Dorothy in *The Wizard of Oz*. He still hadn't made his move.

"Can I ask *you* something?" Mitch asked. He figured now was as good a time as ever.

"Sure."

"Why do you do drugs constantly?"

Syd looked right at him, cheeks drooping, and Mitch saw his own pale face reflected in his dark eyes. "Are you serious?"

"Yeah...I mean, I could see when you were a kid and dealing with...all that shit, but now? You're a famous actor. You've got everything."

"Doesn't feel like it."

"What do you mean?"

Syd exhaled, his mouth a tight O. "You'd think achieving your dreams and more would make you happy. Like you'd never Want again. But it doesn't. I think it's in human nature to Want."

"You say Want like it's capitalized."

"It's the central human emotion. If we don't Want, we lack purpose. Or *feel* like we lack purpose, probably because we attribute feeling shitty to not having whatever we currently Want. So when we get that thing, and we still feel shitty, we wonder why. And it's hard to accept that maybe your entire brain is irreparably fucked because what can be done about that? So we just move the goalposts and find something else to Want instead."

"What does that have to do with drugs?"

"Not sure. I just know I feel less shitty when I'm on them."

"You probably seldom feel shitty then," Mitch joked, and then felt some square-root inkling of guilt, though not the Catholic variety. "Sorry."

"No, you're right." Syd was surprisingly amiable, Mitch noted. Rare form. "They used to make me feel un-shitty, but now they just make me feel normal. I get the sense most people do drugs to feel *ab*normal. That's probably the healthiest relationship one can have with drugs, anyway. But me? When things start feeling *really* fucked up, I take it as a sign I need another hit. And the thing I interpret as 'feeling really fucked up' is just basic garden-variety sobriety."

"Do you think you have a problem?" Mitch asked. "With using drugs?"

"*I* don't have a problem with it. Do *you* have a problem with it?"

Mitch chortled in a sort of obligatory way. "But you know what I mean."

"Yeah," stiffly. Syd turned back to the board and then changed the subject. "So I guess we can both agree that I won."

Mitch let out a second chortle at what he thought was a second joke, but Syd remained stone-faced. "Oh, come on."

"It's true," with the egotistical sharpness that marks a stimulant high. "Seven moves 'til checkmate. You don't believe me?"

An instant's pause. "No. But don't you ever worry you'll end up OD'ing or...?"

"I think it's a possibility," Syd admitted. The whole conversation's tempo felt slower than usual despite Mitch's own sobriety. Besides smoking a single joint behind St. Mary's Catholic Church in the eleventh grade, he had never done drugs. And that one instance had really only been a fuck-you to the God he'd claimed to no longer believe in. The weed had come from a girl in his class, whose name eluded him now. He remembered laughing a lot and leaning lazily against the corroding bricks of God's house, wondering whether He could feel Mitch's mortal wrath as strongly as Mitch could feel his own throbbing heartbeat in the back of his neck. "But I don't worry about it," Syd finished.

"Is it not a massively undesirable state, though?"

"Nah. Neutral at best."

Mitch forced a smile that revealed a happiness he did not feel. The snow wasn't real snow—more like that flurried kind that melts the second it hits the ground. A chunky pile of wet sludge had gathered in the street, and cars left ugly little wheel-tracks in it while they drove by, splashing sheets of dirty, freezing water onto the sidewalk.

"What?" Syd asked, noting Mitch's expression, which must have displayed some degree of horror.

"You are...fucked up, man..."

Syd laughed, checking Mitch with his bishop. "Yeah, I am. Really fucked up." He snorted a rare powderless snort.

So Mitch laughed again. He wished he knew what at.

4

A few weeks after Mitch and Syd's Final Real Good Experience, a serious debacle occurred on the set of *MusicaLaw* between Syd and his costar Ned Wesham. While the debacle's details were somewhat hazy to Mitch, the important and potentially fatal developments were that Syd's public image and stock price were now on the line, and Mitch and Syd's already precarious and mutually deceptive relationship had entered a rapid nosedive.

So Mitch now drove in a kind of dazed panic to the Manhattan General Hospital to ask Ned, who was currently in quite dire shape, for a favor. It wouldn't be a big deal, and if Mitch could successfully sneak into his hospital room, *Ned* would be thanking *him*.

But first, Mitch called Syd, whose amphetaminic voice blared sharply out of the Prius' hands-free speaker (Mitch being the sort of safe and conscientious driver who wouldn't dare take his hands off the wheel). "You're talking to me again? Is the silent treatment over?"

"Hardly. I'm doing you an enormous kindness. Is Ned close with anyone?"

"He has a German girlfriend named Phillipa last I checked, but they're probably broken up by now."

"What about immediate family members? Any brothers or anything?"

"He's got a brother, yeah. He's always talking about him."

"Who lives nearby?"

"Sounds like it. Relatively near."

"Great. What's his name?"

"Uh, Brian, I think."

"Thanks."

"Mitch, I—"

But Mitch had already hung up on him. Hanging up on him felt good—like sending a naughty child to his room to "think about what [he's] done."

Mitch gave the name "Brian Wesham" to the front desk attendant outside the injury ward, who left to go tell Ned's nurse.

When I interviewed Ned for this "novel," he told me he hadn't seen Brian in years and often reminisced wistfully about all the great times they'd had growing up—sitting on their backyard deck watching the night sky, reenacting iconic movie scenes together, developing elaborate joint theories of fuel-efficiency-management in the *Star Wars* universe and contemplating the (in my opinion unfeasible) logistics of publishing said theories in legitimate academic journals, etc.—and wondered where it all went wrong. He and his brother hadn't formally fallen out; they'd more just grown apart over time. Their last encounter had been at his mother's funeral—Ned's mother had died unexpectedly a few years back as the result of a lawnmowing accident, and Ned had assumed the suddenness of her death might force the brothers to hang tightly onto each other in their respective times of needs, but instead, the two grew even *more* distant because their mom had always been the one to schedule family get-togethers—to invite her grown-up sons to her house every Christmas, for example, where the three of them (Ned's father was also deceased) would decorate ornaments. A sort of bubble of sincerity always surrounded that whole affair and prevented either Ned or Brian from making fun of the other for being in his twenties and decorating ornaments without a hint of irony.

So you can probably imagine Ned's indignation when the man who strolled into his hospital room turned out not to be Brian at all but the manager of the guy who'd landed him here in the first place. Ned vaguely recognized Mitch but at this point hadn't even properly conversed with him.

"Who are you?" Ned's voice was scratchy, as the voices of people who've recently been punched in the throat tend to be. "Wait. I know you."

Mitch took a seat at his bedside. Ned was pretty bruised up—had casts on his right arm and left leg and braces on his neck and nose, and one of his eyes was badly swollen, and little pieces of tape had been dispersed across his usually sunken but now puffy face, seemingly at random.

"Brian," Mitch tried. He figured it was worth a try; he couldn't be sure of the status of Ned's eyesight. Ned couldn't see Mitch very well, but his reddish hair in its gratingly mussed style made him immediately recognizable.

"Get out," Ned demanded.

"Fine. I'm not Brian. My name is Mitch Larkin. I'm Syd's manager."

"Yep. Now get out before I buzz the nurse."

"Do you want to make a lot of money?" while Ned's finger hovered over the nurse-buzzer. His hand appeared to have sprouted some weird IV contraption, which Mitch tried not to look at too closely.

"Is this a sales pitch for a pyramid scheme?"

Mitch shook his head and then felt bad for flaunting the fact that he was capable of shaking his head. "No pyramid schemes. I pay you five grand not to break the Syd story or press charges. I can have my lawyer draw up the whole NDA." Hayley's lawyer, more accurately—he'd helped Hayley and Mitch with the bookstore purchase. Luckily, he was thirty years Hayley's senior and thus barely a romantic threat.

Ned told me later that breaking the story had not even crossed his concussed mind until Mitch had mentioned it, but once he had... "Five grand won't even pay my medical bills."

"Yeah, but like..." Mitch shifted nervously on the hospital chair, which was lumpy and uncomfortable but clearly designed with comfort in mind. "You're an actor. You're not exactly hurting for cash."

"Fifteen grand," Ned said.

"Come on, now."

"Fifteen or no deal."

Mitch scooched his chair forward a couple inches so that it nearly touched Ned's bed. "You know, he did the same to me once. Syd."

"Put you in the hospital?"

"Not quite. Didn't even break my nose. He damn near did, though."

"What did he do?"

"Punched me in the face. Over something stupid, too."

Ned gestured with his less fucked-up hand to the general state of his body. "*This* was over something stupid," he said with a sharp laugh, which sounded grotesque coming from a supine, broken-nosed man.

"I bet," Mitch replied, stroking Ned's arm tenderly. Ned yanked it away and then grimaced in pain. "What I'm trying to say is that we've all been there."

"*That's* your defense of him? That he beats the shit out of people all the time? That I should grin and bear it because that's just what he's *like*? I might not even get to do this *movie* now, for fuck's sake. They were almost done filming, but now they've changed around their entire schedule, and if I'm not back on my feet and good as new within *three months*, they're gonna recast me. I'm gonna be in the hospital on *Christmas Day*. You *haven't* been here."

"No," Mitch agreed. "I think I'm just trying to say that, on some level, I know how you feel."

Ned didn't speak for a bit, just breathed loudly. Creaked his head back and forth what little amount he could. "Why do you put up with him?"

"Syd?"

Grunted affirmatively.

"I don't know. I guess...he's nice sometimes."

"That's it?"

"He's really interesting. He's got dimensions to him. Contains multitudes. He's brilliant. I dunno."

Ned clicked his tongue; all other gestures had become too burdensome.

"What?"

"You'll figure it out soon enough."

"No, tell me."

"You know what they say about birds?" Ned paused, and then, seeing Mitch's confusion, "Of a feather?"

"I've never beat up anyone in my life."

"I'm just saying. You wouldn't spend all that time with him if you weren't exactly the same. You're a violent, rotten piece of work too—you're just mature enough and smart enough to dole out your violence in socially acceptable ways."

Mitch tried not to process Ned's words too deeply.

"You came in here pretending to be my estranged brother, for example."

"Estranged? Syd said you two were close."

"Yeah, he would, wouldn't he? Terrible listener, that guy."

"*Endearingly* bad."

There was an awkward silence.

"Well, I guess I'll be leaving." Mitch slapped his knees and stood up. "*With* my money." Began walking away in an exaggerated slow-mo. He'd linger in the doorway for a few seconds if Ned didn't change his mind during the grand exit.

"Wait," Ned said tiredly, almost requisitely. What he did next remains one of his biggest regrets. "I'll take the ten grand."

Mitch turned around at normal speed. "I said five."

"I know you did. I said ten."

"Would you consider eight?"

"No, I would not."

"Right. It's settled then."

It was far from settled, but I'll let past-Mitch dream.

"Please wait until I'm eating solid food again before you start hounding me with shit to sign," Ned added, for good measure.

5

Mitch and Syd sat slouched on Mitch's couch, squeezed cheek-to-cheek into the single cushion's worth of available space, Syd tweaking on CNO. Mitch could tell he thought his intoxication was discreet, but it wasn't—the rapid nictation, the restlessness, the unfocused gaze—and though Mitch had come to accept Syd's drug abuse as an unchangeable yet ultimately unbothersome aspect of his personhood, Syd's caginess about the *frequency* of his use still irked him.

"You gotta slow down on the CNO," Mitch said now. "You're gonna end up in the hospital."

Okay, so he did mind it a little bit, though not for any moral reasons—it was more the fact that Mitch had a lot of money riding on Syd's success. Besides, Syd tended to behave unpredictably when he was high. Violently even, sometimes.

"Why am I here?" Syd asked blankly, his voice a disinterested drawl.

"I can't just want to hang out with my favorite client?"

"I'm your only client."

"What makes you think that?"

Syd glanced briefly at Mitch's face as if making a good and honest attempt to give him the benefit of the doubt and then deciding it wasn't worth it. "It's obvious. Besides, we haven't hung out in ages."

"You've been kinda busy with Rankin."

Syd didn't react or respond—just stared lazily at the carpet, his knees tucked into his chest like a kid playing "popcorn" on a backyard trampoline. He appeared profoundly sad and lonely despite being more loved and popular than ever, Mitch observed, and for a split and lucid second he almost thought he understood why, but then he mentally chocked it up to what Hayley referred to as "Ungrateful Celebrity Syndrome," which had become a sort of all-encompassing, nebulous diagnosis with supernatural explanatory powers.

"Look, what I really need is for you to calm down," Mitch went on.

"I'm about as calm as possible."

He didn't look it—what Syd really looked was *sedated*. Restless but numb.

"You know what I mean. I smoothed over the thing with Ned, but I can't guarantee I'll be able to smooth it over that well in the future. Especially with *Life Imitates Art* opening next week." Mitch made a mental note to properly pack for the upcoming festival—he hadn't begun thinking about what he'd bring to such an event and truthfully didn't understand what a film festival even *was*.

"Why *did* you smooth it over, by the way?"

"Because I care about you."

Syd scoffed, but a trace of a smile instantaneously flickered across his face. "Nothing in it for you then?"

"Nope," taking care not to look at Syd while he said it. If he looked at him, he'd fold.

The room's quiet thundered—the distant thud of Mitch's clothes in the dryer two rooms away, the throbbing whip of the ceiling fan.

"I want to buy back the canvas," Syd muttered.

"What?"

Syd pointed to the kitchen table, his hand shaking from drug intoxication. "I want it back."

"But you got a deal on it," Mitch reminded him. "You even said as much."

"Then you should want to sell it back. You don't even like it."

"*You* don't even like it." Mitch adjusted his position on the couch. His big toes, seemingly the only things anchoring him to the physical realm, dug self-soothingly into the carpet. "*I* love it. It reminds me of you."

"Why do you need to be reminded of me when I'm right here?"

"I don't know. I..." An intrusive daydream popped unprompted into Mitch's head—the image of Syd *not* being there. Of Syd being six feet under as the result of some horrific drug-induced disaster whose details weren't clear, because in the daydream, Mitch was already at the funeral, and he was crying. He truly mourned Syd, in the daydream, which came as a shock to both the literal in-the-moment Mitch and the projected at-the-funeral Mitch. When the pastor called Mitch up to say a few words, and he opened his mouth to speak, nothing came out. Attendees dabbed their eyes and watched him in anticipation, becoming increasingly distraught with the passing of each eternal wordless moment. "I don't know where we'll both be in ten years' time," Mitch said audibly to the real, corporeal, living Syd. "You know?"

"I'll probably be shooting my newest blockbuster, and you'll probably be..."

"I'll be what, Syd? You think you don't need me?" He maintained a gentleness to his voice despite the novel mixture of anxiety, despair, and dread he felt. He prided himself on his ability to affect artificial cool—to give off the wise impression that he knew what he was doing despite experiencing all thirty-three years of his life thus far as a kind of uncontrolled freefall.

Syd hesitated, and Mitch couldn't tell whether this was due to his flair for dramatic pauses, his inability to come up with anything in the moment, or CNO's alleged time-distorting effects. When he finally spoke, he insisted, "I want it back."

Then he stood up and broke into a stride, and Mitch followed closely behind him, attempting to bridge the distance Syd's head start had afforded him, and after a couple silent, panicked seconds of futile chasing, Syd grabbed the staple-laden canvas off the kitchen table and stabbed a hole in it with his overgrown pinky nail.

"Give it back," Mitch demanded, but now Syd stumbled through Mitch's obstacle course of junk, canvas clutched firmly in coke-nailed hand. Mitch had saved all the trash on his floor out of fear it would someday come in handy, and boy was it coming in handy now, slowing Syd down. Unfortunately, it slowed Mitch down too.

"Punching holes in it is fine," Mitch called irritably. "It's kind of the whole premise of the art. Just give it back."

Syd slipped into Mitch's bathroom and slammed the door, but Mitch caught the doorknob just before the latch clicked and pushed against it with his full weight, feeling Syd exerting equal force in the opposite direction. A year ago, Mitch would have overpowered him through sheer body mass, but Syd had recently gone through that second puberty that tends to hit men in their early twenties, and Mitch had never been one to keep much meat on his bones, so the two of them probably weighed the same amount, give or take ten pounds—basically, the door wasn't going to budge either way unless someone let up.

"I'll give it back if you tell me the real reason you want it."

"I like it."

"The *real* reason."

"I fucking *love* it," Mitch tried. "I only said I hated it at first because I was so jealous of your enormous talent."

Syd made a buzz reminiscent of the ones game shows play when someone answers a question wrong.

"Okay," Mitch panted. Trying to open a resistant door was more of a workout than one might expect, but to be fair, Mitch had never run more than a mile in his life. "You want the truth? I am deeply, incurably in love with you, Syd Morris. I fear I might someday lose you. When I sleep with Hayley, I can think only of you. You are the sole object of my desires—I've loved you since the day we met, and I'll love you until the day I die, and if there's one thing I think is emblematic of the connection we have, it's the thing that sparked our first...what's that noise?"

But the question was rhetorical; there was no mistaking the sound now echoing off the bathroom walls—a displeasing tinkle partially muffled by the splatter of liquid hitting canvas.

"Syd, are you—?"

Syd relinquished his pressure on the door, and Mitch tumbled into the bathroom, and before he'd even found his footing on the slippery tiles, Syd had shoved the wet, soiled canvas into his hand.

"Now it'll remind you of me even more." Syd gave him a smug grin that silently said, *Your move.* His pants hung around his ankles, and he seemed in no hurry to pull them up. Mitch struggled to keep his gaze above the belt.

"You're a real prick, you know."

"Never considered it."

"You owe me four hundred dollars."

Grinned again with that annoying, trademark flash of a grin. "Nah. It's not worth nearly that much."

Life Imitates the Life Art is Imitating:[18]
Part 1

Ever since developing an interest in "acting" (and, more broadly, lying), I've repeatedly wondered what exactly makes a performance "good." Just about everyone can identify strong acting, but very few people can explain what it actually *is*. It's not just the ability to convincingly mimic reality—after all, the most impressive performances are more than just convincing; they're haunting. *Un*natural. So perhaps good acting is maintaining a delicate balance between persuasion and entertainment, but if that's the case, then it probably has nothing to do with one's ability to capture "real life." "Real life," I've found, is seldom entertaining.

I keep this question at the forefront of my mind as I embark on a three-hour drive to Atlanta's Slingshot Acting Studios during August of 2024 to take an eight-session, once-weekly class in the basics of meat puppetry. If I still lived in Boston, NYC would have been a mere train ride away, but my recent relocation to Mississippi means Atlanta is the closest performing arts hub, and without any major magazines agreeing to fund this endeavor upfront like they did with "Art Imitates Life," monetary constraints dictate that the class must be within driving distance. So here I am. What follows is a day-by-day journal of my adventures.

DAY 1

The entirety of the eight-week workshop will be held in one cramped classroom, which looks typical except for the tripod and video camera sitting in the room's center and the total absence of desks. Sixteen chairs have been arranged into a great big circle around the camera. A small TV rests atop an empty bookshelf. A spacious window boasts hideous yellow curtains. You get the picture. Before our 5:30 PM class starts, attendees explore all two hundred square

---

18   The aforementioned second sequel to "Art Imitates Life".

feet of this soon-to-be stage and get acquainted, many of them drinking what seems to be coffee (at 5:30?) and/or listening to music on near-ubiquitous AirPods. I don't speak to anyone, nor do I derive any noteworthy journalistic insights from the cascade of small talk that surrounds me. When a flannel-wearing woman of about thirty-five introduces herself as Lana and tells us, with the gentleness of a teacher herding a classroom of kindergarteners, that the session is starting, we all drop into our seats like eager participants in a game of musical chairs.

"We are here today," Lana announces, "to learn how to *act!*"

Many cheers. People are really enthused at the prospect of becoming meat puppets.

"But first, we've gotta warm up our bodies. Anyone know which body part is the key to acting?"

If I were about fourteen years younger, I might have made a crude joke here, but I know better now.

"The arms," someone says.

"The penis," someone else interjects.

"The face," a third person tries uncertainly. I don't quite pinpoint the source of the voice.

"The face," Lana repeats. She puts two hands to her mouselike visage and massages it like Play-Doh, which creeps me out. I consider how faces are just sacks of flesh hanging off our skulls, and aging is caused by said faces sliding slowly off said skulls gravitationally over time. I subconsciously rub my own face in the hopes of propping it up for a bit longer.

"Everyone do like this young lady," Lana says, removing one hand from her cheeks to point at me. "What's your name?"

"Hannah."

"Everyone do like Hannah."

The others begin massaging their face skin, and I can't help but feel a small spark of satisfaction—the vestiges of my brown-nosing school days, perhaps—at doing something right.

"Your faces are malleable," Lana grunts through stretched lips, "and as actors, you'll want to use the whole shebang."

By the time we're done warming up, our faces have been molded and loosened, our mouths and eyes held wide open, our nostrils flared, and our tongues curled up taco style, though I've never been able to do this last one, so my academic glee from earlier has been replaced by that particular dread you get in those recurring nightmares where you've about to take a test on a textbook chapter you didn't study.

We then break into pairs and move into a deceptively innocuous-sounding game called "reflection," for which I'm partnered with a young woman (seriously, like, twenty-one, tops) named Stardust.[19] Lana invites the now-eight pairs to gaze wistfully into each other's eyes and mirror each other's physical movements. This is a bit too traumatically intimate for me, given that I struggle to maintain eye contact with my dearest friends on good days, so the remainder of this first class is a mental blank.

DAY 2

During the part of Day 1 that I must have deleted from my brain's hard drive (and my usually trusty notebook is of no help—I didn't even write anything down), Stardust and I evidently became quite good friends. Today, she's dressed suspiciously like *Batman*'s Harley Quinn, her pastel-pink hair up in high pigtails, her legs in fishnets, her bright blouse complemented by a denim jacket. Before class begins, she sits down next to me and asks me what kind of stuff I write, which means I must have told her I'm a writer. I wonder what other embarrassing secrets I let loose during my social fugue state.

"Fiction, mostly," I say, "but right now I'm working on some nonfiction."

Her face doesn't assume the smug, condescending look people's faces typically assume when they hear I write fiction (as if to say, "That's cute; I go boating on weekends sometimes. But what do you do for your *job*?"). Instead, her eyes light up with youthful naivety. "Fiction is awesome. Ever had anything turned into a movie?"

I lift one eyebrow with the precision of a facial-warmup expert. "What do you think?"

---

19   NEF: Though this is a pseudonym, her "real" name, which is actually a stage name, is similarly stripperesque.

"Probably not. It's pretty difficult, I've heard."

"Yeah."

"But you're probably *great* at acting, then."

"Why?"

"Well, acting is just like fiction. You're trying to bring characters to life."

I've considered this idea before, of course, but her insight still impresses me.

For today's class, we're each invited to memorize a monologue of our choice. I edgily pick Hamlet's "To Be or Not to Be" and feel mildly perturbed when half the class chooses the same one. Stardust performs Konstantin's mother's speech from Chekhov's "The Seagull," and she's not half bad. She's one of the few people here I might Google in three years' time to see whether they've appeared on any cast lists. I tell her she gave a performance every bit as pivotal as a rifle hanging on a stage wall. She takes a couple seconds to get it.

DAY 3

Today, Lana breaks out the camera—a pretty big deal in the acting world. "Performing on a stage is one thing, but performing in front of a lens is completely different," she explains. "You're being watched, but you're being watched much more clinically. The temptation is going to be to look directly into the camera—to watch the watcher. Resist that temptation. One of the biggest early hurdles for actors is developing the ability to seem unwatched in the face of clinical watching."

I soon discover just how correct she is. Despite my best intentions, my eyes naturally follow the camera's lens, and Lana's flukeish first impression of me as someone who knows my shit has fallen into obvious disrepair.

"You're doing good," she says unenthusiastically, alternately watching me and watching the camera watch me.

"'To be or not to be,'" I begin for the fourteenth or so time.

"Are you feeling okay?" Lana asks.

What I'm really feeling is that special type of burnout associated with not immediately excelling at something. "I need a break," I reply as a bead of sweat rolls off my chin. "I'm melting all over the stage."

BETWEEN DAYS 3 AND 4

On Wednesday, I receive a call from the editor of [magazine name redacted], and it's big news. Long story short, the *Life Imitates Art* essay won't run. So I don't know whether I'm writing for anyone but myself at this point, but I've paid for this acting class, and by God I am going to finish it.

DAY 4

I've had a few days to come to terms with recent shocking developments and any associated guilt about my own small and honestly negligible part in what occurred, and in that time, I've decided that my number one commitment is still to the truth, while my number two commitment is to learning how to convincingly and entertainingly lie. Today, we're receiving a crash course in The Method.

"These next few weeks will be an exercise in character-creation," Lana announces, rotating in place to establish spasmodic eye contact with each of us while standing so close to the camera she's nearly humping it. "I want each of you to create a character. Doesn't have to be someone completely fictional, but try to envision a person not wholly like yourself. Then give yourself the internal monologue of that person. It'll take some mental translating at first, but after a while, it'll be second nature."

This sort of thing could turn into escapism if one isn't careful.

"That doesn't mean the character can't share *any* of your traits, however," Lana continues. "Sometimes it's good to have a few anchoring details you can fall back on."

"So you don't want us to be meat puppets?" I ask.

"To be what? I'm sorry."

"Meat puppets. Like..." I remember with embarrassment that I've never heard anyone besides Greg the Cameraman use "meat puppet" in this manner. "Never mind."

She plows ahead as if the interruption didn't occur. "Today's task is simple: live as your character. Embody your character's essence."

The character whose essence Stardust is embodying has a comparatively normal name: Ophelia. She's got nothing to do with *Hamlet*'s Ophelia, but her boyfriend's father nonetheless passed away under suspicious circumstances.[20] To further emphasize that this is NOT A SHAKESPEARE REFERENCE, Ophelia's boyfriend's name is not Hamlet but Bradley.

As I mingle and interface with the characters of my peers, I can't help but bemoan the needless convolution of this whole affair. I barely broke a sweat memorizing sixteen names, but now we're being asked to remember double that, and to keep track of not just which pair of names references which single person but also which of the two names corresponds to said person's "real" self and which refers to the character.

"What sort of character are you playing?" Stardust asks.

"A woman named Hannah," I say, not wishing to add a thirty-third name to my mental blender. "She's a writer."

"Sounds just like your real self."

"Anchoring details. She's written a book that's been made into a movie, whereas I haven't. She's extremely successful, basically."

"So then act like it," Chase says, his arm draped around Stardust's shoulder, his blond hair coolly swept to one side—the hairstyle of someone who fell into a coma in 2008 and just woke up.

"Huh?"

"Carry yourself like someone successful. You're still acting like the you who hasn't had any movie adaptations. The slumped posture, the dreary monotone. [Okay, Chase, I get it.] How would that level of success change you?"

I imagine myself sitting in a crowded movie theater, watching the meat-puppet incarnations of characters I've invented roam around the big screen, their heads so large and high-def I can see their nose-hairs, the characters seeming more real than even myself, the surround sound of the theater a deafening roar. The theater's chairs resemble business-class airline seats and offer a tantalizing "massage" option. I imagine sitting in one of those chairs and watching the char-

---

20   "Patricide," the boyfriend, via his aspiring meat puppet Chase, claims proudly. It's not clear whether he knows what patricide is.

acter-Hannah I just created thirty seconds ago stroll down the pristine hallways of *The New Yorker*'s headquarters, wearing a tightly-fitted purple dress jacket and a silver bowtie, looking realer up there on screen than the now only half-real me in the audience, while she (i.e., the fictional Hannah, on the movie screen) gives orders to underlings and signs mass-market copies of her newest book *Meat Puppets*, which I decide in this moment that I'm going to write, and which, in the universe of the film my half-fictional self is currently watching, will soon be adapted into a film. I watch my chair-massaged half-real self toss thoroughly- and evenly-buttered handfuls of movie popcorn into her mouth, her eyes fixed on that new, filmic Hannah, two years clean from smoking and definitely not currently craving a cigarette, glowing with the youthful energy that comes from success and fully healed lungs, while the mental reel of the real, non-character Hannah standing dumbly in a Slingshot Acting Studios classroom ouroborosizes itself over and over and over again and Stardust/Ophelia and Chase/Bradley watch me watch the film of my mind's eye's film, their own eyes aglow with concern and trepidation.

6

Financial meetings had once been the highlight of Mitch's month, but now that he and Hayley more or less lived together, the novelty had run dry. They'd begun holding the consults at Nelson's again because Mitch had a habit of trying to get through entire meetings without ever once broaching the subject of finances—he achieved this mostly through a series of diverting sexual come-ons Hayley found too compelling to resist in the privacy of their own home but had no qualms about ignoring in the professional business setting of a money-laundering bookstore. So that's where they met today—the bookstore—seated opposite one another at the checkout desk. Two customers browsed the shelves, which was basically an unprecedentedly high turnout, so Mitch was on his best behavior.

"I think Syd's gonna ruin me," he opened.

"How?" Hayley had a fidgety habit of shuffling through inscrutable and neatly-stapled financial packets whenever she was on edge. It put Mitch on edge too—suspended him in perpetual pause while he waited for her to locate some piece of information she wasn't even looking for. "Don't you have insurance?" she asked, referring to the soiled staple art.

"That fell through."

"What do you mean? Did you *lose* the canvas?" She spoke in an aggressive near-whisper. If it's possible to yell in a whisper, this was it. She used this inflection whenever she wanted to signal to Mitch that she'd rather be yelling, but circumstances did not permit it.

"Something like that. Not important. Look—what do I do about him? He's only getting more popular, and his popularity is financial suicide now. I won't be able to pay back the investors if I don't have anything to sell."

"So tank him."

"But I've made him immune to things that *should* tank him, so I'm not sure I even *have* that power. Besides..."

"Besides what?" Hayley folded her hands atop the register.

"It's stupid, but I guess I've just sort of grown to...."

"To *care* about him? Is that what you're saying? You've developed empathetic feelings for one of your products?"

"He's not a product."

"He's a product by definition, whether you care about him or not. You're selling him. You've *sold* him. How much is his stock worth?"

"Two hundred fifty."

"And you usually cut them loose at what? One-fifty? You broke off a near-engagement when Benji hit one-fifty, so what's taking so long?"

"I can't ditch him *now*. I need to recoup my loss. But I don't know *how*. He's mad at me. Suspicious of my motives. He'll never give me another canvas. Hell, I've hardly *seen* him these past few months—he's been spending all his time with Peter Rankin doing who knows what rarefied designer drugs. *He* doesn't care about *me*."

Hayley blinked right as Mitch broke eye contact. "Are you serious? With all that stuff he told you about his family? God, Mitch, you're so oblivious."

"What do you mean?" But he knew exactly what she meant—had simply hoped it was his imagination.

She sighed long and hard, like an exasperated fourth grade teacher after you ask whether you *can* use the restroom instead of whether you *may*. "You're a surrogate *father* to him. You fill some kind of weird parental void."

"But now he's got Rankin. Rankin is more of a father figure than me, surely."

"Are you in the habit of doing...what did you call them...'rarefied designer drugs' with your parents?"

"No, but—"

"Would Syd ever for a *second* think to do drugs with you?"

A fleeting delay. "No."

She made a "well, there you go" gesture with her hand. "He doesn't see Rankin as a father. Rankin is more like a fraternity brother whose parents own a yacht."

"But Rankin is like fifty. I mean, shit, I'm not even *old* enough to be his dad."

"You're thinking too literally. The reality is that, for whatever reason, Syd has assigned you the dad role. He probably did it before

Rankin even entered the picture, and there was no room for a second dad, so Rankin ended up in the friend-slash-colleague bucket."

"So I'm *still* the dad?" Mitch ran a nervous hand through his hair. His forehead's sweat had an irritating tendency to coalesce around his widow's peak. "Fuck. Then what now?"

"Depends on how horrible a person you're willing to be. But it's clearly in your best interests for Syd's stock price to fall."

"Can I artificially reduce it?"

"Not without sending shareholders into a frenzy. Good luck explaining how you lost the canvas to *them*. They'll assume they're being scammed." She lowered her voice back to a non-yelling whisper. "And I don't want to freak you out, but everything you've been doing here is *illegal*."

"Shit, Hayley, you think I don't *know* that? We're in the money-launder headquarters."

"Say that a little louder, why don't you?" she whisper-yelled, nodding demonstrably toward what was now the store's lone browser—a tall, squarely-bespectacled, college-aged guy who looked like the sort to go into coffee shops and hold a book open but not read it and instead wait for voluptuous and intellectually inclined women to materialize in the seat across from him. "What I *meant* is, there's no legal recourse for people to make back their money if you don't hold up your side of the deal."

"That's good, right?"

"Not exactly. What sorts of methods do you think they'll turn to when they can't take you to court? You can bet it's a lot grislier than court. My point is, you don't want to piss these people off. Anything sneaky you do to Syd's stock must not be traceable back to you."

"So making more stock..."

A vehement head shake. "Moronic. Death wish."

"You're invoking death. Pretty serious." She *looked* serious too. Hayley had never before appeared so genuinely petrified. And since Mitch relied on her for constant reassurance that everything would be stable and fine, he was operating on shaky grounds.

"How many shares are out there?"

"Five hundred."

"So at two-fifty a share, that means if everybody sold now, you'd have to pay out…" She mouthed a few indecipherable words while she did some instantaneous mental math, a skill Mitch had always found bafflingly impressive. "…a hundred twenty-five thousand dollars. You don't have that much disposable income."

"So tank Syd. ASAP."

"But the second he starts tanking, shareholders are going to come knocking. You need some way of getting more money."

"But I can't make more stocks, you said."

"Sneakier." She played idly with the corner of her packet of financial gibberish, seldom looking up. "Do you know what shorting is?"

"Sort of." He didn't, really. He'd seen *The Big Short* years ago, and he'd pretended to understand it at the time, but all he remembered now was Christian Bale playing the drums at some point.

Hayley interpreted his "sort of" as a "no." "It's where you borrow shares from someone else and resell them. You'll owe the first person shares, not cash."

"So if Syd's value goes down…"

"You'll make money."

"But nobody would lend *me* Syd shares. They'd know something was up."

"Which is why we've gotta do it through a third party," Hayley said, grabbing a copy of *Oedipus Rex* from the college-aged hipster in the one-person checkout line and scanning it. "We don't sell many of these," she commented.

"Wanna discuss it further over lunch sometime?" the kid asked her.

She turned back to Mitch. "And I know just the person."

The potential accomplice Hayley had in mind was her old high school friend Lindsay Stewart, who was, by Hayley's estimation, not exactly the pointiest needle in the haystack. Hayley had attended a small high school in rural Illinois with a population of four hundred, so her friendship choices had been limited, she explains defensively. The reason she picked Lindsay for the stock-shorting mission is because Lindsay loves to hear herself talk—"it's excruciating, almost"—and the more she talks, the dumber she sounds. Since the idea was for the stock-borrowee to feel assured that the borrower had no clue what any of it meant, Lindsay would be perfect. Plus, she'd contacted Hayley a few months earlier to tell her she'd just moved to upstate

New York for some new job Hayley can't remember the specifics of, and ever since then, she'd been pestering Hayley about possibly grabbing coffee sometime, and Hayley had been diplomatically worming her way out of the commitments and now feared Lindsay might fear she didn't even want to be her friend anymore, so this meeting could serve multiple purposes, Hayley supposed.

"What if she fucks up?" Mitch asked while he and Hayley sped across the countryside, the one-lane, medianless highway appearing more plastered than carved out—dropped down from heaven to cover a small strip of otherwise ubiquitous corn.

"She won't."

"Right. It's just that like a minute ago you were going on about how stupid she is." He had a point.

"We'll have a script. She can *read*, at least. The plan is airtight."

Here was the plan: sit down for coffee. Pretend to listen patiently to Lindsay's life story. Ask her for a favor. Make her a new profile on Mitch's stock trading server. Give her the number of one of the other stock traders, handpicked by Mitch: a big, gruff guy named Paul who owned forty Syd shares—Syd's largest investor by far—and always showed up to trades completely hammered. He'd ask how she got his number; she'd tell him he gave it to her at the last open trading session, and he'd say something like "Must've blacked out." Paul wasn't the shiniest shoe either. This would be a case of the blind leading the blind while being artfully puppeteered by the sighted.

Lindsay Stewart, whom I managed to track down, is a bubbly and cheerful young lady reminiscent of many I've had the displeasure of knowing. I won't shit-talk Lindsay—she's really the singular participant in these shenanigans who remains morally untainted—but people like her are exhausting to be around not because of any misdeeds on their part but because they make you painfully aware of what a downer *you* are by comparison. When she, Hayley, and Mitch met at a large coffee chain whose workers had a big strike a few years prior and to whom I don't want to give any positive press by naming, Lindsay hugged her old friend tightly. The whole place smelled of slightly burnt, watery coffee (my addendum). When Lindsay and *I* later met, she invited me into her home, which was small but cozy and spotless to a degree that seems impossible unless cleaning your own house is your full-time job.

Hayley doesn't remember what Lindsay blabbered on about for the first forty-five minutes of their lunch date while Mitch scarfed down a club sandwich, a French fry basket, and a large triple-chocolate muffin and then spent the rest of the meeting poking the remaining muffin crumbs with his fork. But I can bet it's similar to what she told me, which I made a point of taking careful notes on—it was the least I could do. The general gist of her monologue is reproduced below:

When Lindsay graduated from Peoria High School in 2006, she thought she wanted to be a school counselor. She abhorred the disinterested flippancy with which public high schools' counselors treated their jobs and wished for nothing more than to make an actual difference in kids' lives. So she graduated with this plan in mind. Here, she goes on a small tangent: her high school let students customize their graduation caps, so hers featured a printed screencap of this niche sci-fi cult classic *Sgt. Nebula*, which after three installments is now being serialized, if you can believe it, and you can bet she's going to be one of the first to watch the new show when it finally stops getting delayed and hits a god-awful streaming service I won't do the favor of mentioning either—substitute in your own most hated—and she plans on reviewing it on her Tumblr blog, which, she knows Tumblr is kind of a thing of the past, but believe it or not there are still a lot of thriving communities on there, and her blog has a modest following of 1768 people. (She checks her Tumblr page now and sees that her follower count has dropped to 1765 and muses bitterly on whether she said something to piss those three people off—she hates losing followers and not knowing why.) Anyway, she managed to get into the University of Illinois Urbana-Champaign and began a psychology major but unfortunately found the required classes to be total snoozefests, which threw her into an existential crisis regarding what she really wanted to do with her life. She ultimately decided on dental school, and she was blessed to open her own practice in central Illinois. This was about 2014ish. It was at this dental practice that she met the love of her life—one of her patients, Mark. The two dated for a few years and were even engaged to be married, but then one day Mark just up and left. No explanation whatsoever—he just left. She felt, in that moment, that she could have really used a therapist herself (and I can't help but agree, sitting here listening, trying not to check the time but feeling confident that I could be making good money right now if I simply had a counseling degree) and contemplated returning to her original professional dream after what she now concedes was a long but necessary detour, in terms of her own personal self-discovery journey. She knew one thing for sure, and that was that she couldn't continue being a dentist—not here, at least, where at the mere scent of burning, drilled teeth she'd be transported Proustianly back to the first time Mark sat in her chair, appearing almost angelically aglow, bathed in the romantic light of the dental lamp (part my addendum, part not; guess which is which). So, long story short, she went back to college and passed all the boring, regrettably mandatory psych classes and finally got a job school-counseling in upstate New York, which she thought perfect, not just because her good friend Hayley was a financial advisor in NYC, last she checked, but also because it meant she could remain far away from Mark and all latent reminders of him.

After Hayley listened patiently to what I assume was some iteration of the above, she told Lindsay that she needed help—she and Mitch wanted to borrow stocks, but Mitch had had a run-in with this guy at his corporate law job, so the guy would never lend him stocks directly. The shares would come from a company called Syd Morris. And Lindsay did, at the time, believe Syd Morris to be the name of a company, though now she of course knows better, and she acknowledges that it was a bit silly of her not to suspect anything, what with Mitch being the way he was—bad vibes, this guy. She bets that if she'd brought her crystals to the lunch meetup, they would have been visibly vibrating from all the sinister and negative energy bouncing around, because when dissonant auras hit each other, they create micro-vibrations that can only be felt by crystals. I haven't asked any crystals for corroboration, so you'll have to just take her word for it.

Lindsay dialed up Paul and read from a Hayley-authored script in Hayley's closest prosaic approximation of Lindsay's own voice, asking to borrow forty Syd shares. Paul asked why, and Lindsay looked at her script's decision tree and replied that, get this: she knew Syd's value was increasing, and she'd read somewhere that borrowing stocks is a good move when a company's value is increasing, and she intended to make some money.

I never got around to interviewing Paul, but I can imagine that by this point he was absolutely gleeful, probably figuring what are the chances of being approached by the one stock-trader on the planet who got the whole basic functionality of stocks completely backward?

The website required proof of identity before transactions could be fulfilled, in order to minimize potential rigging or fraudulent behavior, so Lindsay held her driver's license up to her webcam (after first bemoaning that the picture was *really* bad, and she had to suffer with this license for six more *years*; can you believe it?), and the camera decided it was valid, and that was it. Lindsay was ten thousand dollars richer and forty stocks in debt. She offloaded the shares and debt onto Mitch, and then it was all over.

"I have a bad feeling," Lindsay said, closing her laptop, which was adorned with cliché and feel-good stickers espousing inspirational quotes—stuff like "Dance like nobody's watching" and "You miss all the shots you don't take" and "Yesterday is history, tomorrow is a mystery, and today is a gift—that's why it's called the present."

"What do you mean?" Hayley asked.

"I feel like I've gotten involved in stuff I shouldn't have."

"Put it out of your mind," Mitch told her. "You literally don't even have to *think* about it until it's time for me to pay back the stocks."

Lindsay didn't make eye contact with him—didn't respond at all, in fact. Mitch feared she disliked him almost as much as he disliked her.

"It's true," Hayley reiterated, figuring Lindsay'd be more likely to believe it coming from her. "I'll let you know when Mitch is ready to pay them back. It'll be quick and painless."

"What if he doesn't?" Lindsay said quietly.

"Huh?"

"Pay them back. What if he never does."

"I'm *gonna* pay them back."

"Do you trust us?" Hayley asked her.

Lindsay winced politely.

"Do you trust *me*, at least?"

Nodded.

"Then there's nothing to worry about. Everything is going to be fine."

7

So now that Mitch had washed his hands of Syd—shorted his stock and made the most difficult phone call of his life—Syd needed to fail. He needed to crash and burn, and his stock price along with him. And Hayley's encouragement, though the begrudging encouragement of someone who had told him so (and even told him she'd told him so) time and time again, reassured him that this was the right move.

Mitch didn't even know why she still stayed with him. Financially speaking, he needed her more than she needed him. On the physical attractiveness flagpole, he'd always placed himself right at half-mast. And he had no delusions about being a considerate lover—tended to treat sex the way most men treat fleshlight use, immediately pulling out after coming and then lying on his back in sweaty, post-orgasmic bliss, forgetting that a whole other person had been involved in making him feel the way he'd just felt.

But if she insisted on staying with him, the least he could do was not bankrupt her, which was why Syd needed to fail, which was why Mitch now sped down the highway to Ned Wesham's house with the intention of deliberately backtracking something he'd previously taken great pains to engineer.

Ned was doing a bit better now, at least physically. When he answered the door, he looked exactly like he'd looked before the event, save for a barely noticeable, white hairline scar under his right eye.

"You again," he said, the statement more a bland declaration than an expression of outrage. He swung the door shut in Mitch's face.

Mitch, having anticipated such a reaction, caught it mid-slam and reopened it. He and Ned stared each other down for a few seconds. Mitch noticed that, though he appeared surprisingly physically healthy, something in Ned's eyes had died. His usually gelled dark hair was greasy and disheveled, and he wore the droopy expression of a prisoner of war.

"I've come to make you an offer," Mitch said.

"I'm not giving back the money."

"I don't want anything back. This is for you," which was true. Well, half-true.

Ned scanned Mitch's face slowly with eyes that were still relearning their proper functions.

"I'd like to come in," Mitch asserted, cringing the whole time—assertiveness caused him great discomfort, believe it or not. He'd mostly gotten used to it the way he'd gotten used to feeling guilty, but in times like these, he wondered why he hadn't chosen a career path that didn't necessitate regularly harassing people.

Ned didn't say no, which Mitch interpreted as a "yes." His house was dirty, but the dirt seemed new. The place didn't look like that of someone who didn't mind mess but of someone who'd once gone to great lengths to stay clean but whose cleaning routines had gradually, progressively fallen by the wayside. Miscellaneous crumbs peppered Ned's counters. About half his stove shone so spotlessly you could see your reflection while the other half appeared sticky and grimy, as if Ned had begun wiping it down and then figured, ah, what's the point. Given what I know about Ned, I can provide further insight into this strange ambience: he was depressed. He was also recovering from a pretty major ordeal. He'd hoped the depression would fade with his injuries; it had not.

"I want to talk about Syd Morris," Mitch continued.

"Surprise. How did you find me here?"

"Your agent."

"I told her not to let you contact me."

"I used another fake name."

"Are you completely shameless?" Mitch noticed that Ned's left eyebrow had another white scar just deep enough to warp the skin's surface, creating a subtle, hairless slit. A more fashionable man than Ned could own that look, Mitch thought.

"You got a bunch of money from me," Mitch reminded him.

"Yeah. And now you've come to take it back."

"No, I've come to ask you to defect on your side of the deal. Mind if I take a seat?" Ned's couch possessed the faint imprint of a human body—like someone had slept on it recently.

Again, no answer. Mitch sat.

"It's legally binding." Ned said everything in the same declarative, disinterested tone. He can occasionally be probed into animation if you push the right buttons, but Mitch never managed it. The only time I managed it was today, when I broke news that just about made him leap out of his oversized pants (Ned's lost a lot of weight this past year) in glee. "You'll sue me and spend about as much on lawyer fees as you paid me. The courts will rule in your favor. *I'll* also lose money from the lawsuit. It'll be a lose-neutral-win. But as long as you have me beat, right?"

"Lose-neutral-win?"

"I lose, you break even, the lawyers win."

"Ah. Not a fan of lawyers, then?"

"Is anyone?"

"Lawyers, I presume."

"Until they need one." The corner of Ned's mouth twitched.

Mitch gently patted the sunken cushion to his immediate left. "Take a seat, handsome. Chill with me a while." When assertiveness failed, seduction was his next best bet. "It's your house, after all."

It didn't feel like that to Ned, however. His house had been violated, much like his body. Nothing was his own anymore, except the money Mitch had paid him to stay mum, but now that too seemed like threatened property.

"I'm trying to destroy Syd," Mitch explained.

"Some manager."

"I'm not his manager anymore."

"What happened?"

"A lot," Mitch said. "Including the, er," signaling with his eyes to the general vicinity of Ned's entire face. "I mean, you look good," he saved, after Ned shot him the glare of someone who wants you dead and has the means to pull it off without a legal hitch.

"So *now* you care about that?"

"It was wrong. *I* was wrong for not caring upfront." Explaining his stock dilemma to Ned would take too much time, and Mitch couldn't shake the impression that Ned didn't like him. Ned, at this juncture, was imagining putting Mitch through a kind of *1000 Ways to Die*-inspired obstacle course where an onsite team of paramedics revives him after each deadly hurdle before sending him onward to the next one.

"Surely *you* want Syd to fail too. So just go public. Tell the world what he did. I can arrange for reporters to line up outside your door if you merely say the word."

Ned nodded a few great, gyroscopic nods. He was dealing with some whiplash issues, still. "So what's the catch?"

"No catch."

"Except there is. What's in it for you?"

"Change of heart, like I said—"

"Considering you're possibly the most amoral slimeball on the planet, excuse me if I find it a bit, um, *difficult* to believe that you suddenly restructured the entire way you live your life. You're not motivated by ethics. Most people are. You aren't. Nothing to be ashamed of. Well, I think it's pretty damn shameful, but whatever lets you sleep at night. Do *not* try to take me for some kind of fool, though. You're no different from before. If you were, you wouldn't have committed fraud to get in touch with me. Again," he added. "The only thing that's changed is where the money is." Ned clasped his hands together across his stomach, as if in casual prayer. He still had not sat. "So where's the money now?"

"In your pocket, I presume, unless you've spent it already."

"The *metaphorical* money [sic]," Ned amended, glaring at Mitch sharply. "The money so large it ceases to be an earthly entity and enters the indefinite realm of infinite space. I've been led to believe what you gave me was only a tiny fraction of the real goods."

"You've been misled, then. I don't have any money. I'm actually struggling a bit financially." That was the wrong thing to say, and Mitch knew it immediately.

"*Oh*," Ned exclaimed. "*Oh*, so you're worried Syd is a *liability* now, is that it?"

It was, pretty much. "No."

"I bet that's it, yeah."

"I just want you to speak your truth." Mitch found himself wishing he possessed Syd's bullshitting abilities. Syd would be able to come up with the right line—the perfect combination of words to really sell Ned on the idea. He'd sold more outrageous stuff than this.

But Ned shook his head in that same delicate way he'd nodded.

"You don't want to speak your truth?"

"I want to be left *alone*. If I don't see you or that devil Morris ever again it'll be too soon."

Now Mitch's head swam with slimily amoral ideas. He could call the press anyway. He could sock Ned in his good eye. He could contact Syd and arrange another meeting between him and Ned.

"Aren't you worried?" Ned asked, his voice dripping with a hint toward the propensity for possible animation.

"About what?"

"Morris. You're on his shit list too now, are you not?"

"I wouldn't..."

"Yeah, you saw what happened to me. And I didn't do half of what you've done. Imagine what he could do to *you*."

"He wouldn't—"

"Why wouldn't he? You're just too delightful and charming or what?"

But Mitch had never so much as considered that Syd might come after him. If he were going to, he likely would have by now—Syd wasn't much of a planner. He acted solely on impulse.

"I wouldn't be so sure," Ned went on, his voice now dripping with slightly more than a hint toward the propensity for possible animation. "Especially if you're gonna keep playing with fire. You know what they say about little boys who play with fire."

Mitch did—he'd been a pyromaniac as a child, after all. When he'd begun altar serving, his parents had doused him with praise, believing him to be saintly and devoted and on a fast track to the pearly gates, but his real, secret reasoning was that he longed to carry candles and watch in reverent awe as their small flames melted the wax around them into clear goo. He liked to swipe his prepubescent fingers through the flames' centers and build tiny matchstick houses and barns and set those constructions alight in the back of the church while the priest admired his holy garb in a long mirror, seemingly unaware of Mitch's volatile presence.

After one Mass, Mitch had licked his fingers to extinguish a candle, longing for that familiar delightful sizzle as the fire succumbed to his superior willpower, but he didn't use enough spit and pinched the flame for just a little bit too long. A sharp pain started in his fingers and then seemed somehow—impossibly—to sear all the way through his body like an electric shock. He pulled his tiny hand away and shook it out while jumping up and down in the typical manner of kids who have been hurt but are trying not to cry, his skin irritated and red.

The candle burned on.

8

During the later stages of my in-depth interview with Hayley Duker, she tells me about the time she and Mitch wound up at a gun store, where Mitch intended to buy a gun for the purpose of murdering Syd.

"Self-defense," Hayley corrects me. "In case Syd came after him first."

Hayley adamantly assures me that Mitch never intended to kill Syd, though I have my doubts, given what happened later.

"So you were perfectly cool with the gun thing?"

The impending purchase bothered her, but she wished her worries away, like she did with most of Mitch's more bothersome quirks. The previous vigor of their sex life had hit a standstill after Mitch and Syd's falling out, and since then, she'd been noticing troubling idiosyncrasies in Mitch that she'd previously been oblivious to.

Anyway, on this fine day, which was sometime in June of 2024, the pair headed to the AmmoLation Gun Shop in Saratoga Springs, NY. Mitch told Hayley the purchase would look less fishy if he brought a woman with him. It annoyed her the way he said, "a woman," as if any woman would do.

"I don't know about this," she told him as they pulled into the parking lot. Mitch tended to pull as far into parking spots as was physically possible, so the bottom of the Prius's bumper made an unpleasant crunching sound as it scraped against the high curb. Hayley wondered how Mitch had become the default designated driver—after all, her skills far eclipsed his, so was it just like a masculinity thing? Come to think of it, was his insistence on buying a gun a masculinity thing too? This isn't a rhetorical question, she says now—it's just been so *long* since she's been able to talk to someone, woman-to-woman. She asks whether I also feel these pressures to like, surrender myself to the male will. I say no, not really, but to be fair, whatever childhood socialization protocols most women go through seemed not to have worked on me. For all intents and purposes, I barely count as a woman, I say.

"You'll be fine," Mitch assured Hayley. "They're suckers for people who are passionate about home defense. They'll probably dupe us into buying five or six guns."

"We are *not* buying five or six guns."

"Two, at most."

"No, one. One at most."

The inside of AmmoLation resembled an old-fashioned fishing lodge or some other type of whimsical refuge for those who want to live on the outskirts of society and take matters into their own hands, independent of government considerations—like if Henry Thoreau had shipped himself out to Walden Pond with nothing but the clothes on his back and his three hundred trustiest semi-automatics.

"It's a subconscious projection thing," Mitch whispered to Hayley, signaling broadly to the whole atmosphere of the store. "They want you to feel like if you buy a gun, you can live someplace like this."

"How can I help you folks?" the guy working there asked, resting a nonchalant size-thirteen boot on the check-out counter. He was bearded and rotund, wore denim overalls, and affected a fake southern accent.

"Looking for a gun," Mitch replied, his eyes darting around.

The worker let out a condescending huff like *How did these poor naïve liberal elites manage to wander into my gun shop in the first place?*

"I somehow got it in my head that the guy's name was Cletus," Hayley says now. She gives a slight smile, her eyebrows working. "But I don't know where that impression came from, because now that I say it aloud, it sounds ridiculous."

But "Cletus" is easier than "the guy working there," so it'll have to do for pseudonymic purposes.

"What kind of gun?" Cletus asked, stroking his squarely-trimmed beard in a positively East-Coast manner.

"Handgun," Mitch said.

"Type of handgun? Revolver? Bolt-action? Break-action? Semi-automatic?"

Now he was just showing off. "Uhhh..."

"What type is ideal for preventing home invasions?" Hayley

piped up.

Cletus grunted. Turned around and scanned the shelves for a few seconds before delicately grabbing one. "Kill Bill[21] nine-millimeter," he said, holding it out with flat palms. "Great for control. 'S what all the cops use."

Mitch picked it up with a lack of delicacy that made both Hayley and Cletus flinch. "Got a mirror or anything?"

"A mirror?" Cletus repeated, his face blank.

"Wanna see how I look firing it."

"Uh, no."

Mitch pointed it at Hayley with a bent arm. She instinctively ducked.

"You see this coming, what do you do?" lowering the barrel so that it once again targeted her.

"Don't point at people," Cletus urged, far more weakly than you'd expect from a gun shop worker.

"It's not loaded."

"Fair enough."

Hayley observed how easily Cletus bent to Mitch's will. At the end of the day, Cletus wanted to sell a gun, or several, and he wasn't about to say anything that might jeopardize that goal.

"Mitch became a completely different person when he held the gun," Hayley tells me. "Or maybe a more intense version of who he was. I'm not sure. Maybe I should have known better."

I tell her a song by a really famous and heavily trademarked band has that title.

"How is it for beginners?" Hayley asked Cletus, regaining composure. Mitch was now preoccupied with closing one eye and fake-firing at select gun displays while muttering, "Bam."

"Not ideal," Cletus admitted, making a visible, concerted effort to ignore Mitch. "You want a more beginner-friendly one, I'd go with the Chekhov 30."[22] Cletus somehow knew the precise location of every gun by heart. "Also nine-millimeter. Modular back strap and in-

---

21   This was not the gun's real name, as you've probably guessed.

22   Not a real gun brand either.

tuitive, easy-to-operate, manual safety. No external hammer. Simple to fire."

About fifty percent of his statement was comprehensible to Hayley and Mitch, who now realized they'd waded into metaphorical waters too deep to stand in comfortably. Or at least, Hayley got that sense. Mitch reveled in the masculine power fantasy of holding a deadly weapon.

Cletus all but yanked the first gun out of Mitch's grasp and replaced it with the Chekhov, which Mitch weighed in his hand the way he assumed a gun connoisseur might. He held it up in another performative gesture of aiming.

"You'll want a straighter elbow than that," Cletus told him with the air of someone who's been holding back a critical comment for several minutes.

"Show me," Mitch urged.

Cletus held out his palm like *well give me the gun then*, and Mitch pointed with his free hand to the spot at his immediate left. "Show me," he repeated.

Cletus sighed and traversed the counter. You could tell he viewed the counter as a sort of impermeable barrier between Seller and Customer. Hayley, by this point riveted, watched while Mitch held his elbow deliberately limp and Cletus grabbed said elbow with a poorly-repressed disgust and tried to reposition it.

"What about my grip?" Mitch asked, eyeing his hand demonstrably.

"That's wrong too."

"Show me."

"You gotta have your fingers like—I mean—just give me the gun, man," the southern accent becoming less pronounced with every word.

Mitch adjusted his grip into another unnatural and clearly incorrect position. "Like this?"

"No, just—"

"I'm a physical learner," Mitch said, beaming with repressed mirth. "One might say touch is my love language."

Cletus took a sudden, wary step back.

"Gun language," he amended.

Cletus sighed again, his sighs becoming progressively louder and more like screams, and grabbed Mitch's gun hand, fixing his eyes unblinkingly on the opposite wall as if afraid meeting Mitch's gaze would turn him to stone, and maybe that simile isn't too far off. Hayley's annoyance grew. She couldn't for the life of her understand why Mitch was flirting with the obviously heterosexual hick at the gun shop. She'd thought he had eyes only for her.

"I've been meaning to ask," I ask, "whether Mitch's bisexuality…"

"I have no idea," she replies, anticipating the question. "I know he loved me. Or I thought he did…." She looks down at the freshly Swiffered floor. "But the men? It's hard to say. It all seemed so transactional with everyone else." Everyone except one person, I wanted to add.

Mitch resisted each of Cletus' attempts to reposition his fingers. "Am I getting close?" he asked innocently. Hayley laughed.

And she tells me that, for better or for worse, one of her most enduring memories of her former lover Mitch is of him standing there grinning while Cletus the Gun Shop Owner uncomfortably and eye-contactlessly touches his hand with his own and Mitch tries, against all reason, to goad him into keeping it there for just a little bit longer.

9

Rest assured: this is the last section of this novel/biography/memoir/uncategorizable bookish compendium that will feature a call between Syd and Mitch. This call was the first in a long time—the first, in fact, since Mitch had cut Syd off. Syd had shown impressive restraint up until now.

Mitch picked up—he almost didn't, in which case things would have turned out a lot differently—but alas, he picked up, reluctantly, cautiously, I think partially in the hopes that Syd would convince him to come back around.

Upon Syd's first utterance, a weak "Mitch?", Mitch could tell that he'd passed his default state of moderate intoxication and entered the dangerous category.

"What, Syd?"

"Mitch...I think I overdosed."

"On CNO?"

"CNO, some heroin. A few sleeping pills. Some tequila. Sleeping pills. Did I say heroin yet?"

"You took all those things?" There was, of course, a good chance Syd was lying—he was a hell of an actor, by this point—and while Mitch desired nothing more than to partake in what he pictured as a *Scooby-Doo*-esque unveiling of Syd's true motives, the alternative was too dire. Sure, he wanted to destroy this guy's public image, but he didn't want him *dead*. "How long ago?"

"Like ten...twenty minutes."

"Well shit, Syd, have you called an ambulance?"

A few seconds' pause followed, which Mitch experienced as a Schrödinger's Cat-type situation. "I called *you*," Syd said, as if he hadn't fully understood the question, and if he'd really ingested all those substances, perhaps he hadn't.

"But an ambulance too, right?"

Another pause that seemed to warp the entire time-space continuum. "Mitch? Do you love me?"

"I don't…"

"I need to know that you love me."

"What you *need* is to go to the hospital. I'm calling nine-one-one."

"Don't bother with them," Syd slurred. "They can't fix me. You can fix me. Come over."

"I can't fix you, Syd. What the fuck am *I* gonna do?"

No answer.

Mitch tightened his grip on the phone. "Syd? Are you there?"

"I'm not going anywhere, silly billy. Relax." Syd let out two weak, short laughs. "I'm gonna be right…here."

"Okay, just…hang tight."

"Mitch?"

"Yeah?"

"I was wrong. About it not being an undesirable state."

"Huh? About what?"

"Like we talked about before. Overdosing. It *is* an undesirable state. I don't wanna die like this, Mitch." The statement sounded more like a plea than a whine.

"You won't. You're gonna be fine." Mitch wished he had the acting chops to sound convincing.

"Okay. I'll see you soon."

"I'm not—" but then the situation's crushing urgency hit him, and he hung up.

Mitch called the ambulance with arthritic stiffness—it was as if a new set of bureaucratic middlemen separated his brain and his muscles. He spoke to the female operator with an affected slur reminiscent of Syd's, giving her Syd's name and address as his own, telling her that he'd taken a substantial amount of heroin, CNO, alcohol, and pills about twenty minutes ago, all the while thinking that if Syd was jerking him around he'd have him killed. Or the cops would, for putting in a fake 9-1-1 call. He supposed either way it would work out.

"Syd Morris? The famous actor?" the operator asked, her whole vocal demeanor altered, as if she'd briefly forgotten she was supposed to be in emergency crunch-mode.

"I'm not sure how *famous*…"

"Yeah, that sounds like you," a proclamation that bewildered Mitch. "We'll have someone right with you, Mr. Morris."

Mitch exhaled slightly. "Thanks."

I'll jump in here and give Mitch a bit of privacy, and besides, nothing much happened until he received a phone call a couple hours later, at which point he, having had some time to decompress and contemplate to what extent he'd be culpable if Syd died, found his formerly bureaucratic limbs freshly greased and rejuvenated.

"Hello."

"Hi, is this Mitchell Larkin?" a female voice asked. She sounded young but put-together.

"Mm. Who is this?"

"Manhattan General Hospital. We have one Sydney Morris here—"

Mitch shot up from the couch as if his ass were spring-loaded. "Syd? Is he okay?"

"His condition is stable. He had a pretty major drug overdose, and it was touch-and-go for a while, but he's in the ICU, and we don't anticipate any long-term damage."

Mitch let out a long gust of air he hadn't realized he'd been holding in for the past however-long-it-had-been—each minute had felt like days. "Thank God."

"You may visit him if you like."

"You're allowing open visitations?"

She chuckled dryly. "No, sir. You're his emergency contact."

Mitch gaped. "Yeah," he said. "Okay. Sure."

He didn't intend to ruminate too heavily on the implications of his first post-breakup encounter with Syd taking place in a hospital. All he knew was that if he—Mitch—was Syd's emergency contact, then Syd really had no one. Guilt was becoming harder to process as a neutral emotion.

Mitch hadn't ever been hospitalized—possessed a strikingly immune phenotype and had never gone under the knife for *anything*, not even the removal of his wisdom teeth, which had grown neatly into his mouth, baffling his dentists. Still, he knew from his recent escapade as a hospital visitor that waiting rooms tended to get chilly, so he threw a faded Arctic Monkeys sweatshirt into his passenger's seat and fired off a text message to Hayley, which read: *Headed to hospital. Syd had drug mishap. Might be a few hours.*

On some level, Mitch hoped Hayley would drop everything and come wait with him. Rub his shoulders, which had never felt so tense. Tell him little niceties like "This isn't your fault" and "There's no way you could have known" and maybe even the uber-delusional "There's nothing you could have done differently."

But Syd would live. And this would relieve Mitch, at least for a bit—at least until the unfortunate turn of events that would force him to take a hard and contrary stance on the whole whether-Syd-lives business.

The inside of the hospital was a maze-like collection of right-angled halls with a repellent combination of beige tiling and beige wallpaper that resembled the inside of a human intestine. It wasn't cold—if anything, it was stuffy and suffocating and felt like death. Literally—on the other side of any of these walls, someone could be dying. This place concretized the last stage of human life—provided refuge for those who wanted their demise to be as clean and managed as possible.

Despite his best efforts to find the ICU, Mitch somehow wound up in the urology unit, and after the chirpy young woman working the desk gave him detailed directions ("Take a left at the end of the hall and then an immediate right, and then take the elevator up to floor 'M,' and then take a right and then there should be a few doors, and it's the third door on the left but the fourth or fifth door in total, and once you're in there, there's a lobby area and a check-in desk, but the check-in desk is sort of tucked behind a wall a bit, and the cardiology check-in desk is in there too, so make sure you go to the rounded, dark brown one and not the mahogany one"), he understandably made a wrong turn at some point and found himself in the gastroenterology unit. He was getting closer though—was at least on the correct floor this time. The older gentleman at the gastro desk kindly helped him get his bearings.

This sort of logistical stuff usually gets omitted in fiction. Unless a hospital hallway breeds narratively relevant events, fictional stories typically feature a contemplative image of the protagonist in the car before abruptly cutting to his entrance into the correct ward, at which point he declares, winded and out of breath for reasons I can assure you have everything to do with unwilling hospital tourism,

"I'm here for ______."

"I'm here for Syd," Mitch declared, winded and out of breath from unwilling hospital tourism.

"Last name?" the woman (this one older and motherly) asked.

"Morris. Sydney Morris. And I'm Mitchell Larkin. I was told I could visit him at some point."

The woman clicked through a few pages on her computer—receptionists were always clicking through nebulous, secret things on their screens. She wore a tight ponytail and smelled faintly of lavender. "One moment please," she said, holding a manicured finger in the air. And then she disappeared into that ubiquitous hospital void where doctors and nurses and receptionists go to sort out confidential business.

Upon her return, she simply stated, "He's sleeping. Would you still like to see him?"

Mitch nodded without much contemplation.

"One moment please."

And then he waited. He hadn't thought about the Chekhov 30 in quite some time.

10

Sometimes, when the night was heavy and Mitch's bed comforter was heavier, he awoke in a panicked sweat attributable to multiple causes.

But mostly guilt, he figured. Guilt more than any kind of temperature considerations. The temperature consideration stuff was a red herring, or a metaphor, or some other literary device he'd learned about in high school and not thought about since and was definitely too tired and guilt-wracked to think about when he woke up this morning.

He pitied himself for it—the guilt. After all, he didn't deserve it, and he certainly didn't deserve this negatively-charged, Catholic-esque guilt he thought he'd long ago mastered not feeling. It's not like he'd killed someone.

The real cause of Mitch's strife, I think, was that he missed Syd. He missed having an equal—someone who thwarted his schemes by scheming back. In his previous relationship dealings, he'd resembled a dog playing with a limp, dead squirrel. Now he was more like...a dog who had tried unsuccessfully to catch a squirrel for years, become self-conscious about its own squirrel-catching abilities, decided to blow the squirrel's head off with a gun (the dog has opposable thumbs, in this universe of simile), and then not even toyed with the pulped squirrel afterward—it wouldn't be right, given the circumstances that led to its death.

Anyway, point being, Syd comprised a larger-than-usual portion of Mitch's brain space this morning. His clock, its glowing red numbers the only visible light in the whole room, read 4:06 AM, and a shadowy, seething menace filled the air, and as Mitch grabbed the Chekhov 30 pistol out of his desk drawer and spun it around his finger (with the safety *on*—he was no moron), he couldn't help but sense that there was something else stirring—one more trick up the endless and physics-defying sleeve of the man who'd given him way more trouble than he'd signed up for.

But he'd sign up again in a heartbeat, Mitch would. He'd go straight back to that little Times Square stand advertising dorky, stapled canvases and ask Syd once again for his hand in whatever would allow them to be inseparable for the next two years. This revelation scared him—made him fear he'd lost sight of what was meaningful about the Process. The Process had made him rich, and any good financial advisor would tell him not to mess with his single, fickle source of income.

If Hayley weren't still fast asleep next to him, he'd ask her. He'd ask her about the guilt thing too. Being with her had somehow become less about romance and more about the fact that she was his sole confidant.

Mitch's typical schedule nowadays was as follows: Wake up in the morning's wee hours, panicking. Spin the Chekhov and imagine a fanciful scene in which it comes to good use.[23] Brew a cup of black coffee. Drink it. Brew another. Drink it. Wait for Hayley to wake up, usually on the tenth or eleventh cup of coffee. Beg Hayley to quit her

---

23   The scene usually went something like this: Syd, having learned what was going on the entire time he and Mitch were consorting, comes after Mitch with an axe. In a couple swift chops, Mitch and Hayley's front door is completely bashed in. Hayley is clutching Mitch damsel-in-distressedly, whimpering for him to do something (author note that this would be extremely out of character for Hayley, but this doesn't disturb Mitch's fantasy). Syd is standing there in the doorway with the axe above his head. It's storming. A bolt of lightning hits the field outside, way too close for comfort, illuminating the murderous evil in Syd's eyes for just an instant, but that instant is terrifying, and the lightning strike strikes fear in Mitch's troubled but brave heart. Fear and a bit of arousal, Mitch being someone who has always secretly longed to fire a gun at a human target but never been in a situation where that sort of action was necessary or advisable. Until now. Syd struts measuredly and murderously toward him, axe still raised. Mitch, quick on his feet, pulls the gun out of his holster (Mitch didn't own a holster, but these fantasies sometimes made him wish he'd just buy one already), aims with two hands, and fires straight at the menace's heart. The menace staggers but doesn't fall. He keeps advancing, now more zombily than anything. Mitch shoots again, this time at the face's dead center. Hayley screams as Syd's skull pops and disintegrates with a satisfying but horrifying Kennedian *splat*. Syd's headless body advances for a couple more steps before his knees buckle, and he falls throat-forward onto the ground, axe arm outstretched, blood pouring from his decapitated neck. Hayley kisses Mitch, and the two of them head to bed, and the fantasy fades to black with the kind of "you know what happens next" implicative wink often employed in PG-13 movies (though the scene leading up to that point is delightfully R-rated with a body gore volume high enough to cause a national shortage of fake blood).

financial advisor job and stay with him at home so they can wallow in misery together. Listen to Hayley remind him that the two of them will be in financial ruin once the stock scam catches up with them and she needs her job now more than ever. Ignore the assertion because it only induces panic. Hallucinate disgruntled stock owners outside his window like shapes on Plato's cave wall. Maybe go to the shooting range if he's feeling it. Google "Syd Morris" and read as many articles as he can stomach. Wait for Hayley to return and cook him dinner. Talk to Hayley about the guilt he feels over Syd. Commiserate with Hayley about what a bad investment Syd turned out to be. Apologize to Hayley for making such a bad investment. Have sex with Hayley but feel kind of empty. Go to bed.

But today, there was an additional, unexpected entry in this sordid sequence: receive a phone call from Syd.[24] Given what his and Syd's last conversation had been, Mitch was almost afraid to answer his phone, but he reluctantly picked up, if only because he still missed the sound of Syd's voice, which this time was clear and crisp and surprisingly lucid.

Syd didn't greet him. He didn't ask him for anything. He just said, "I've been cast in a movie."

Mitch gathered his thoughts, feeling the eerie sense of inner calm that accompanies pre-tornadic weather. "What movie?"

Syd's response was one that I can't print here—the movie's production company is famously litigious, despite (or perhaps as the result of) having more money than God. Suffice it to say, it's part of a franchise that has been trapping many up-and-coming indie directors and actors. Being cast in it brings wealth, fame, and an ongoing contract that spans an indefinite length of time. Its films consistently do well with the twelve-to-fourteen-year-old demographic, as well as some mentally and emotionally stunted adults. I'll go ahead and pseudonymize the film in question as *Captain Wilderness: Escape from Alaska.*

"Pretty major role too. I'm the reason the heroes almost don't escape from Alaska. Oh, and I know all about your little stock busi-

---

24   Okay, so I was lying about the no-more-calls thing. As you might expect, I've become a pretty good actor as of late.

ness," Syd went on before Mitch had time to properly react to the *Captain Wilderness* thing. "Some of your buyers do too. You're in deep shit, man. You're in like a shit anthill. Except you're one of the ants, and I'm a little kid stomping all over your hill. You're fucking *dead*, man."

Mitch didn't say anything—somehow felt dehydrated on twelve cups of coffee.

"The news is dropping next week. Publicly. I'm giving you special advance notice because...oh, I don't know. Because I just love you so much, I guess."

Mitch's mind now managed to be both totally empty and totally full—full of *something* but nothing resembling words. A cloud of electrostatic noise.

"Come on, man, aren't you gonna fight back? You pathetic piece of shit. You absolute loser. You—"

"Careful," Mitch said. Even mustering the energy to project his voice at a normal level felt like yelling. "Most people still don't know who you are."

Syd let out a high-pitched, hyenic laugh. He was definitely tweaking, now that Mitch thought about it.

"*Nobody* knows who you are," Syd spat back. And then he hung up.

Mitch slumped down on the sofa. His house felt depressingly empty—had felt this way ever since Hayley had made him throw out all his useless junk piles.

Hayley. He would call Hayley. He removed his phone from his pocket, shaking violently. Hayley would know what to do. And if she *didn't*, well, then...

"What about 'I am meeting with clients from nine to five' don't you understand, Mitch?"

"I know, I know. There's just been a...development in the Syd case."

"Can it wait?"

"He's been cast in the new [redacted] movie. *Captain Wilderness: Clash of Nebraska* or whatever."

Hesitation. "And you believe this?"

"What choice do I have?"

Muffled, to someone else: "I'm sorry. It's another client. Stock trouble. I'll give you extra time at the end." To Mitch again: "I don't think I can help you."

"But this affects you too." He lacked the soundness of mind necessary to object to being called a "client."

"I know. I just don't have an answer, Mitch. What do you want me to say?"

"Come up with something! This is your job."

"I'm sorry that this didn't end well for you. For us. I suppose another 'I told you so' would be a step too far. Is that okay? Is that enough? Can I get back to earning actual money now while you get back to losing it so we can at least break even?"

Silence.

"I'm hanging up now."

And she did.

But Mitch did have *one* path of recourse, he thought, his pointer finger itching for the cool spin of a Chekhov 30 firearm. It was messy and last-resort and not the sort of thing he could loop Hayley in on, but it was *possible*.

If Syd had been telling the truth, and the announcement was really happening next week, his stock price would skyrocket. And if it did, buyers would be rushing to sell their shares back before Mitch could so much as utter the word "bankrupt," and when Mitch failed to pay out the money he owed, shareholders would come after *him*. They were already talking to Syd, apparently.

So it was decided: the only way to prevent this disturbing development was to get Syd recast. And the only reason [redacted] would dare recast him was if he were dead.

No, he wasn't proud of it, but what choice did he have? Subjects' stock prices were determined by the rate of accruing celebrity buzz, which meant they couldn't fluctuate posthumously, which meant this would still be Mitch's safest gamble. He couldn't see any other option that didn't end up with *himself* dead, and the gun *had* been bought for self-defense purposes, after all.

The Aftermath

Most prison-tourism experts would likely tell you that a maximum-security prison should not be the first kind you visit, much like Mount Everest should not be the first mountain you climb. They'd probably be right—the fact that I'm here now, journalistic materials in hand, ready to exploit a sordid story for literary profit, feels dirty. Perhaps it *is* dirty. I'm not even sure why I was invited—when I sent the letter asking whether I could visit the maximum-security wing of the Fishkill Correctional Facility (I think my note actually said "murder wing," which should have been enough of a faux pas to get me dismissed from the outset), it was a long shot. It *still* feels like a long shot—like at any moment, the warden who's currently leading me down a poorly-lit hall past legions of sunken-faced, orange-suited men is going to wake up from his stupor and say, "Wait a second. Where are we? Who are you? Who am I?" Maybe I too will wake up to find myself alone in the comfort of my double bed in my roomy apartment with shades on the windows instead of bars, where I'll spend a few reflective minutes admiring the sheer journalistic balls of my dream self.

The warden's[25] silence only makes the whole thing eerier—he could utter any number of statements to put my mind at ease, but he seems to consider my nerves or lack thereof a matter of little consequence.

When we enter the actual murder wing, it's ghostly silent and spectrally absent of human presences. Two prison guards lead a single uncaged man down the hall's invisibly-delineated oncoming lane. The prisoner's face is unshaven, and his hands are cuffed, and each prison guard dwarfs him by about fifty percent.

"I'm surprised he invited you," the warden says now, referring

---

25   In order to create a fictional aura around what was truthfully a very real and harrowing experience, I'll refer to the warden only as "the warden," since fictional wardens are seldom afforded the privilege of first names.

to a different prisoner. The warden is a tall, clean-shaven man—so clean-shaven that I can see each of his pores in minute and harrowing detail. I almost wish I'd left my glasses at home.

"Why's that?" I ask.

The warden stops walking for a second. Turns his entire upper body. Looks down at me. "He doesn't take kindly to visitors."

That was not among the many mind-easing statements he could have uttered.

Apparently noting my discomfort, he emits a jarring, straight-faced laugh. "Relax. We haven't had any visitors killed in here in *years.*" Pauses. Laughs again. "Oh, *man.* You should see your *face.*"

I remain silent for the remainder of the walk, hoping the warden will follow suit.

The murder wing's visitor area strongly resembles those depicted in movies—a long, bleak row of cubbies, each featuring a transparent, smudgeless pane of glass with an old-fashioned, white, corded phone hanging next to it and an identical phone inside its corresponding cell.

"Alert me when you're done," the warden says flatly, and then he leaves me alone with the murderer.

The disheveled murderer appears more sad than dangerous, with eyebags so deep his face looks hollow and thin hair that has seen better days. His orange jumpsuit is buttoned one hole off from what nature intended.

Looking at him now, some of my fear subsides. This guy wouldn't try to kill me—I'm positive of that much. I find it hard to believe he ever killed *anyone.*

I pull out his cubby's chair with a nauseous creak. While I take a seat, he takes one opposite me, mirroring my every move. Watching him feels like watching a dark and Lynchianly altered reflection of myself. I place my list of interview questions onto the counter, my hands trembling. He leans forward, trying to snag a glance. I adjust the tiny microphone hooked to my left ear and double-check that the tape is running.

I pick up my phone. He picks up his phone.

I clear my throat.

Part IV:
...and the Start of Something Else

1

Mitch was not the first person Syd punched—far from it. By the time he met Mitch, he was already a de facto punching expert—had enough experience hitting people to know just how much force would induce bleeding without bone-breakage. He'd use prissy, low-force bops to give punchees a taste of what could come, much the way dogs nip before they bite. But in high school, he didn't yet possess this Zen precision of power. Back then, hitting someone was a total crapshoot.

Take, for example, the first semester of his freshman year, when his mom still had custody of him, and his then-stepdad Glen was still alive, and Syd socked and broke the nose of one Thomas Newson, who had done nothing to deserve it besides be his annoying sniveling freak self, but in Syd's defense, he was going through a bit of a psychoemotional turmoil at home. That morning, Glen had revealed plans to adopt him and become his *real* dad, which elicited all sorts of muddled feelings in Syd. On one hand, Glen hadn't given any indication that he'd be anything less than a stellar father, but on the other, he played saxophone in a jazz band called Glossy Fuse, which was just about the squarest occupation Syd could imagine. Telling your high school peers your dad is a jazz saxophonist is basically masochism with an extra step.

Syd's mom rarely spoke and never reacted and thus didn't have much to say about the punching incident besides "Did it have to be the nose?" Her indifference to her son's outbursts was honestly part of his problem; she didn't exactly disciplinarily deter him from punching more kids in the future, which he would—two, to be exact. She also told him that she shouldn't even be driving right now, the implications of which were self-evident.

"Is Glen still going to adopt me?" Syd asked his mother when they arrived home. Glen was practicing alto saxophone loudly in the guest bathroom, which he maintained had the best acoustics in the house.

"I assume so," his mom said.

"Even though I'm a juvenile delinquent?" Syd slipped his backpack off his shoulders and dropped it onto the floor the way kids who never really took a solid stance on the object permanence issue often did.

"Why don't you ask him?"

So fourteen-year-old Syd burst into the guest bathroom right in the middle of one of Glen's most tasteful, complicated licks and announced, "I'm suspended for punching."

Glen removed his mouth from the saxophone. He had very round lips and a graying beard that formed a happy trail down the middle of his neck.

"Do you really want to tell all your stupid jazz people your *son* punched a guy?" Syd pressed, because Glen's lack of any comprehensible reaction discomforted him—he'd come to expect as much from his mom, but Glen was supposed to *care* about him.

His stepfather stood up, sax in hand. Patted Syd's shoulder. "Want to learn some stuff about music?"

"Aren't you gonna say anything about what I just told you?"

"Glossy Fuse actually needs a piano player." Glen's avoidance, Syd would later understand, stemmed not from apathy but from a desire to withhold from him the one thing he most desperately craved— mistreatment. If Syd could get Glen to mistreat him, he'd have a tangible objection to the adoption thing. Right now, his reasoning was nebulous, and Syd, being no idiot, detested nebulosity and cognitive dissonance above all else.

"I don't play piano."

"That's okay—I'll teach you."

So Syd and Glen sat side by side on the dusty bench of the family's brown upright piano, and Syd's annoyance at Glen's non-response to the punching revelation faded into the recesses of his mind.

Glen held his saxophone in one hand and placed his other on the piano. Pressed a key with a flat-fingered, chicken-pecking motion that told Syd his stepfather didn't know his way around this particular instrument.

"This one's A," Glen said. The note's timbre reminded Syd of the color red. "Here's B." B sounded more like navy blue—fully distinct from A.

"Why do they name them with letters instead of colors?" Syd asked, his mind a kaleidoscope of imagined noise. His mother had disappeared to wherever she was always disappearing to for hours at a time.

"I suppose they *could* name them after colors," Glen conceded, "but then you'd have to keep track of which order the colors came in."

This made no sense to Syd, but he didn't object.

"Notice when I play middle C"—pressed an adjacent white key on the piano, which sounded turquoise—"that I can make that same note on my sax." Glen blew into his saxophone, and the two notes blended seamlessly into another turquoise—inexplicably richer but unmistakably uniform.

"I can even do it with—" Glen played the red note on his sax, so Syd instinctively pressed the piano's corresponding key to recreate that beautiful monophony.

Glen yanked the saxophone out of his mouth with the force of someone who'd discovered it was actually a snake. Half the red dissipated. "—how did you do that?"

"Do what?" Syd asked, still holding down the red key. "I just did what you did."

"How did you know which note I played?"

"You played it earlier."

"But how did you remember the pitch?"

Syd didn't answer, confused as to why it wouldn't be obvious.

"Turn around," Glen ordered now, his eyes alight.

And I probably don't have to dramatize what came next. Glen played some more piano notes and asked Syd to identify them by color. Then he started repeating notes to check the consistency of Syd's designations, and then the still-entranced Glen explained to Syd with a gleaming excitement what perfect pitch was and how it would make him a great jazz improvisor because he'd intuitively know which notes would sound good with which other notes. Glen told Syd that if he kept practicing, he might one day be able to perform with Glossy Fuse, and this made Syd feel good, but also bad, because Syd wanted more than anything to hate this guy, but Glen had not, in all Syd's six years of knowing him, gifted him with a single concrete hateable trait.

"I've got it with dates, you know," Glen added.

"Got what?"

"Synesthesia. June is pink. July is yellow. December is a bright gray."

"Is that how you remember my birthday?"

Laughed. "I'd remember *your* birthday either way, Syd. That's how I remember the birthdays of people like...King Charlemagne."

"Which is when?"

"April second, seven forty-eight. Pretty close to yours, interestingly enough."

Syd's mouth fell open. Glen could have been bullshitting, he supposed, but he didn't think so. "I've got that with music?"

"Perfect tonal recall, yep. Very rare—you should make something of it."

So, feeling rare and proud for once in his life, Syd swung open the master bedroom door, where his mother stood hunched over her nightstand snorting coke, and at the sound of her son's indiscreet, unceremonious entry, she stumbled around as if drunk rather than wired, nearly knocked the reading lamp onto the floor, and then finally stood up gawkishly, blocking as much of the nightstand as she could reasonably manage with her tiny, underweight body.

"I've got perfect pitch," Syd said, though the emotion that prompted the statement had admittedly lost some verve.

His mom gave him the smile adults give when they've been interrupted in the middle of important tasks. "That's great, Syd." Took a step forward and attempted to guide him out of the room by the shoulders. "Let's go."

"Can I use your bathroom?" he asked, remaining defiantly still.

His mom rocked back and forth from foot to foot a few times. "Sure."

So Syd rushed into the master bathroom with the unpleasant haste that usually indicates a desperate need to shit, sat patiently on the closed toilet until he heard his mother's footsteps recede, and then sneaked back out to her nightstand and snorted the familiar white powder she'd left there. Within seconds, he was so far gone he found himself wishing Glen would adopt him after all.

2

Syd didn't even need to ask why his mom lost custody of him—it was glaringly obvious. Weeks prior, CPS had asked him a bunch of questions, the general thrust of which had been whether he often witnessed his mother consuming illegal substances, and he hadn't seen any reason to lie—had figured that since Glen wasn't his biological father anyway, he could now either become an emancipated minor or track down his real dad and live with him. And Glen had not spared Ms. Ashley Morris, neé Burcham, in his deposition—had detailed all the hotel rooms he and Syd had fled to, all the band rehearsals he'd cancelled to pick Syd up from school because Syd's mom was unconscious or otherwise unfit for operating large motor vehicles, all the times she'd operated large motor vehicles anyway, all the shifts she'd missed and department stores she'd been fired from for substance-related reasons, all the times Glen had found substances left out in the open for Ashley's teenage son to consume (though Glen *didn't* know about all the times Syd had actually consumed them). But she wasn't *always* like this, Glen added—a few years ago, the drug abuse had been mere background noise, but now it was more like an annoying, persistent, saxophoneish drone.

In short, this was a pretty clear-cut case of parental neglect and not a particularly unique one. True stories tend to be less interesting. Still, the officers kept looking salaciously up and down from their notepads while they attended to the sordid tale, occasionally affecting expressions of outraged horror lest Syd and Glen suspect titillation.

Glen and Ashley had informally separated months ago but now decided to make that split official. Syd watched in numb indifference as Ashley dragged suitcases across Glen's hardwood floor, and Glen said Please don't drag suitcases across my floor or you'll scratch it, and Ashley said Don't tell me what to do, and Glen said I'll do as I see fit, and Ashley said It's bad enough that you're taking my son away, and Glen said You're *giving* your son away, and that's when it dawned on Syd that he wouldn't be a true emancipated minor after all—would instead be taken into the custody of a saxophone-playing loser who collected *Star Wars* trading cards.

Okay, so he didn't exactly think Glen was a loser—the two had grown somewhat closer in recent months. Soon after Ashley had moved out, Glen had taught him to play chess, and within weeks, Syd was already beating him. Syd's facility with the piano had also taken off, just as Glen had promised it would. During the arduous custody battle, Glen had begun bringing Syd to his Glossy Fuse rehearsals and letting him practice with the band—probably just to get him out of the house away and from the drugs, but Syd nevertheless appreciated the gesture.

In the meantime, Syd's drug consumption had ramped up. After losing access to his mother's coke, he'd turned to a dealer at his high school named Alexander, who went by "Xan," likely as a calculated marketing move. Xan was about seven inches taller than Syd but of similar overall mass and wore Sex Pistols beanies pulled as far down on his forehead as one could conceivably pull a beanie without blindfolding oneself. Syd paid Xan with stolen money from Glen's wallet—concert tips, mostly—and for discretion's sake, he never took more than fifty dollars at once, and no big bills. He snorted so much coke in the months following his mother's loss of custody that he quickly grew bored of it, at which point Xan told him about this little-known designer substance called CNO that was, like, totally off the walls—would make coke seem like baby aspirin by comparison, would make you, like, totally *phreak*. Thus commenced Syd's most enduring habit.

Syd performed poorly in school, mostly out of lack of effort—his complex and opaque adolescent ethical code dictated that he avoid all homework and assigned readings. He read voraciously on his own, though—everything from McCarthy to Heidegger to Ginsberg to Hunter S. Thompson. He particularly appreciated Thompson for his gonzo-journalistic style and often envisioned himself as the subject of a Thompsonesque escapade.[26] Besides, ethical code or no, he didn't much enjoy the books his teacher assigned and always flipped to the end without so much as glancing at the middle: Gatsby dies. Boo

26 Seriously.

Radley isn't a menace but a misunderstood weirdo. The pigs are no different from the men.

The one exception to his school-reading aversion was Salinger's *The Catcher in the Rye*, which he enjoyed so much he made it his personality for an entire year. He picked up a cigarette habit primarily because of Holden Caulfield, though he took great pains not to smell like smoke, regularly changing his clothes and applying cologne. "Does Holden wear suffocating quantities of Axe Body Spray?" Glen asked him on one occasion. On others, Glen expressed concerns about Syd's *Catcher* obsession. Too much misery and despair in there. "Besides," he added, "you should take a look at the sorts of people who love that book. Delinquents and criminals, all of them."

Syd seldom saw his mother and found that he seldom missed her, but he began to develop curiosities about his real dad, Stanley, whom he hadn't so much as heard from since the age of seven. Syd hardly remembered him, but if his mother's account could be trusted, Stanley had conveniently won a million dollars in a small-sweeps lottery right smack-dab in the middle of the divorce proceedings, at which point a huge legal quarrel had ensued over whether Stanley would be required to split the money with Ashley. Syd had vague memories of sitting on the steps of his parents' old house, just like in the movies, and listening to them yell what he remembered as a random assortment of inordinately large numbers back and forth at each other. However, Stanley's lottery loot had given him the upper hand—he used some of it to secure a good divorce lawyer and, after a legal settlement uncoincidentally allowed him to keep the rest, fled to Aruba to get out of paying child support. Once there, he allegedly began living like a drug-addicted one-percenter as opposed to the upper-middle-classer his new net worth now showed him to be on paper. Syd had no idea whether he was still in Aruba or had moved somewhere else once he'd gone broke—his father had cut off all contact.

But one day in late 2016, in the midst of an improvisational keyboard-sax duet, the crushing weight of Syd's uncertainties became too cumbersome, and he stopped playing mid-phrase.

Glen followed suit. "Everything okay?"

"Do you think I could contact my dad?" He didn't know what had prompted the question, but asking it felt like scratching an itch he'd deliberately left alone for months.

"I'm your dad."

"My *real* dad."

"I'm your real dad."

"The guy whose sperm went up my mom's pussy and made me."

Glen winced—he was quite prudish for a professional musician. "I..."

"Where does he live?"

"I don't know."

"But could we find out?"

Glen hesitated.

"I want to write him a letter," Syd decided, though the statement sounded alien once he'd said it.

"I don't..."

"Let me guess—you won't help me. You're jealous."

"No, I just don't want you to be disappointed." He nervously tooted his sax a few times—G, F, B-flat. "You know, *my* father was a piece of work too. So I know what these types are like, and they tend not to change.... But we can try," he added decisively. "I'm willing to help you try."

Syd's excitement was tempered by a familiar disappointment at Glen's inability to do anything properly cruel or unfair. "Okay."

He pulled up a chair at Glen's office desk while Glen clicked through online database lists of Stanley Morrises on his desktop computer. One entry looked promising—this Stanley was forty-three years old and living somewhere in Montana, though finding out his precise address would require a modest fee of $49.95.

"Are you gonna pay?" Syd asked.

"These things are scams," scratching the back of his head as he often did during ponderous dilemmas. "There's gotta be a free one somewhere."

But they had no such luck.

"We should just pay," Syd insisted, guiltily wishing he hadn't spent far more than $49.95 of Glen's money already. He sniffed, his septum stinging. Glen shot him a glance of mild suspicion.

"Fine, I'll pay."

"You will?"

"Yeah." He sounded uncertain but resigned. Like the prospect of disappointing Syd was worse than whatever formless evil he feared contacting Stanley might unleash.

While Glen typed his credit card info into the database's check-out page, Syd sprung from his seat and grabbed a sheet of cardstock paper from the printer, his hand vibrating with premature writerly glee (and CNO intoxication). He felt so full of words and sentiments he feared he might explode. But when he sat down at the kitchen table and placed pen to paper, his hand refused to move. He sat there for several minutes, stiller than he'd been in years. He just couldn't figure out what to say to a man whose sole defining characteristic was that he'd abandoned him.

He managed to write *something*, though, and Glen helped him address the envelope, and Syd licked it eagerly—he'd always somewhat enjoyed the harsh sweetness of an envelope seal—and just like that, the letter was ready to go.

"Thank you," Syd said, realizing with a pang of near-guilt that he'd never thanked Glen for anything before in his life.

His adopted father blinked a few times. His eyes developed shiny, reflective coatings but didn't shed them. "I'll mail it tomorrow when you're at school."

✻   ✻   ✻

The following Friday, Glen's band invited Syd to perform with them. They were gigging at one of those high-class restaurants with meals that cost triple digits per person and feature intricate ice sculptures and curtained stages and waiters who fold napkins over their arms—in other words, the type of restaurant that serves jazz music's primary audience. Glen's bandmates patted Syd on the back and wished him luck while they set up their instruments' PA systems. Syd, still riding last week's politeness streak, thanked them effusively for letting him join.

"There's no 'letting,'" said not-quite-elderly, balding trumpetist Alan Greensboro, while he and Syd lugged the electric keyboard to its stand, Syd walking carefully in reverse with the careful reverse walk that all reverse-walkers use when lugging heavy equipment. Alan was about a head shorter than Syd and looked more like he was raising the keyboard in a peace offering than carrying it. "You earned it." He got this look in his eyes like if he had a free hand to pat Syd's back with, he would.

"Yeah," guitarist Bonnie chimed in. She was maybe mid-thirties, curvy, and always wore tight-fitting dresses. She crouched down and tinkered with the guitar pedals while Syd tried not to ogle.

"This is the start of something good," Glen assured Syd. "Enjoy it."

And it did all seem a little too perfect. Syd's initial resistance to Glen's unceasing generosity, he knew now, had not been out of personal hatred but stubborn suspicion—he'd be suspicious of anyone who tried to enter his life as a father figure, because the only other man who'd done that had walked out. But now he was making amends with that man too. For once, he felt cautiously optimistic. If he weren't already hopelessly addicted, he might have even considered getting sober.

"Is this working?" Glen asked, his mouth nearly kissing the microphone. His amplified voice emerged as a fricative-heavy crackle, definitively answering his question in the affirmative. Still, he tapped the mic a few times. Performers love to tap microphones a few times even when those microphones are obviously working. It's a little ritual for them, like the way football enthusiasts wear lucky jerseys to big games and hopeless romantics throw pennies into fountains.

"We've got a special guest with us today," Glen said while the rest of the band played a simple chord progression. Syd winced at the abject cheesiness of it. The dim spotlight of the classily low-lit stage penetrated Syd's epidermis, heating the back of his neck. His forehead sweated under his red hunting hat. "This is my fifteen-year-old son, Whimsy Sydney." Syd had not consented to the nickname but nonetheless felt a bit warm and fuzzy at the declaration, and the raucous applause that followed, and the fact that there hadn't been a hint of sardonicism or irony or shame in the tone with which Glen had said "son." Syd hadn't thought about CNO in hours and wouldn't think about it again for several hours more.

"Tickle some keys for us, Syd."

So Syd improvised a blues riff—one based on something he'd been practicing over the past week, which was based on a sax riff Glen had improvised, which was based on a Duke Ellington lick Glen had transposed into a different key and replaced half the notes of. That was the thing—improvisation wasn't *really* spontaneous composition. Spontaneous composition didn't exist. Everything was based on something.

But audiences didn't understand that sentiment, so these folks went about as wild as a bunch of venture capitalists and lawyers and CEOs on their second glass of eighty-dollar wine can ever be expected to go.

And when Syd joined in with the band, something odd happened. He'd been anticipating nerves—had gotten nervous about his impending nervousness and nervous about his nervousness about his nervousness, etc.—but once he started playing, the audience disappeared. They faded into a sea of nondescript points of color—a blank sheet of melted, dimly shrouded gray. The music carried Syd. He could exchange wordless expressions with any of his bandmates and instantly know what to do. *This* was where the real composition happened—in the multitude of ways in which the parts Syd had already come up with interlocked with the parts his bandmates had already come up with and got scrambled around and permutated. When it was Syd's turn to solo, he received more applause than the others, probably on account of his age, sure, but he still felt *wanted* in a way he'd never felt wanted before. That feeling of wantedness would be short-lived, but he'd spend the rest of his life chasing it.

After the concert, the six of them—Glen, Syd, Bonnie, Alan, drummer Casey, and bassist Khaleel—took their equipment van through the McDonald's drive-thru. Syd sat up front next to Glen, tapping his fingers pianistically on the dashboard.

"How much?" Glen asked the drive-thru girl, who wore a low ponytail and appeared to be of high-school age. Syd grinned at her from the passenger seat, but she wasn't looking far enough to grin back.

She muttered something in response.

"*How* much?" Glen leaned so far toward her his head stuck out the van window. "Stop that," he told Syd, swatting blindly at his drumming hand.

"Fifty-two ninety-four, sir."

Glen pried his wallet out of his jeans' pocket. Syd had noticed that all his jeans were at least one or two sizes smaller than what was recommended for his waist circumference, probably for complex jazz-style reasons.

"Our credit card reader is broken," the girl added.

"All right, let me just..." Glen began digging around for cash. Syd's heart caught, and his conscious mind took a few seconds to catch up with his instincts.

"Weird," Glen said, his face's components arranging themselves into an unreadable improvised combination.

Syd reminded himself first and foremost to breathe, second and secondmost to breathe quietly.

"I could have sworn I had more..."

"I got some," Khaleel offered from the van's third row. "We got a lot of tips."

"Those were mostly for Syd, and..." Glen re-counted what money he had. "I just *know* there were more Washingtons in here." He side-eyed Syd, who couldn't see himself but safely assumed he was doing a piss-poor job of acting innocent. Glen scratched his head for a few seconds. "You know what, Khaleel? Yeah. Pass me some of those tips."

The drive-thru girl observed the exchange as passively as it went down.

The rest of the drive's awkwardness was so palpable that the nauseous sounds of Glen's bandmates masticating came as almost a relief. Syd didn't so much as touch his own meal. Glen said nothing and looked at no one. His bandmates gave no indication of noticing that anything was wrong.

Syd almost wished Glen would confront him about the money then and there, publicly. Just let it all out—tell his friends what a pathetic junkie Whimsy Sydney really was. Tell them how their whole idea of Syd as some brilliant, sensitive, musician guy was just image-curation Glen employed to protect his own ego from the shame of having a damaged son.

But he didn't. When they got home, Glen sat Syd down gently. Took a seat opposite him at the kitchen table, his hands folded prudently atop it. "You already know," he said after an agonizingly drawn-out wait for a confession.

Syd nodded, but he didn't cry. He *wished* he could cry or even simply feel guilty for the stealing and the CNO. If he felt guilty for *anything*, it was making Glen think he was someone he wasn't.

"So here's what's going to happen," Glen continued. "I'm going to keep all my money locked in a safe deposit box, which I will nail to my wall. You will not be given the code. I will *change* the code regularly so you can't just try every combination over an extended period of time. You will get off the drugs immediately. Does that sound fair?"

Nodded again, not meeting Glen's eyes, his own hands clasped tightly under the table. "It's just…"

"Yes?"

Syd laughed a couple times, unable to comprehend the full absurdity of talking to his nerdy adopted dad, who he could tell hadn't touched so much as a cigarette in his entire life, about his deepest, darkest open secret. "Getting off is hard."

"What do you mean?"

"I mean it sucks."

"You should have thought about that when you got *on*, shouldn't you have?"

"Sure. But I think more of a taper rather than a cold turkey…"

But Glen was already shaking his head. "I'll send you to rehab if you really need it, but you are not to consume another speck of whatever you're consuming under this roof. Do you understand?"

Syd nodded a third time.

"And I'll make sure of it—believe you me."

Nodded. Glen's wretched passivity was agonizing. A *real* dad wouldn't be this laid-back about his son purloining cash to fuel a drug dependency. A real dad would beat him or ground him or put him up for adoption. Syd didn't know what the catch was. He'd been looking for a catch ever since his mom had brought Glen home for the first time, and Glen had gotten down on one knee so that he met Syd's eyes head-on and asked Syd about his *Star Wars* pajamas, which had featured a picture of Darth Vader with one side of his face in the shadows, the other illuminated by a red lightsaber. "Who's that?" Glen had asked. Syd had known even then that there was zero chance Glen didn't recognize Darth Vader—he'd likely been bombarded by so many images of Darth Vader in his Gen-X youth that he saw the figure in his dreams. This suspicion was confirmed when, a few months later, Glen showed Syd his shiny, silver, "super rare" Darth Vader trading card—only one per ten thousand, he declared proudly. After that, Syd found himself not really even liking *Star Wars* all that much.

"Dad?" Syd asked now. He'd never called him Dad before.

Glen perked up for an instant but then seemed to suppress his glee. "Yes?"

"Hit me," finally looking him directly in the eye.

"What?"

"Punch me in the face."

Sighed. "I'm not gonna do that, Syd."

"No, I'm serious. That's what you're *supposed* to do." The impetus for the request eluded him—perhaps he just wanted to feel *something* besides sadness and self-loathing and fear.

Glen sighed again and looked down at his lap.

"Do something *active* for one moment in your fucking pathetic life, huh?" Syd demanded, raising his voice. "Be *angry* at me!"

"I am angry," Glen replied calmly.

"Then fucking *act* like it, you *phony*!" Syd stood up, removed his hat, and pointed to his left eye. "Sock me in the face, right here."

Glen would never commit a premeditated act of violence, Syd knew, but he also knew that his own worst fights had been the impulsive ones. The ones where the anger inside him had grown so unruly it had forced its way out in a single paroxysmic burst.

"No."

"I'll settle for you just, like, throwing or breaking something in my presence."

"No."

"Or even just yelling at me."

"What good would that do?"

No answer.

"Exactly. Are we done here?"

Nodded one last time.

"Good. Then go do your homework and get out of my hair."

3

Syd's sixteenth birthday party wasn't even his own, really. At least fifty percent of it belonged to drummer Casey's son Luke, who would turn fourteen later that month and who was infinitely more popular than Syd. Syd knew his relative lonership was the *real* reason he wasn't getting his own party—no one would come. His overall vibe, with his black coats that would be of the trench variety if those weren't banned at his school and at most schools around the country, put people off.

Syd and Glen knew that this was not just a birthday party but a rough celebration of Syd being six months clean from all substances, which he was—Glen remembered the exact date he'd quit. But to Syd, the milestone felt more like a punishment than an achievement; he hadn't gotten any real say in the matter and still couldn't go twenty-four hours without craving a hit. Sobriety *had* become the norm, though, and things were mostly good. He could admit that much to himself—that things were the best they'd been in a long while, even with his mom theoretically still in rehab and his real dad failing to respond to his letter. Other than these minor technicalities, things were good.

The party took place at Casey and Luke's house, which had a spacious living room and a nice little backyard deck. Eighth graders flooded the deck and surrounding grass, and Syd skulked around, longitudinally dwarfing them all by several inches. You wouldn't expect a two-year age gap to amount to much, but when you're talking about the two most critical male pubertal developmental years, it's the difference between looking like a boy and looking like a (disproportionate, baby-faced, facial-hairless) man.

For the party's entertainment, Luke had requested an "edgy clown." Edgy clowns, Casey explained to Syd while looking repeatedly to his son for confirmation that he was getting it right, were clowns that dressed a bit grunge and terrorized party guests. Syd didn't quite get it, but the middle schoolers went wild for this guy, who wore giant black shoes and a black squeaky nose and an electrified-looking mad scientist wig and across whose forehead the words "I BITE" had been scrawled in black facepaint.

The backyard's air felt thin and cold—more so than Syd had come to expect from April. As the sun set, it only felt thinner and colder. The frigidity seemed to concentrate at the back of his neck, and straightening his jacket collar did little to insulate him. Cold was truly one of most uncomfortable sensations a body could feel.

Syd coldly observed the way the kids sat at attention, accepting the clown's dodgeball-throws with the same unironic glee younger children might afford a traditional clown. And yet, if Casey or his accountant wife Margaret were to bring a "real" clown out right now, the kids would all whisper edgily to each other and groan and maybe throw things at *him* instead of the other way around. The quote unquote "ironic" nature of the edgy clown spectacle falsely reassured these kids that they were in on the joke—"I can enjoy this *edgy* clown because I think normal clowns are stupid, and he does too, and my participation in his act is a performative acknowledgement of how stupid we all find this lurid affair we're currently subjecting ourselves to under the guise of self-aware acknowledgement." Syd stood behind the seated crowd, explaining this theory to Glen while the clown occasionally shot him death glares, seeming not to care that he was a Birthday Boy. His crinkled birthday hat sat slightly off to one side of his head so that no one suspected him of enjoying the birthday hat tradition.

"For my next trick," the edgy clown announced. A lopsided, drawn-on Hitler mustache covered his top lip. "I'll make this balloon into a dog." He whipped a long, black balloon out of his unfrilly, black, edgy clown sleeve.

The kids booed performatively.

"Just kidding," the clown predictably amended. He stretched the balloon and then launched it catapult-style at a braided-haired girl in the front row, whom it nailed solidly in the right eye.

"Ow," she said, rubbing the injury site. A few boys in the back laughed and pointed. The girl sitting next to the balloon-launch victim put an impassive arm around her shoulder as if to commend her for her sportsmanship.

"His entire act is just throwing different types of objects at people," Syd whispered, while Glen nodded unenthusiastically. "But these little freaks eat it right up. 'Look at us,'" he mocked. "'We're too cool for regular entertainment, so we have to develop derivative meta-entertainments that pretend to rebel against the normal kind without even saying anything of substance.'"

"Can't you just *enjoy* yourself for once?" Glen asked him. "Or at least let *others* enjoy themselves?"

"I *am* enjoying myself." Syd removed a toothpick from his coat pocket and chewed it—a habit he'd taken up recently as an unsatisfying substitute for drugs. "I *enjoy* criticizing innocuous things."

He heard a car pull into the front driveway, signaling Margaret's return from the cake shop, and his stomach gave an anticipatory groan.

"Well as long as you're self-aware," Glen replied in a snarky tone that made him sound unconvinced of Syd's self-awareness. But Syd knew himself better than anyone—he was so self-aware he was *aware* of his self-awareness.

"Multiple levels of awareness going on in here." Syd pointed to his crinkled-birthday-hatted head. Glen scratched his chin.

"For my next trick," the clown said (this was how he preempted every trick), "I'm going to need a volunteer. How about one of our Birthday Boys?"

Glen nudged Syd. Syd shook his head. Luke turned around, his hair and face soaking wet from a recent water ballooning, and his face assumed a supplicatory expression that said, *I did the last one.*

Syd spat out the toothpick. "Fine." As he edged his way through the seated crowd, he tried to predict what would get thrown at/ sprayed onto him—surely nothing too dangerous or it would be a liability issue. Maybe some silly string. Ketchup. A live turtle. There was no telling.

The back gate's latch clicked open, and Margaret cautiously hefted a large Pfeffer's Bakery box into the yard. Syd experienced a moment of relief at the fact that not only would the show soon come to a magnanimous close, but he'd also soon be eating cake—a Spider-Man-themed chocolate ice cream cake, to be exact. Its bright blue frosting sparkled with unnatural vibrance, and several Spider-Mans (Spider-Men?) had been printed atop it in a variety of poses. The cake's final form was a compromise between Luke (who'd requested a Spider-Man cake) and Syd (who'd requested ice cream cake and didn't particularly care what was printed on it since it was just going to be cut up and eaten anyway). Casey and Glen hurried over to help Margaret set the cake onto the wooden backyard table, which had caught splashes of water and Cheez Whiz from some of the clown's messier antics, and the three of them tried several possible placements before resigning to the fact that the bottom of the box was probably going to get a bit wet and Cheez Whizzy no matter what.

Syd made it to the front of the crowd and gave them a broad, artificial grin. The eighth graders' expressions varied from glee to fear, and Syd noted with a bit of malice that some of these kids were actually *scared* of him. Their parents had probably told them to beware of tall, sketchily-dressed boys.

"For you, Birthday Boy, I've got a *very* special surprise," the Hitler-clown said, bending over to open his duffle bag, which had been ripped and then duct taped back up again in a bunch of deliberate and edgy places.

"Let me guess, a pie?" Syd asked before being rudely and stickily informed that he was correct. The clown didn't so much smash the pie in his face as hurl it discus-style. It consisted mostly of whipped cream and tasted faintly of lemon.

And then Syd, impulsive as ever, made the split-second decision to give the clown a pieing of his own and, blinking cream out of his own eyes the whole time, grabbed the only pieable thing in sight, aka the ice cream Spider-Men cake. It hit the clown with a cold, satisfying *splat*, and the kids erupted in a few seconds' worth of raucous laughter before realizing that the cake they'd been about to consume was now spread out inedibly over the entire surface area of the clown's face and his Slipknot shirt and part of his frillless clown coat and his edgy hair.

Syd's reaction too transformed from vindictive glee to regret. "Aw, shit." He spat out some pie.

The clown wiped his face clean with a black-nail-polished hand. "This isn't how these things usually go."

"What's his problem?" a boy in the front row whimpered.

"He's an asshole is what," answered a kid who had eagerly volunteered to be both dodgeballed and Cheezed.

"I'll go buy another cake," Glen said tiredly.

"You don't hav—" Syd began.

"I'm not doing it for *you*," he snapped. "It's for Luke."

"I'm sorry," Syd said, his voice breaking a bit.

"Don't apologize to *me*."

"I'm sorry, Luke."

Luke picked at the sole of his sneaker and gave no sign of hearing him.

"You know, I tried *so hard* with you," Glen went on, emoting forcefully with his hands. "I tried so hard to...to make you the type of son I'd be proud to have or to fix you or—"

"To *fix* me?"

"That's not what I meant."

"I'm *not* the type of son you'd be proud to have?"

"Now you're twisting my words. See, you're always doing that, Sydney. You're always trying to make me out to be a bad guy. Why? Because Stanley is? Is that it?"

Syd's eyes throbbed with uncomfortable, wet thickness.

"Do you think I'm like Stanley?"

Syd shook his head.

"Have I given you *any* reason to believe I bear even the *remotest* resemblance to Stanley?"

Shook his head again.

"Do you think that, if you had sent *me* a letter, I would have replied?"

Began to shake his head and then realized that the "correct" answer to this one was affirmative and nodded.

"So then what's your endgame? Huh? What are you trying to prove?"

Syd didn't answer and didn't know. The middle schoolers watched the exchange with silent attention. The ice cream-faced clown made a show of cleaning up his edgy materials while nevertheless eavesdropping keenly. Syd wished he had another cake to throw.

"Do you have *anything* to say to me right now?" flecks of spit hitting Syd's sticky face.

Shook his head.

"You're always calling *me* passive, right? 'Do something active for once in your life,'" Glen mimicked in a high-pitched childish whine. "Right? Isn't that what you said to me?"

Nodded as subtly as he could without remaining completely still.

"Then why are you just *standing* there? Do something! Don't you have any *aspirations*? Any *goals*? Or are you exclusively defined in terms of what you're not? Because *that*, Sydney..." He let loose a few staccato chuckles with the sort of breath control only woodwind players possessed. "...that is a *sad* and *lonely* and, yes, *passive* way to live." He pulled his car keys out of his coat pocket, chin drooping. "I'm going to buy Luke a new cake. You're welcome to eat some too, when I get back. Maybe then we can talk this over and decide what exactly your deal is. Happy fuckin' birthday, kid." It would be the first and last time Syd heard Glen curse.

Because Glen never returned from his trip to Pfeffer's, as you've probably guessed by now. But you probably *haven't* guessed, and may even be wondering, in what riveting manner he died. If this were a work of fiction, I'd come up with one, and an immensely satisfying one at that. But in real life, tragedies are seldom exciting.

What happened next on Syd's end is so monotonous as to not require dramatization. He sat at the wet, Cheez Whizzy table and waited. He watched parents trickle in through the back gate to pick up their disgruntled, cake-deprived kids. A few moms made empty promises to buy their children replacement desserts on the ride home. Some attendees pointed at Syd in what he assumed were answers to parent questions along the lines of "What absolute douchebag would throw a cake at the party entertainment?" No one wished Syd a happy birthday. Luke had vanished to his bedroom to play his new Nintendo Switch and hadn't been heard from since. At one point, the evening cold became too much for Syd to stand, so he relocated to the kitchen table indoors. At another, later point, Syd asked Margaret how far away the cake shop was, and she told him not far—like a fifteen-minute drive. Come to think of it, Margaret added after a short pause, Pfeffer's closed at five PM, and it must have been about that time when Glen left, so she doubted he'd even made it through the door.

When all the guests had gone, Syd asked Casey and Margaret

whether they'd like to go looking for Glen. He wasn't answering Syd's text messages or calls, and Syd worried something bad had happened. If Casey and Margaret shared that worry, they didn't let on. The clouds outside were spitting one of those light New York drizzles that could turn into a storm at any instant. Which it did, with a demonstrative crackle, just as Casey grabbed his coat.

The cloud-darkened sky and heavy rain gave the drive to Pfeffer's a foreboding aspect. A black curtain seemed to encase the entire Earth. The sound of rain hitting tempered glass mingled with the hiss of Casey's wipers throwing it onto the flooded road. Overall visibility was murky—about as murky, in fact, as Syd's memories of this night would later be. What happened next is something he'd do his best to forget.

They entered the Pfeffer's parking lot and saw that the place was indeed closed, but Glen's Ford Focus was parked out front. Syd leapt out of Casey's car and began sprinting toward the shop before they'd even parked. He sensed, innately, that something tragic had occurred inside. The rain fell so hard he couldn't see where he was headed. He kept his eyes squeezed shut, opening them only occasionally to get his bearings. His wet and pie-coated hair dripped down his cold neck and into his coat collar, soaking his shirt. Puddled rainwater splashed into his shoes and drenched his socks and made his cold feet feel even colder. He shivered, wondering whether anyone else on Earth had ever felt this cold.

The front door of the cake shop was clearly locked, but Syd tugged at its cold metal handle a few times to make sure. Casey called out to him in the distance. Syd squinted and tried to look back but could see only a wet, cold, dark blur. The rain was so constant and total he felt like he was being pissed on by a dozen hypothermics at once.

Then Syd saw it—the cake shop's broken window—and for a second, time passed at regular speed. The window had shattered the way punched windows tend to shatter. It wasn't a particularly large window—probably only two by three feet. Drops of blood stained the few remaining intact glass shards' jagged spikes. Immediately indoors, a puddle of rainwater expanded rapidly, and off in the distance, where the flooding hadn't yet reached, a bright red splattered trail led to the freezer.

Syd's breathing became shallow. He debated whether to proceed. He could stand out here in the pissing rain forever and never have to find out what happened. He could head home and pretend nothing was wrong. Margaret yelled something from the car that may as well have been gibberish but likely had to do with the fact that—hey, they'd tried, and the shop was closed, and shouldn't they head back? Syd climbed through the broken window.

Though no longer rain-blinded, he squinted as he followed the red trail, afraid he might see too much. He grabbed the bloody handle of the freezer and tugged it open with the weak force of someone whose brain's wires are plugged into all the wrong sockets. Inside the freezer, slumped back against a tower of ice cream buckets, lay a bloody-fisted, blue, motionless Glen.

You and I can probably deduce much of what happened while Syd awaited his father's return. At 4:47 PM, Glen sped down the highway, racing the clock, listening to the smooth jazz station, seething at the glib defiance of his adopted son, the jazz forming an out-of-place musical backdrop for his anger and indignation—whatever amount of those emotions Glen had the capacity for, anyway. The sky rumbled with pre-storm thunder. The radio's signal turned to static mid-bass solo.

At 5:01 PM, Glen arrived at Pfeffer's. He tugged at the shop's cold handle. He cupped his hands and peered through the tinted window. And then, in a rare moment of activity and defiance and with a one-track mind that told him Syd would give three arms and a leg to hear *this* story—who was passive *now*, huh?—he punched out the glass. His hand broke and bled, but he didn't really feel it. He climbed through the jagged opening and hurried to the freezer, dribbling blood all the way. He stepped inside and admired his selection of cakes with the cool nonchalance of someone who has all day to make a decision. But then the door, which locked from the outside, slammed shut behind him, and he was trapped and alone and much colder than Syd had ever felt.

Perhaps then he used his unbloodied hand to call Syd, but his phone just gave that mute empty ring cell phones give when they can't find anything to connect to. Maybe he watched his struggling phone screen with motionless indifference, feeling strangely calm when it declaimed that his call had failed. Syd too felt strangely calm, sitting outside on the cold porch miles away—or numb, perhaps. Soon Glen began to feel numb as well—first in his hands, and then in his feet and ears. He sat down and leaned against the ice cream bucket tower, which now felt no colder than the seat back of a cushy office chair. After a short while, he tried his phone again, dialing an ambulance this time. Still nothing. His touchscreen had somewhat stopped working because it no longer recognized his fingers as human fingers. He found it near-impossible to believe that these stiff fingers were the same ones that hours ago could play nimble jazz riffs—the same fingers that had taught Syd piano and tousled his hair after he'd done a good job in last year's show and pointed emphatically and harshly at him during what Glen was beginning to accept was probably their last ever conversation. Some part of Syd knew that too, by now, but the knowledge manifested as merely a weird gut discomfort he couldn't quite place. They both prepared for their aspirational reunion by devising rhetorically impressive statements of extravagant oration, rehearsing the words in their heads, imagining fighting back tears while declaiming to a passive, silent, nodding other. For Glen, this was his only real recourse—nothing else to do besides wait for someone to come to his rescue.

He grew delirious as the cold penetrated his skull. He thought he saw the freezer door swing open, an aura of fuzzy angelic light expanding gloriously to reveal a rain-soaked, dripping Syd, his coat unnaturally wrinkled and stuck to his body like a flimsy T-shirt. And then the two of them were back on Glen's piano bench, and Glen tried to speak but couldn't even move his mouth, but that was okay, because Syd played something soulful and technically proficient and indescribable to anyone who hasn't been on death's front porch, and the music said everything Glen would have.

✳   ✳   ✳

Syd saw his mom at the funeral, but their interactions felt false and overly formal. They smiled at each other and occasionally made meaningless small talk about the weather or Syd's classes while people Syd had never met in his life gave them two-handed handshakes—a kind of sturdy clasp from both sides—and apologized with such profuse drama you'd think they'd killed Glen themselves. The cause of Glen's death hung unspoken in the atmosphere and toxified the funeral and afterparty's very oxygen. Syd couldn't quite suss out people's grasp of the subtler details but wondered what they knew or suspected about his own part in the disaster.

Glen's will hadn't been updated in years, so he'd left most of his belongings to Syd's mom. Some money was supposed to be placed in a trust fund for Syd to access once he was no longer in Ashley's custody—presumably when he came of age. Glen had left the house to both Ashley and Syd and specified that it be sold when Syd turned eighteen and that the spoils be split evenly three ways between Ashley, Syd, and a charity called Musical Mandalas. Glen had spoken about the charity on many occasions, but Syd had always shown deliberate disinterest. He regretted that now.

At the will reading, Syd sat a respectable distance from his mother. The biggest question the estate-executor had was who should *really* get the house, since Ashley's loss of custody for non-coming-of-age reasons rendered many of the terms under which Glen had drafted the will more or less void. A grueling judicial process followed, and all inaccuracies here on my part are due to the fact that Syd himself could only make sense of its broader strokes and none of its intricacies. After all was said and done and many dollars had changed hands, courts decreed that Syd would become an emancipated minor and the de-facto temporary owner of the house. Since he was sixteen and had a 1.9 GPA, he also dropped out of school after completing the tenth grade.

The next couple years passed in a muddled blur. At some point, not coincidentally almost immediately after Syd received the now-liquid funds Glen had intended to keep solid until he turned eighteen, Syd contacted his old drug dealer Xan, who'd also dropped out of school not long ago. They met up at Village of Walton's shady, rundown park—the one nobody ever brought their kids to because drug-addict bums tended to hang out there.

"How do I know you're not a cop now?" Xan asked, while he and

Syd swayed gently on adjacent swings, Xan chain-smoking and occasionally discarding cigarette butts into the potentially flammable mulch at their feet. He'd beefed up since Syd had seen him last—his body was sturdier, his head rounder, his beanies no longer coming down quite so low on his face. He now looked positively capable of beating Syd up.

"Come on."

"No, really." Xan exhaled bovinely through his nose. "First you say you can't buy from me anymore because you're gettin' straight or some shit, and then I don't hear from you in months. Now you're back. What changed?"

"My fuckin' dad died, all right?" Nodded at the box of cigarettes, hoping Xan would take a hint.

"Ask nicely, you fuckin' animal."

"Sorry. May I bum a cigarette?"

Xan narrowed his eyes before forking one over. "I'm adding fifty cents to your purchase." He gave Syd a light while Syd leaned dizzily against his swing's crunchy, rusted chain. Xan's lighter's design was the Monster Energy Drink logo. "But what do you mean your dad died? I thought he walked out on you."

"That's my other dad."

"You got two gay dads or something?"

"No, I…it's not important. But he's the reason I was clean. He was honestly kinda fascist about it."

Xan shook his head in amused disbelief. "Bet it's a relief he's dead then, huh?"

Syd coughed on his first puff, the smoke burning his throat and some sort of new, painful guilt burning his chest (though that may have also been the smoke). He'd always derived a sick rush from poking fun at Glen but couldn't stand it when others did.

"Sorry," Xan muttered while Syd continued coughing. "*Man.* You're out of practice."

"It's okay," Syd lied, regaining his composure. "It's okay now." He wasn't totally sure whom he was talking to or what he was referencing.

Syd had thought getting back on CNO would bring him some much-needed relief, and it did, but it also brought that same familiar, painful, grief-ridden, chest-burning guilt. He imagined metaphorical ghost-Glen looking over his shoulder and clicking his tongue in dis-approval every time he bent over for a hit. If Syd ingested enough sub-stance, he'd sometimes believe it literally. I suppose it just comforted him to think that Glen wasn't really gone. That he lived on in some currently-inaccessible realm, and Syd would talk to him again once he figured out how. And that, when their paths finally reconvened, Syd could explain, properly and definitively, that Glen was in no way responsible for how Syd had turned out and that Syd appreciated him. He could say he was sorry without injecting his apology with the cyn-ical, sardonic martyrdom he'd injected into every conversation he'd ever had with Glen.

The one place he *didn't* snort CNO was the house, for he still balked at the prospect of breaking his promise to remain drug-free under Glen's roof. Instead, he took the stuff out to the yard, or to the aforementioned park, or, on particularly cold days, into the garage, which, luckily for him, wasn't connected to the house and therefore didn't truly count as "under the same roof." These loopholes amount-ed to meaningless technicalities, he knew, but they granted him a per-functory reassurance that he hadn't completely failed Glen.

When Syd turned eighteen and the house went up for sale, it got snapped up almost immediately by a young family with two toddlers, so Glen's old bandmates Khaleel and Bonnie came over to help Syd pack his belongings into moving-truck-friendly tote boxes. Bonnie brought her girlfriend Evelyn, who said about three words the entire time but packed more efficiently than any of the others. Khaleel told Syd his husband sends his regards.

"Ever think about taking up the sax?" Khaleel asked, pulling one of Glen's altos out from his closet, unlatching its case, and holding it up, just in case Syd didn't know what a saxophone looked like.

Syd shook his head while piling office supplies indiscriminately into a box.

"Why not?" Bonnie asked. Syd had become too depressed to find her sexually appealing anymore.

"Just, uh, didn't want him to think I was only doing it just be-cause he was," which was the lame truth.

"Not really a problem anymore, though," Khaleel pointed out. Bonnie smiled. Evelyn packed. They acted no differently from how they had before the accident, Syd noted bitterly. Two years had healed all their grief-wounds.

"I guess not," Syd agreed.

"He really loved you, you know," Bonnie added.

Syd didn't say anything.

"He loved you and was proud of you," she repeated, cramming a lid onto an overfull tote by sitting on it.

Syd could tell she thought she was comforting him, but his chest felt the way it might if he'd just smoked an entire pack of cigarettes in one big mammoth huff.

"I think I speak for all of us here when I say," Khaleel said, exchanging quick alternate glances with Bonnie and Evelyn, "you'll always have us, if you want us." But Syd could tell the statement was more obligatory than sincere. That what Khaleel really meant was, *You can call us on holidays, and we can talk stiffly about something trivial and emotionally untaxing, and as long as we don't have to think about you for the other 360 days of the year, we can superficially maintain our own selfishly virtuous ideals.*

"Thanks," Syd said, his smile feeling weighed down by a gravity far stronger than Earth's.

After a few uneventful minutes of packing, Syd discovered something bizarre—a photo album with a blue, striped cover. Only the first few pages had been filled—with pictures of Glen's band, pictures of Ashley and Glen, pictures of Ashley and Syd and Glen, pictures of just Syd and Glen. The oldest photo in the album was of a younger Glen and Ashley playing a piano-sax duet. Syd hadn't known his mother played piano; she'd certainly never played in front of him. The most recent photo had been taken after Syd's concert debut as Whimsy Sydney—Glen was squeezing Syd's waist firmly, the latter's forehead shrouded by the red hunting hat he hadn't taken off for all of 2016, his eyes glowing underneath it. His skin glowed a bit too, from the sweat. Syd and Glen smiled in a zero-gravity-type way. They were the only ones in focus among the dimly lit crowd that surrounded them. Syd distinctly remembered Alan snapping the picture with his Stone-Age blackberry phone. The caption read, *My Whimsical Son.*

Syd's eyes now felt simultaneously wet and dry, like they were trying to decide which extreme to commit to. He wished, more than anything, that the album could have been completed—that he could have spent enough years with Glen to fill it. He longed to sit next to his dad on their faded couch while Glen thumbed through the pages and described the context of each photo in excruciating detail and Syd outwardly rolled his properly-lubricated eyes but internally felt fulfilled and untroubled and like this was exactly what adolescence was supposed to be. Glen had never shown him the album when he was alive, and Syd didn't blame him—he'd probably feared ridicule of the malicious and non-teasing kind. His fear was probably well-founded, and he probably would have responded to Syd's inevitable jeers with a warm, hurt, passive "never mind."

Syd closed the album and lifted it into his open tote, but when he did, a thin envelope fell out. He instantly recognized his own writing—a painstakingly-printed, barely legible "Mr. Stanley Morris" with his biological father's Montana address scrawled below it. The letter, which Glen had promised to mail when Syd was at school, had been neither stamped nor postmarked.

"Find any old treasures?" Bonnie asked.

Startled, Syd tossed the envelope into the box. It spun Frisbee-like a few times before getting lost among the loose papers. "Nope."

"You okay?"

"Do I seem okay?", which is probably the wrong thing to say when you're trying to convince people you're okay.

"You seem a bit shaken up."

"I'm fine," he said, hoping that, if he couldn't trick his dead father's bandmates into believing it, he could at least trick himself.

When Khaleel, Bonnie, and Evelyn had left, Syd snorted a line of CNO off Glen's newly barren mattress and delighted in the nauseous burn that spread throughout his nasal cavity, the pain finally—mercifully—giving him a real, physical reason to cry.

Life Imitates the Life Art is Imitating: Part 2

My first four acting classes were far from colorless—I tried and failed to get camera trained, loosened my facial muscles, performed a suicidal Hamlet monologue, learned some earthshattering news, imagined watching an idealized version of myself watch an idealized version of *her*self, and met a couple really cool young people. In the interest of what I've now deemed my tertiary goal: making friends—third only to being honest and learning to lie, respectively—I've gone out to eat with Stardust and Chase before class on…

…DAY 5.

We've chosen a diner called Momma's Kitchen. It's got the ambience of a cheap restaurant that wants to seem expensive—white walls, cushioned booths, hanging lamps, framed photos that look like Getty stock images, etc. Stardust says this is her favorite place to eat in all of Atlanta, and I have to admit it's pretty tasty for budget food. The fried chicken is crispy. The mac and cheese is silky smooth. The cornbread is not dry. Stardust and Chase remain in character for the entire meal and politely correct me each time I accidentally address them by their real names. Whenever I try to make conversation, they ask me who I'm talking to, referring to themselves in the third person (e.g. "Where do you go to college?" "Where does *Stardust* go to college? Or Ophelia?" "Stardust." "She goes to GIT."). By the end of the meal, in what must be a tremendous character study, they're both tongue-deep in an impressively naturalistic make-out session, and now I'm the weirdo third wheel watching them. I offer to pay, but Chase detaches his face from Stardust's for just long enough to inform me that his dad is an investment banker. I ask whether he's referring to Chase's dad or Bradley's, the latter of whom, I remind him, was patricided, and he appears to short-circuit.

Today's class features some more method acting—we're asked to recite a generic, in-character monologue I'm ninety percent sure

Lana wrote up just last night. The monologue pertains to a mundane gasoline purchase, and some of my more annoying classmates claim they're unable to perform it due to character inaccuracies ("Fraser would never buy Regular," an older man named George complains. "He's exclusively diesel-only."). Lana passive-aggressively rewards these sorts, commending them for ironing out even the smallest and most useless details of their characters' personalities. I feel a bit silly for not considering which type of gasoline the fictional, film-adapted Hannah would use.

DAY 6

Today, things get weird.

When I enter our classroom and take my usual seat, I notice Stardust is crying. I ask her what's wrong, and she says, "I just can't believe she actually *did* it." Chase pats her comfortingly on the back.

"Did what?" I ask. "Who?"

Stardust sniffles a few times and sighs. Dabs her eyes, careful not to ruin her makeup. "So a while back, there was this girl who was really bitchy to me."

I nod with the true empathy born of experience.

"And the other day, she came up to me during Advanced Theater Methods and basically called me a slut. I wanted to *slap* her."

"And did you?"

Stardust bites her lip and shakes her head. "No. I did something worse."

"It wasn't worse," Chase insists. "There's no way you could have known." Looks up at me. "There's no way she could have known," in case I missed it the first time.

"What did you do?"

Sniffs again. "I told her to kill herself."

"And she did?" I ask, all my repressed guilt and apprehension from the past few weeks now rearranging my internal organs into a variety of unnatural layouts.

Stardust nods and then bursts into a fresh bout of tears. They're really flowing.

"Well, I suppose you can't be held responsible," I say. "She probably had some other stuff going on."

"That's what I've been telling her," Chase replies. "She just won't listen."

"You can't be held responsible for others' actions," I repeat, more firmly this time, somewhat to myself as well.

"The thing is," Stardust continues, "I haven't seen the note, but..."

"But what?"

"Well, apparently she, like, mentioned me." She speaks in that squeaky cry-voice that tends to afflict young, well-off women.

"She must have really wanted to twist the knife in."

Stardust shakes her head, pigtails batting her face. "She said—" Inhales deeply. "She said—" Sobs some more and buries her face in her hands.

"The basic thesis of the note was that this girl had been depressed for a while," Chase explains, "but she'd never attempted suicide because she'd always thought *others* wanted her to stay alive. So she claimed Stardust's statement had been the thing that..."

"Right," I mutter, the last of my comforting niceties fully exhausted.

"And, scene," Stardust proclaims, instantaneously regaining her peppy composure. She stands up and takes an elaborate bow.

I blink a few times, stupidly. "None of this was real?"

She and Chase shake their heads in mutual glee.

"I mean, it's real for *Ophelia*, but in terms of it happening in this actual reality...not so much." Stardust giggles.

"That was really fucked up, you know that? Lying to me like that?"

"It's called *acting*."

"Well, give me a warning before you start *acting* next time, yeah?" But now I'm half-laughing too, and my organs are returning to their natural places. "I mean, you were crying for *real*."

She nods, her eyes shiny, a few last meaningless tears rolling off her chin.

"How the fuck did you make that so convincing, huh?"

"Vulnerability," sitting spunkily back down. "That's the key to acting. It doesn't need to be *true* vulnerability, but if you aren't afraid to make yourself look bad or unlikeable, they'll figure you'd never lie."

I can't even tell you what we did in today's class.

DAY 7

Ever since Stardust alerted me of her meat puppet status, I've been keeping my distance. Spending too much time with meat puppets is like spending too much time with compulsive liars—you start to doubt the most basic aspects of their personality. You begin wondering whether previous statements that seemed innocuous were fabricated just for the fun of it. You develop the paranoid fear that maybe it's not possible to ever truly know anyone at all. Meat puppets are more dangerous than your standard compulsive liar, though, because they display no tells. They've had all the tells trained out of them.

Today, I'm hoping to have the tells trained out of me by practicing some in-character improvisation. I slightly regret choosing this Hannah persona—a bit boring—and wish I'd picked a character a bit more like that of my scene partner Jared.

Jared is playing a goth music venue owner-slash-serial killer named Fang who murders his venue's headliner after every concert. He has no reasonable answer to the question of why Fang isn't a prime subject when murders keep occurring at his venue, or the equally valid question of why artists keep agreeing to *play* at a venue that offers them a one hundred percent statistical chance of gruesome death, or the even more pressing question of Isn't systematically killing your own musical acts sort of a bullet in your own foot, business-wise? But logical inconsistencies notwithstanding, I anticipate a fun improvisational exchange. The dynamic we've agreed upon is that I'm a clueless journalist writing a news piece on the "murder venue," and Fang is one of my interview subjects.

"When did these murders begin?" I ask journalistically.

Fang rubs his neck murdererishly. "Gee, I don't know. The first one was in twenty-seventeen, I think."

"And you didn't report it to the police?"

"Didn't know it was a murder, at first."

"What about after the authorities found the bodies of each individual member of Polyrocket Technodick buried in the junkyard behind this venue? You *still* had no idea?"

"Is this an interrogation, ma'am?"

"No, sir. I'm not a cop."

Fang pulls an invisible gun out of his pocket and fake-shoots me squarely in the chest.

"What was that?" the real Hannah asks bluntly.

"What my character would do. You're dead."

"Yeah, but if I'm dead, we can't really do the scene, can we? We can't do a character study involving two people if one of them is dead."

Jared shrugs. "Let's start over then."

We start over exactly seven more times during today's session, each instance ending with an identical invisible-gun murder.

"*Again*, dude?"

"Who am I to change my character's very nature?"

Etc.

DAY 8

This is it. My final attempt at vulnerability. My last shot at becoming a meat puppet unless I want to pay another $465. Today, we're getting back out in front of the camera to perform yesterday's improvised dialogues. And I'm feeling pretty good—after the embarrassing catastrophe of Day 3, I placed my old, no-longer-functional digital Kodak (don't even ask where I found it) atop my bedroom dresser and have been practicing the art of appearing unwatched every morning and night for the past five weeks. I am nothing if not prepared.

Jared/Fang is less prepared. While the murderous, scene-killing Fang of yesterday at least managed to address me directly—almost uncomfortably intimately—he now solely addresses the lens.

"Remember, the camera is invisible," Lana reminds him. Fang and I face each other on metal stools in front of a plain white background—the alleged standard for filmed improvisations.

Fang turns his head back toward me, slowly, as if prying himself away. "What made you decide to interview me?"

"Just wanted to—" I clear my throat. "Just wanted to ask—sorry." I'm still faltering. Because it's not the *camera*'s watchful eye that throws me off, I discover in one devastating revelatory burst—it's the *thirty-one* prying eyes[27] of my peers and teacher, who are alternately watching that camera watch me and watching me directly. Just about anyone would fold under the weight of this much watching, I figure, and now I'm sweating again.

"Just relax," Lana says.

"I am relaxed," I snap, louder than I intended. "Sorry."

"Look, acting isn't for everyone. Like I said, this is the biggest hurdle."

"I *am* going to be an actor," I insist, perturbed that she seems to think I'm in some way uniquely defective, even in the presence of Can't-End-a-Scene-Without-Murdering-Someone Jared.

"Okay..."

I arise dramatically from the stool. "I need a break. Some fresh air. Maybe a cigarette." I still smoke a cig or two a day, despite vowing to quit over a year ago. I probably won't finish this book thing I've told myself I'm going to write either. I'm not so much a human person as a pathetic compendium of unrealized goals.

"Who's next then?" I hear Lana say as I storm out, seething at her and Fang and Jared and most of all myself.

I stand at the perimeter of Slingshot Acting Studios' parking lot in the balmy Atlanta air, smoking my once-or-twice-daily cig and bemoaning my inability to become a bona fide meat puppet. I can't even play *myself* convincingly, for fuck's sake. Who was I to *ever* think I could play someone else?

The back door swings open with a vacuum hiss, and Lana steps outside. She says, "I just wanted to say I'm sorry."

"It's fine." I toss the cigarette butt onto the ground and extinguish it with my foot, thinking *I* should probably be the one apologizing. "It's all totally, completely fine." But given my gritted teeth and watering eyes, I doubt she buys it.

"Look, if you feel like this class wasn't helpful for you, we occasionally offer refunds...."

I focus intently on the smooshed butt. My hair, which I trimmed very short about a year ago and haven't cut since, blows in my face, looking all kinds of uneven.

---

27   (my classmate Heather wore an eyepatch).

"It was helpful," I say, holding my eyes open widely to prevent tears from escaping.

"Well, that's the important thing. That you learned something, even if—"

"And...scene," I straighten my shoulders.

"Huh?"

"I was *acting*. I know my way around a camera."

"This whole day...?"

I nod.

She chuckles. Pauses. Chuckles again. "Man, I can't imagine what your internal monologue must have been like. That was a *really* convincing performance."

"Thank you." I bow slightly, my back aching with that familiar mild pain that hits all mid-twenties Americans and brings with it the crushing epiphany that your childhood is truly and definitively over. "But was it *entertaining*?"

"Kinda," she admits through nervous laughs. "I mean, I felt *bad* for being entertained, but it was *dramatic*. How long...have you been in character for? Like, was it just today?"

"That's the question, right? How long indeed? And if I told you, would you even believe me?"

"What do you mean?"

"Well, I could *still* be acting, right?"

"So if you *saying* you were acting...was acting...does that mean the scene itself was real?"

"Maybe."

Because good acting, I've decided, is just negative space. It's whatever is untrue, backwards, mind-fucked. It's the justification for paranoia. It's fiction that pretends it's not.

Which is why, after this final class, I feel no cognitive dissonance calling myself an actor. I still have a long road ahead before I can become a truly convincing one, but these past eight weeks have molded me into at least *part* of a meat puppet—a plant-puppet, maybe. And I think that's the best I could hope for; after all, it's not like I'm trying to make a living at this. Thus, to you, my dear esteemed readers, watchers, whatever the fuck you are, I can finally say,

Scene.

4

Syd, being somewhat of a natural human-repellent, had always struggled to make friends. And he didn't outgrow this difficulty the way many childhood loners do—if anything, his solitude only deepened with age. People often find strangely-behaved kids endearing, but when you're twenty-two and still brooding in corners during lunch breaks, other adults naturally assume there's a good reason.

Such was the case when Shannon Marshall's movie *MusicaLaw* began shooting in December of 2023. Shannon adhered to a strict directorial doctrine that prohibited uninvolved parties from entering the studio, so besides dropping Syd off and picking him up, Mitch was conspicuously absent on set.

Syd watched in confused awe as his costars grouped off into cliques within a day of meeting each other. Whenever he attempted to join one of these groups, they didn't shun him or throw food at him the way your stereotypical high school clique might, but their behavior nonetheless shifted. They artificially interrupted their real conversations to ask him trivial questions ("How long have you been acting?" "Who's your favorite actor?" "What's your favorite role you've played?"), and after a while, the whole charade felt more like a patronizing interrogation than a genuine social interaction. And that was the *best*-case scenario. Usually, they just ignored him, and when he tried to jump in, they either continued ignoring him or gave him the type of look people give weirdos who attempt to jump into their conversations. Syd had a whole mental flowchart of possible reactions to various social faux pas, and no path led to the formation of worthwhile friendships.

But for some reason, within *MusicaLaw*'s first couple weeks of shooting—maybe it was in the spirit of Christmas Charity; Syd didn't really know—he managed to make one friend and a few tertiary acquaintances. The friend's name was Ned Wesham.

Ned had a lot more screentime than Syd and was slightly more famous. He was also about six years Syd's senior. But given the nature of their characters' relationships—Syd played a perfect-pitched music lawyer at a law firm called Ehinger & Kobow, while Ned played his strict and borderline-abusive boss—they spent many hours together, began to tolerate each other, and, eventually, actually grew to somewhat enjoy each other's company. Or Syd enjoyed Ned's, at least. I never got a realistic read on how much Ned liked Syd *before* the incident.

Ned's clique consisted of himself and three female costars—Annabel, whose straight hair/bangs combo resembled a blonde rebel helmet from *Star Wars*; Philippa, who spoke with a light German accent on the rare occasions she spoke at all; and Rachel, who reminisced about her college track-and-field career with the same starry-eyed longing with which normal, non-actors often reminisce about their college track-and-field careers. Syd immediately sensed that Ned was a bit of a womanizer and liked to keep a squad of potential suitees on deck at all times—on the first day of filming, for example, he had a girlfriend named Tracy, of whom he spoke positively and often, but they split acrimoniously about a week later, and after not even three days of bachelordom, he was spotted (not by Syd, but word got around) canoodling with Philippa on set between takes. Many of these dynamics played out in the break room—a cramped, repurposed middle-management office whose single table looked as if it had been delivered there pronto from a cafeteria. A giant poster of Soderbergh's *Schizopolis* hung on the wall and watched Syd uncomfortably while he ate lunch.

"Are you gonna date Rachel or Annabel next?" Syd asked Ned one fine afternoon, not particularly caring that Rachel and Annabel were seated right there at the table with them. He bit into his meatball sub, inadvertently ejecting a meatball.

Rachel and Annabel looked synchronously to Ned for just the slightest instant before feigning outrage at Syd.

Instead of answering the question, Ned replied, in his traditional inanimate monotone, "You got anyone, Syd?" Philippa ran her hand repeatedly through Ned's hair, which was a bit too short to run one's hand through comfortably.

"I've got Mitch; he's a full-time job," Syd replied. To his disgust, he often caught himself name-dropping Mitch in casual conversations, mainly because he didn't regularly interact with many other human beings besides Peter, with whom recall of his interactions was foggy.

"Who's Mitch again?" Rachel asked.

"He's dating his manager," Ned explained, picking at a tower of fried rice with his fork, Philippa still mussing his hair with rhythmic regularity. Syd wondered whether Ned ever tired of having his hair mussed.

"We're not *dating*," Syd said quickly. "I mean, he wanted to date me at first, but now—"

Ned set down his fork and adjusted his posture slightly. "Oh God," he drawled. "That's great."

Syd couldn't tell whether he was being laughed *with* or *at*.

"You've gotta get laid," Ned went on. "Annabel, he's your type, isn't he?"

"Not really."

"Why not?" Ned asked.

Annabel's mouth moved wordlessly while she searched for an optimally tactful response. "Too young."

"What about Rachel?" Syd suggested. Though he had no real interest in Rachel, he enjoyed observing the intragroup tensions between Rachel and Ned, Ned and Annabel, Ned and Philippa, and Philippa, Annabel, and Rachel.

Ned scanned her briefly, his eyes lingering unsubtly on her track-enhanced legs, and then shook his head. "Nah. She's *way* out of your league."

Philippa removed her hand from Ned's hair and swatted his arm. Annabel developed an unusual interest in her chow mien.

But when Ned wasn't teasing Syd or his own loyal band of eligible bachelorettes, he liked to ramble about his family. These ramblings bored Syd, who mostly tuned them out and nodded during dramatic pauses. If he'd been listening, he would have learned that much of Ned's unconventional romantic behavior was attributable to loneliness—his parents were both dead, and he didn't really talk to his brother anymore. You already know the deal—Ned told me many of the same anecdotes I imagine he told Syd.

During *MusicaLaw*'s final week of filming, Syd and Annabel's acquaintanceship developed into something of a low-grade friendship. A scene in which their characters devise a conspiracy to get Ned's character disbarred was slated to film last, so they spent a lot of one-on-one time practicing. All the while, Annabel continued to hang clingily and groupie-like onto Ned, despite her seeming annoyance with him. When Ned went off with Philippa, she often muttered snide comments to Syd that had nothing to do with Ned's obvious *real* offense—his placement of Annabel below Rachel on the eligible-bachelorette food chain—and instead pertained to small, superficial quirks.

"His left pant leg is always tucked into his sock," she pointed out while Ned stood contemplatively at the vending machine about fifty feet away. "Ever notice that?"

Syd noted blandly that she was indeed correct.

"You won't snitch on me though, right?"

"I won't snitch that you noticed his pant leg was tucked into his sock?"

"Yeah. Embarrassing, right?"

"Uh, yeah. I guess so."

"As long as you won't snitch."

And he wouldn't—not only because the observation was so boring as to compel near-immediate disregard but also because he had no real desire to get mixed up in the petty politics of his few almost-friends. Annabel, however, interpreted this indifference as loyalty, which earned him points on what he imagined as a detailed Excel-spreadsheet ranking of her friends, complete with numeric totals broken down by proprieties and transgressions.

"I find the best way to do this scene is to imagine I'm like *really* angry at Ned," she told Syd that final week, while the two of them ran lines in the practice room.

"Is that difficult?"

She cleared her throat, her script rolled into a lidless cylinder at her side. "'He's a senseless brute. Don't you want to *do* something? Or are you just gonna sit around on your ass like you always do?'"

"Oh, uh," Syd said, caught off guard by her sudden transition into rehearsal. "'I just don't know how I feel about risking the only job I've ever had,'" he recited.

"'*Please*, a track record like yours? You'll get snatched up by another firm within weeks. It's really *me* we have to worry about.'" She placed a hand on his shoulder and met his eyes. "'If I'm not worried, you shouldn't be either.'"

"'I think I just favor a more, uh, passive…strategy.'"

Annabel dropped her arm to her side. "What's wrong? Why are you so wooden?"

"Gotta warm up," Syd lied.

"Bull." Annabel continued staring at his face—she'd only broken character below the neck. "This is bringing up some real shit for you, isn't it?"

Syd didn't reply, which was a reply in and of itself.

"Tell me."

"Why? I don't even know you, really."

"And that's a *problem*, isn't it? We're never gonna deliver convincing performances if we can't be honest with each other."

"I'm being honest about not wanting to talk about it."

"What if I told you something about me first?" She dropped into a practice room chair, which told Syd they were going to be here a while, so he took a passive seat next to her.

"When I was twelve, my parents got divorced," she began, and Syd perked up, now under the selfish suspicion that the two of them might have more in common than he'd initially thought. "Huge, messy, ugly split. She got primary custody, but I always preferred my dad. And *he* always preferred my brother, who was two years younger. It was a bit of a familial love triangle. Nothing weird though," she added when Syd raised an eyebrow. "Anyway, I always resented my brother for this, and I started a fistfight with him during chess club this one time."

"You got into a physical brawl during *chess* club? What did he do to provoke it, capture your queen or something?"

"No real injuries, but we each threw a few punches," she continued, ignoring his interjection. "He hadn't hit puberty yet, so I kicked his ass. The school called my mom to come pick us up early. She told my dad. I guess part of me wanted that, but I didn't know it until much later. At the time, I wasn't sure *what* I wanted. I was more or less just improvising.

"The punishment my dad decided on, the next time we visited his place, was that our birthday allowances would be donated to charity, if you want an idea of the sort of upper-class disciplining that went on at my house." Syd sat back in his chair, rapidly losing interest. "For the first time in her life, my mom agreed with him. Blake—that's my brother's name—and I were livid. We decided to steal money from our dad to get back at him." Syd moved back to the edge of his seat, once again intrigued. "You're probably assuming we took the money and got caught and punished again. I *wish* it were as anticlimactic as that. It was actually kind of like something out of a movie. I think one of the reasons I began acting is because I felt like my entire life was a film already, so I figured why not get paid for it? You know?"

"So what happened?" Syd asked, not especially interested in hearing her entire life story and not especially adept at hiding it.

"Turns out my dad had connections to the mob." A momentary, out-of-place giggle. "Yeah, like the fucking Irish mob. From, like, *The Departed*." She pronounced it like "The Depahted." "And that the big suitcase of cash we ransacked—which should have been a tell in and of itself, a big suitcase full of cash, but what did we know? we were kids—that the suitcase was actually money he *owed* to the mob, which felt like an *engineered* coincidence, and while we didn't steal it all, we took just enough that when my dad showed up to some abandoned lot to hand over the loot, the mob had reason to believe he was skimping on them and popped him off." She held up a hand with two fingers outstretched and made the motion of a gun recoiling.

Syd sat in awed silence for a few seconds. If he were a bit more discerning and less emotion-driven, he may have remembered that Annabel *was* a professional actress and thus a professional liar and that nothing she told him should necessarily be believed, but Syd, like most people, defaulted to taking his fellow humans at face value. We kind of *all* have to do that—there isn't any other way to live without dying inside.

"Your turn," Annabel said, slouching her shoulders in a show of relief. Syd's own cushioned chair felt metallically hard—seat cushions this thin didn't serve much purpose if you weighed more than thirty pounds.

"Okay," Syd said, taking a deep breath, and then he told her. He told her the true story of his parents and Glen and the birthday party that went wrong.

"Huh," she said when he finished. "So we were kinda *both* responsible for our fathers' deaths, in a way."

"I wouldn't say I was *responsible*...." Syd's chest grew hot.

"You must be, like, really traumatized by clowns then."

"I guess. I—" Syd laughed in what he hoped was a self-conscious acknowledgement of the lame uncouthness of the admission that followed. "—I beat one up last year."

Annabel's posture returned to its earlier, non-relieved state. "Really?" she said. "*Really?*" she repeated, more drawn-out and exaggerated this time.

Syd would remain oblivious as to Annabel's personal investment in this anecdote—he didn't even know her full name, in fact, which made her immensely difficult to track down and forced me to wait until *MusicaLaw* was released (to mixed reviews) before I reached out. If he *had* taken note of her surname, he would have recognized that it was Olsen and, upon hearing of her brother Blake, may have puzzled out her nepotistic connections to not just the acting industry but also the professional klown one.

"Yeah. I feel like if I even so much as *see* a clown, I'll—" He made a few quick boxing motions.

Annabel refused an in-person interview with me and was fairly short in her email correspondences, but she did provide some details that allowed me to piece together the subsequent days' occurrences, albeit not until after I'd repeatedly reassured her that she'd be anonymized in my forthcoming "novel" and that she was in no way legally culpable for what had happened to Ned (and even if she *were*, he wouldn't be pressing charges, so don't even worry about it, I said). The general gist of her story is that she told Ned it would be funny to prank Syd by showing up to the studio one morning dressed as a clown. She led him to believe she'd do the same. She'd already spoken to Rachel, she convincingly lied. The prank's crux, she explained to Ned and then explained herself explaining to me, was that when Syd saw their clown outfits, he'd be confused and wonder whether there was some kind of memo he'd missed out on. She conveniently omitted Syd's hatred for and history of violence toward clowns when she proposed the idea and did, she confessed in email, ultimately hope Syd would throw a punch or two in Ned's direction—she still held an understandable grudge over his earlier slight, after all.[28] Having accurately identified Syd as the bastard who'd roundhoused her brother at Kayla's birthday party in 2022, she was perfectly happy to toss *him* to the metaphorical wolves as well, if it came to that. Syd and Ned were both dead to her, she said.[29]

So when Ned strolled into the studio in full traditional clown garb on the last day of filming, Syd interpreted the gesture as not just a betrayal on Annabel's part but a sign that Ned had never really been his friend and that the whole time Syd had *thought* he and Annabel were in low-stakes cahoots against Ned, Ned and Annabel had been in *high*-stakes cahoots against *him*, merely waiting for an optimally convenient piece of information with which they could damage him, and the totality of Syd's lifetime sum of clown-hatred escaped in not so much a single burst as a prolonged gush—Syd kicked Ned until he hit the floor, at which point he kneeled on top of him, pinning him, and punched him so hard in the face that his clown nose and a couple teeth went flying off into the object-impermanent distance, and he continued hitting him with the full intention of breaking and hopefully shattering his nose before kneeing his ribcage until he heard one snap, not stopping the onslaught until Ned was coughing up blood and Annabel and Rachel were attempting to pull him off and Philippa was jabbering loudly in rapid-fire German off to the side—it wasn't until *then* that Syd looked into the bruised, rouged eyes of a barely-conscious man he now knew he could fully kill if he wanted—like, a few more punches and he'd be dead, Syd predicted—and begrudgingly relented.

28   By the way, did Ned ever mention her? she asked when I told her I'd been in contact with him. I harnessed my newfound acting skills and told her she may have come up. I suppose this footnote, if she reads it, will serve to let her down easy.

29   Was I sure I didn't *remember* her name coming up when I talked to Ned? she followed up.

5

Life Imitates Art premiered at the Sundance Film Festival in the third week of 2024, just a couple months before Mitch terminated his working relationship with Syd. Hayley had been unable to get off work, so it was just Mitch and Syd flying cross-country as a pair, and Syd, debilitatingly self-conscious and figuring their age gap was too narrow for a father-son relationship to be believable, found himself repeatedly and unpromptedly assuring flight attendants that they weren't romantically involved (e.g. "Pretzels or peanuts?" "Pretzels. We aren't a gay couple.").

"Why do you keep saying that?" Mitch asked after the third or fourth time. Ripped open his bag of peanuts with his teeth.

"Because we're not."

"I know, but why do you think anyone *else* cares?"

Syd wasn't fully sure—just felt an increasing uneasiness around Mitch. Besides, he saw the way these Utah natives looked at them. Mormons, probably. It might not take much to send them on a Holy Crusade, and Syd's newly-heightened awareness of his *own* capacity to beat the shit out of anyone else on a moment's notice made him safely suspect that the same was true of others.

Syd had never seen a mountain in his life, much less looked out onto a vast, snow-covered mountain range while waiting to view a full-length feature film starring himself, so his arrival in Park City, Utah felt a bit surreal. He and Mitch met up with Peter Rankin at the opening night dinner, which took place in the Basin Recreational Fieldhouse and featured a concert pianist and round tables with frilly cloths and a catering menu boasting options far more decadent than anything Syd had encountered in his life thus far. He'd never eaten lobster, for example, and Mitch had to gently inform him of the proper consumption method. Mitch also told him what to do with the cloth napkin his utensils came wrapped in—making it into a floppy origami hat was apparently not SOP.

"You've got some money saved up, right?" Peter asked. Syd sat on his right, and his wife Gerry sat on his left, not saying much but poking delicately at her steak and occasionally making silent facial gestures that could mean any number of things. "You're telling me you've never eaten anywhere fancy?"

"I only know how to live poor." And it was true. What was also true, however, was something he didn't want to mention within earshot of Mitch (who sat on *his* right, aggressively biting into a corncob while following exactly none of the etiquette instructions he'd just tried to instill in Syd): he was buying more CNO than ever before.

Despite his many years of substance abuse, Syd could count on one hand the number of times he'd been drunk. This was mostly a taste thing—cheap beer didn't go down well, and the sheer quantity required for intoxication had always made him wonder what the point was. Today, however, with a bowtied server refilling his champagne glass on a whim and the champagne tasting better than Syd had ever thought alcohol could taste and TSA guidelines prohibiting the transport of suspicious white powders, he felt his thoughts all melting together into an unrefined mental soup as the pesky, annoying sobriety that had afflicted him for hours faded into comfortable oblivion.

"*Sergeant Nebula*," he said, leaning his head on Peter's shoulder. "I was watching the trailer.... God, it's stupid. Am I a hack?" He hacked something up. "Am I a washed-up hack-been? Has-been? Has-not-yet-been? Is-never-going-to—"

"Pull it together," Peter muttered, pushing him off with the gentle haste of an airplane passenger whose row-mate is dozy. Syd slumped forward onto the table, chin resting on folded arms. Etiquette had left the realm of consideration. A mildly buzzed Mitch stared alternate daggers at him and Peter. Ola Benson pursed her lips in a show of suppressed contempt.

"Hey Ola, wanna fuck later?" Syd suggested, noting her distaste.

Ola answered, "Nope" without any deliberation. Peter said, "*Syd*!" Mitch watched the floor.

"I get it; I get it," he slurred. "You're 'method acting,' right? You gotta pretend you're not interested in me because that's what your *character* would do."

"That's not—"

"Yeah, well, filming is over, all right? You've done your duty. Now let's have some fun."

"It wasn't acting," Ola said sharply. "That part wasn't, I mean."

"Did a pretty unconvincing job for someone who wasn't acting." He didn't even *want* to sleep with Ola, was the thing—just wanted to sleep with someone, he thought drunkly, his psyche toeing the surprisingly thin line between horny and suicidal. Anyone at all would do.

Syd's heavy drinking persisted throughout the week. At the screening of *Life Imitates Art*, he brought a bottle of wine into the theater, where he, Mitch, Peter, and Gerry sat in a row in the same formation as opening night. Syd got drunker and drunker as he watched his onscreen alter ego go madder and madder with desperate lust. He drew drunk mental parallels between himself and the fictional, progressively-more-bloated art dealer who inhabited his body. When the artist died by his painting's hand, Syd got drunkly spooked at the sight of the fake blood pouring from his head and the utter absence of all signs of life in his eyes. He got an involuntary drunk vision of himself, dead, just like that. Mitch tossed clumps of popcorn into his mouth, fully engrossed. Peter's face arranged itself into a wide smirk. Gerry smiled sort of despite herself and massaged Peter's shoulders. When the credits rolled, everyone stood and clapped. Syd stood too, taking a moment to find his footing. He followed Peter onstage for the director Q&A, while Mitch tagged closely behind.

"Can I help you?" Peter asked Syd.

Syd shrugged, still clutching the wine bottle. He downed another swig.

"It's just me for this part. The actor Q-and-A is later."

So Syd stumbled back into the plebian audience, feeling sorry for himself, the delayed sting of Peter's apathetic nonchalance intensifying to an uncomfortable sizzle.

While Peter and a couple tech guys tried to set up the stage's microphone, a woman approached Syd with a confident stride that told him she meant business. "That was *really* good," she said, holding out her right hand. Syd moved the wine bottle to his left and shook it. "Why hadn't I heard of you until now?" She was thin with dark hair and high cheekbones, wore a button-down white blouse, and looked to be anywhere from zero to five years older than Mitch.

"Dunno. Why haven't you?"

"I'm Layla," she introduced. "Layla Graham. I manage a few up-and-coming indie actors. I'm guessing *you've* heard of *me*." Though subsequent events will likely shed doubt on her latter assertion, I can confirm that the non-pseudomized version of Layla Graham is indeed a talent acquisition agent.

Syd burped. "Nope."

She smiled professionally. "That makes two of us, then. I was wondering whether you'd be interested in a business relationship," intermittently directing her gaze to Syd and Mitch, the latter of whom had been following Syd everywhere for the entire week and was being a bit of a clingy bitch, if Syd was being honest. Syd shot a quick glance up at the stage, where Peter tapped the wireless microphone delicately and showed no signs of planning to invite Syd to accompany him. "I don't usually take on new clients, but I'm willing to make an exception."

"Nope. Got a manager." Syd pointed to Mitch, whose hair looked so disheveled as to be purposeful and who wore ripped jeans and a Dead Kennedys shirt under his trusty faux-leather jacket, which Syd had to admit looked shockingly in vogue given the cold outdoor weather and mountainous location.

"Oh, this is your *manager*?" Layla extended her hand toward Mitch, who blinked at it as if she'd just offered him a piece of roadkill.

"We're good."

To Mitch: "Well, maybe this is for the best. I wouldn't want my personal feelings to get in the way of my managerial ones." To Syd: "But watching you made me absolutely breathless."

Syd was still sober enough to recognize flirting when he saw it.

"Let me know if you ever change your mind," she finished, once again to Syd and Mitch both, but obviously more to Syd. Syd polished off his remaining sip of wine. As she walked away, she turned around and mouthed, *Catch you later*, definitely only to Syd.

"What a blowhard," Mitch opined once she was out of earshot. Syd gave a slight groan, wanting nothing more than to piss Mitch off and freshly aware of a foolproof method by which to do just that.

The keys to Mitch's rental car sat visibly in his coat's roomy right pocket, and Mitch himself appeared fully preoccupied with watching Peter, who was currently describing his inspiration for *Life Imitates Art*—a trip to Amsterdam's Van Gogh Museum, during which he'd stared for several minutes at a painting of a skeleton smoking a cigarette—you know the one; just Google "van Gogh skeleton smoking a cigarette" if you don't, he added—and realized that his art could literally kill him. That this artist business was no joke. He'd always thought of himself as his movies' master, but (he chuckled) really, they were the master of him. Mitch's awe-paralyzed face remained zeroed-in on the stage, allowing Syd to dislodge the keys with no trouble at all. Mitch laughed at something funny Peter said that Syd missed because he was so focused on the keys. But now Syd was free.

"Where are you going?" Mitch asked. Syd stopped in his tracks with a questionable degree of suave.

"Gonna mingle a bit."

"Without me?"

Mitch was like a toe wart that kept growing back, even after multiple cryogenic treatments. "Well, first I gotta shit. Might be in the bathroom for a while. I'm guessing you don't want any part in that."

Mitch hesitated long enough for Syd to suspect him of contemplating it. "Nope."

"Good, so we're on the same page then."

Syd spotted Layla in the crowd and dangled the keys at eye-level. Somehow, she knew exactly what he was asking. The two of them snuck outside together and then broke into a run, flying through the crisp, cold parking lot air back to Mitch's rental, their breath fogging.

"This is exciting," Layla panted. "I've never missed a Q-and-A before."

"Me neither," Syd replied, failing to add that he was a Q&A virgin. Divulging too much about himself would only change her mind.

He unlocked the white car—so white it almost glowed in the dark—and started the ignition for temperature reasons. They crammed themselves into the narrow, restricted backseat, her on top, which Syd figured must be a bit unconventional. He reached under her shirt and fumbled with her bra, trying in vain to unclasp it—a common fictional cliché but one that, like many clichés, is mostly based in truth. His intoxication didn't help his coordination.

"Hold on," Syd said, right as Layla unzipped his pants and stuck her hand through the fly.

She froze. "Yeah?"

"This is my first time. Can we take it slow?"

"This is your first time?"

Syd nodded.

"Why?"

"Never got around to it."

She removed her hand. "Okay. So do we just kiss first or what?"

"Whatever you usually do when you take it slow."

"I don't usually take it slow."

"Fine, then just do what you normally do but like slowed down fifty percent."

She stuck her hand back into his pants and began moving it with an exaggerated lethargy. It felt good. Syd kissed her. She tasted like expensive champagne. The sound of the car's exhaust formed a white-noise backdrop to their moans while the vehicle rumbled beneath them. Syd, smooshed awkwardly against the door, developed the inklings of a backache. He closed his eyes and knew in his bones that this was where his life peaked. That the nebulous aspirational pleasure he'd spent his whole life chasing was unattainable. So enjoy it while you have it, he told himself, chanting it like a mental mantra, his very thoughts seeming to slur, while Layla removed his pants and then her own and attempted to—

A harsh knock sounded. Syd and Layla froze. Syd craned his neck and peered through the window. Mitch was standing outside in the freezing night air, hands in his now-empty coat pockets, looking red-faced and utterly pissed.

"What's *he* doing here?" Layla shrieked, fumbling with her slacks. Syd hastily pulled his underwear back up.

"It's his car."

"I thought it was *your* car."

"I'm not old enough to rent a car."

"How old *are* you?"

"How old do you *think* I am?"

Mitch swung the door open so swiftly Syd nearly tumbled out. Syd buttoned his jeans with some difficulty, bobbing on the balls of his feet in his socks, the cold now feeling not just uncomfortable but oppressive.

"He's *drunk*," Mitch exclaimed to Layla. "He's *blackout drunk*."

"We both are," Syd said defensively. "I'm not even that drunk." And he hardly felt it anymore. Drunk, that is. "I'm not blacked out."

"Get out," Mitch ordered, pointing a cartoonish finger at Layla.

She fled, head hung in the posture of a bullied schoolgirl.

Mitch grabbed Syd by the shirt collar and shoved him up against the car. Syd had never seen him this mad—not even the day he'd beat up Ned, which was indisputably a much worse offense. "Stealing my *keys*. Having sex in my *car*. What the fuck are you *doing*?"

"I was trying to get laid," his voice breaking like a busted radio signal. For the first time since the day they'd met, Mitch terrified him.

"And why did you think *now* was the right time for that?"

"I didn't wanna be a virgin forever."

Mitch let go of his shirt and took a step back. "You're a *virgin*?"

"Thanks to you, yeah," gradually relaxing his shoulders. "Got really close to losing it."

"You mean being a *movie star* wasn't enough to get you laid?"

"I don't wanna talk about sex with you."

"That's not how this works. You don't get to pickpocket me and fuck strangers in my car and then decide you don't wanna talk about sex."

"Your *rental* car."

Mitch shoved him in the chest, though not hard enough to push him over. A sober or CNO'ed Syd would have struck back harder, but he'd discovered this week that alcohol made him less, not more, quarrelsome. "So why did you do it?"

"I *wanted* to, okay? Is that not enough reason?" A creeping nausea of either physical or metaphysical origin was mounting within him.

"Of *course* it's not. If that were really it, you would have gotten laid a long time ago. So why'd you *really* do it? Huh? Got something to do with me?"

"Jesus, you're such a narcissist."

"Well? Then what is it? She's like fifteen years older than you, for fuck's sake."

"You're not my boyfriend, and you're not my dad, so I don't need to dignify you with a response," Syd said, trying to keep his voice level but shaking all the while—he'd anticipated some anger, sure, but *this* Mitch looked positively murderous. His fatherly cadence superficially resembled Glen's on that fateful April afternoon but possessed a bone-chilling coldness Glen's had lacked.

"Not even after I—" Mitch lowered his voice, even though nobody else was within three hundred feet of them. "Not even after I covered your ass with that Wesham thing?"

"I didn't ask you to do that."

"But you'd probably be in jail now if I hadn't. Do you have the remotest conception of the sheer *power* I have over you?" raising his voice to a premature-hangover-inducing pitch and volume. "I could make your life *hell*."

"But you wouldn't," Syd replied, his face somehow growing hotter while his skin temperature dropped.

"What makes you think that?"

"Because you love me."

"*Do* I, Syd?"

"I don't know. Do you?" Drunkenness tended to make Syd repeat questions back to their askers instead of answering them.

"Prove it."

"What?"

"Prove I love you."

Syd didn't quite understand the question and almost wondered whether his manager was intoxicated too. "Just now, when you thought I was drunk," he said finally. The wind whistled. His head throbbed. His stomach churned. "You yelled at Layla because you thought I was too drunk to fuck. You were looking out for me."

"I wasn't looking *out* for you. I was just trying to scare that bitch off."

Syd couldn't decide whether to believe it. He got a paranoid, drunk vision of a two-years-younger Mitch meticulously orchestrating their entire relationship in pursuit of some nefarious goal, followed by another one of Mitch rigid, blue, and dead in an ice cream freezer. "I'm sorry," he said. And then he leaned over and puked in one swift impromptu motion. The spew narrowly missed the back wheel of Mitch's rental.

Mitch let out a long exhale that left a thin path of steam in the frozen air, keeping a close watch on the inert vomit as if afraid it might disappear and respawn on his windshield. "It's okay."

Then, in spite of all his efforts to remain composed, Syd cried, snot congealing coldly on his upper lip. "Where's Peter?"

"What do you need *him* for?"

"Just wanna talk to him."

"Probably still answering audience questions." Mitch clapped Syd's shoulder fatherlyly. "But let's head back. Wouldn't wanna freeze to death out here."

6

One of the most shameful televisual endeavors Syd took part in during his short acting career was the aforementioned cult sci-fi TV series *Sgt. Nebula*, a revamp of the critically panned but commercially lauded movie trilogy of the same name. Syd played a half-alien named Scybe, and his costuming included a Skywalkerish robe and lots of pale-green *Frankenstein*esque makeup and a couple *Shrek*-like horns, and though he wasn't the star—had not gotten another starring role in anything since *Life Imitates Art* and was starting to doubt his acting abilities as a result—he received just enough screentime to squeeze into the theme-song credits.

Now, more than ever, as he sat at a Seattle Science Fiction Convention booth signing autographs alongside his only three colleagues who didn't have filming conflicts—the five-foot, eleven-inch Amanda Browning, aka Sgt. Mellie Nebula herself, bane of the Dasein of frustrated nerdy virgins everywhere; the stocky, thirty-some Ryan Grasso, who played a tin-mannish cyborg named Prion; and an annoying elementary-school girl named Grace Winter who portrayed a "common field gremlin," which role, in Syd's opinion, she effortlessly embodied—he felt like a sellout. But pulpy, special-effects-ridden TV shows didn't pay very well, so perhaps he hadn't even earned *that* honor. And it wasn't like girls fawned over him the way guys did Amanda, who, Syd enviously noted, was at least afforded the privilege of dressing like a *human*, albeit a scantily-clad one. The un-air-conditioned convention building felt hotly pressurized and smelled exactly how you'd expect a building full of BO-infested nerds in the middle of August to smell.

Right now, about thirty minutes into their three-hour shift, Grace sat crouched under the card table, tugging Syd's alien-robe's sleeve with incessant repetition. "I wanna go *home*," she whined, stretching the final consonant into a hum.

"What do you want me to do about that?" Syd said through gritted teeth as he signed a *Sgt. Nebula*-themed postcard for a high school girl in Mellie Nebula cosplay.

"I wanna go *home*," she repeated, continuing to tug his sleeve.

"Quit it." He slapped her hand. She pulled it away and affected a stern pout. "Go harass Ryan instead." Pointed to his immediate right.

Ryan shot Syd a dirty look, his silver makeup caking a bit. An overweight man with glasses and a neckbeard was describing his masturbatory fantasies to Amanda in stark detail: he and Mellie are the last remaining passengers on the Flubron Space Shuttle when it runs out of fuel. They both accept that they're going to float off into the cold vortex of infinite space and suffer slow starvation-deaths and never return to the planet of Yarz. They grab onto each other for (literal) dear life. He has a boner (my addendum). She does not have the female equivalent of a boner (my additional addendum). They figure, well, if they're both going to die anyway then why not—etc.

"Thanks for being a fan," Amanda told him sweetly, signing his forehead on request.

"I'm never washing my face again," he exclaimed, craning his eyeballs upward in a futile effort to peek at the damage while walking straight past Syd, Grace, and Ryan without even acknowledging them.

"To be fair, I don't think he washed his face much before this either," Syd told Amanda.

She laughed.

"You should've drawn a dick on his forehead."

"I was tempted."

Syd laced his hands behind his head and leaned back in his squeaky chair, utterly convinced for just one precious moment of emotional weakness that Amanda wouldn't *dare* contemplate drawing a dick on *his* forehead.

One female fan who must have chugged about thirty cups of coffee before coming here really wanted to chat with all four of them. She barreled through strings of questions without waiting for answers. She presented exactly eight different pieces of *Sgt. Nebula* memorabilia to be signed in turn, one of which was her old high school graduation cap. She asked Syd & Co. to follow her Tumblr blog. She said there was tons more stuff she'd left in her car because she didn't want to overwhelm them, but she'd happily fetch it on a moment's notice. Like seriously, just say the word, and she'd run out to the parking lot and grab her two large cardboard boxes full of memorabilia.

"I've been meaning to ask," Lindsay continued in the same breath as her last question ("What's your makeup regime, Amanda?"), while Syd signed her limited-edition Scybe bobblehead, "do you have any relation to the *company* Syd Morris?"

"There's a company called Syd Morris?"

Lindsay nodded unsuspectingly. The man waiting behind her in line affected the subtle, annoyed gestures line-waiters affect when the person in front of them is taking far too long.

"Keep it moving," Ryan said, laughing to cover his own annoyance.

"Never heard of it," Syd told Lindsay, handing the bobblehead back.

"It's just—I own stock in a company with your name. Funny."

"It's not a *company*," the subtly-gesturing man cut in, exasperated. He was skinny and round-faced and lisped slightly when he talked. "It's a person—him." He pointed at Syd.

"Move along," Amanda urged Lindsay, smiling in the same patient but obviously fake way she'd smiled at the chronic masturbator.

"Wait," Syd demanded. Trying to make sense of their statements felt a bit like trying to solve a Rubik's Cube blindfolded without knowing somebody had disassembled it and oriented one of the corners wrong. "What on earth are you people talking about?"

"People buy and sell stock in your name," the man explained, lowering his voice. "It's not exactly legal, but...I thought you were aware. It's all facilitated by that one dude."

The analogic cube suddenly fixed itself. "Mitch Larkin?"

"Yeah."

"Mitch doesn't *sell* the stock," Lindsay attempted to correct him. "He borrowed mine after I borrowed it from someone else. Or was it me who borrowed it from Mitch? I can't really remember."

. "He's shorting?" the lispy guy asked.

"He's huh?" Lindsay said.

"Keep the line moving," Ryan said again.

"Why would he be shorting? Once he sells all Syd's stuff..." The man turned his gaze to the filthy-carpeted floor and fell silent.

"What stuff?" Syd asked, his heart pounding so hard it threatened to rip his spandex.

"The stuff you gave him. As part of the 'relationship.'" He put air-quotes around the last word.

"I haven't given him shit," though now Syd was thinking back to all the times Mitch had asked for or bought or tried to steal his staple art. "And I have no 'relationship' with that fuck."

"Language," Amanda said, eyeing Grace.

Syd stood up. "I'm going to use the men's room," he lied, not even attempting to sound convincing. Ryan and Amanda exchanged quizzical glances. Syd pointed to Lindsay and the lispy guy (whose name he never got but whom I'm going to refer to as Chester) and then to a reasonably deserted corner. "Meet me over there."

Syd weaved his way through clusters of cosplayers while Lindsay and Chester followed, most likely out of their own selfish desires to get to the bottom of this mystery and have some shot at recovering their money (in Chester's case) or dignity (in Lindsay's). Once they made it to the corner, Chester gave Syd a detailed rundown of the stock operation from start to finish, Lindsay contributing her own relevant tidbits to help complete the picture and confirm what Syd already knew in his heart to be true. As he listened to their story, his stomach indefinitely freefell through his torso and murderous impulses flooded his brain.

"Why were you betting on me like a horse?" he inquired once they'd finished.

"Mitch tricked me," Lindsay said. "And Hayley—she's my friend, and she's innocent. He tricked her like he tricked you and me. He's tricking everyone, I guess."

Syd believed the first part—knew that if he for whatever reason wanted to dupe somebody into making poor financial decisions, Lindsay would be his go-to. He turned to Chester, who broke eye contact and tapped his thumbs together meterlessly.

"I thought you had great potential, and I wanted to earn some money," which Syd also believed—if he were lying, he would have invented a more flattering excuse.

"It doesn't matter," Syd told them, though he didn't really feel it. "What matters now is that we all wanna see Mitch's downfall, yeah? You, guy, he stole your money. And you, lady, he made you look like an idiot." Lindsay opened her mouth to object. "And me..." Syd didn't have enough lung capacity to list everything Mitch had done to him and didn't think he could make a reasonable effort without smearing his alien makeup.

"I don't think we have any legal footing, given the nature of the thing," Chester admitted.

"You gotta think bigger."

Chester blinked for a few seconds, like he was undergoing a full factory reset. "Well, now Mitch wants you to burn out, right? So you gotta, like, not burn out."

"And what do you think will happen if I don't?" Syd asked rhetorically. "Do you think Mitch will admit he was wrong and pay everyone back what they're owed?"

Both shook their heads. "But beyond assassinating the guy," Chester said, "I dunno what else..."

"What if I scored big?" Syd suggested in an instantaneous spurt of inspiration. "Like, what if I got cast in one of those *Captain Wilderness* features?"

"I love *Captain Wilderness*," Lindsay contributed.

"Do you think there's a chance of that happening?" Chester asked him.

Syd took a deep breath—his first real one in several minutes. "I think there's a chance of me making Mitch *think* it's happening."

"A new one is in pre-production," Lindsay interjected, somehow winded from *not* speaking. "They're announcing the cast next month."

Syd's mouth formed a rictus like the Grinch's when he first got the idea to steal Christmas. "Maybe I can give Mitch a little preview of the cast list."

"By telling him you're in it?" Lindsay said.

"Yes."

"By lying to him?" she followed up.

"By acting. Tricker becomes trickee, am I right?"

"What's a trickee?"

"You guys spread the word about the stock scam. Tell everyone he's borrowing his own stock back. Tell them he's floundering. *I'll* tell *him* I just made it bigger than he ever could have dreamed."

Ryan, watching them from across the room, now made a "get back over here" motion with his shiny hand, but the gesture looked unnatural—like reality itself was tinged with abstraction. Reality hadn't felt fully real to Syd since his overdose. He'd been unconscious for so long it seemed like part of him still hadn't woken up.

"When he hears about *this*, he'll shit bricks," Syd went on. "I bet he'll kill himself on the spot. And if he doesn't?" Looked at Lindsay and then Chester, right as the final dying kick of the CNO he'd snorted before the meet-and-greet forced all the oxygen back into his lungs. "I'll take care of that."

Part V:
The End of the End

1

So now you know most of what led up to Mitch Larkin's decision to put his Chekhov 30 into the pocket of his faux-leather jacket and head due east to the swanky suite he'd helped Syd move into just five months prior. He hadn't told Hayley anything; she was working late and would only worry. It was raining, just like in his fantasies. The sort of ominous, leaden rain that tends to fall when someone is about to die.

While Mitch idled in Manhattan's infamous traffic, the rain on his back window forming a thick, wet shroud that made the scene through his rearview resemble a Nell Sullivan painting, he noticed that the black Ford Escape behind him had been tailing him for quite some time and was possibly even *following* him, as in *on purpose*. At first, he chalked his suspicions up to paranoia, but after taking a convoluted detour down several deserted streets and being tailed the whole way, his apprehension began to mount. After all, Syd knew about the stocks, which meant some of the traders had spilled, which meant they were talking to Syd, and, much like *Mitch* knew *Syd's* address, *Syd* also knew *Mitch's*, and what his car looked like, and what *he* looked like, and how he drove. He'd done his absolute best to keep his emotional guard up around Syd, but some details had slipped through the cracks.

Mitch, now putzing down a one-way residential street with the Ford Escape still following close behind, suddenly sped up. The black car accelerated in turn, not even trying to remain inconspicuous. Only about half a mile to go before Mitch reached Syd's apartment, and his pursuer still hadn't let up. He could turn around, he supposed, but what good would that do? The last thing he needed was a murderous stalker on his home turf.

The black car accelerated again in a seeming bid to pass him despite the road being far too narrow for that. Mitch sped up even more, now going upwards of fifty, his heart rate speeding up right along with him. The menacing black car dinged his back bumper, and Mitch's wimpy Prius shot up onto the curb with a couple sharp bumps. For good measure (though Mitch found it slightly overkill), the car impacted him again, this time from the side and much more emphatically. His driver's window shattered. He slowed to a stop. His airbag exploded and hit his chest with something between a *smack* and a *splat*. His wipers continued wiping.

Before Mitch had the chance to get his bearings or gather his thoughts or even catch his breath, a burly, ski-masked man pried open his dinged door from the inside, dragged him out, and kneed him in the stomach. Mitch crumpled, the gun in his pocket a distant memory. A blow from a completely different direction struck his chest and sent him toppling backward, and though Mitch now had ample self-defense reasons to fire the gun, he couldn't summon the mental or physical energy to do so, and by the time it dawned on him that maybe shooting these guys wouldn't be the worst of ideas, one of them was stomping on his hand with a sickening, squelching crack while Mitch helplessly watched a fist close in on his face. A searing pain flooded his temples for just an instant before he blacked out.

When he woke up, he was lying on his back on the curb of an alley. His car was nowhere in view. Every square inch of his body screamed out in agony. It was no longer raining, but the air felt as damp as the ground.

His leather jacket was scuffed but intact. His phone, which he now pulled out of his jeans pocket with his unbroken left hand, displayed the telltale spiderweb lines of a cracked screen but still functioned fine—according to his maps, he was about three blocks from Syd's place. Perhaps the thugs had dragged him here after they'd beaten him unconscious, he thought, brief memories returning to him while others spontaneously dissipated. He wondered why they hadn't finished the job. Maybe some people simply lacked the capacity for murder. Maybe that was the reason Syd hadn't killed Ned.

Syd. What Mitch really wanted was to see Syd. His reasons for wanting this weren't totally clear even to him, but he knew he wanted it. And Syd wasn't far. He could have him, if he wanted him. And he did.

He sat up, his limbs seeming to catch new fire, and made a one-handed phone call.

"Yes?" Syd said upon picking up.

"I've been beat," Mitch told him weakly. "Some guys beat me up."

"Did you call an ambulance?", his voice oddly measured.

"I called *you*."

A sigh whistled through Mitch's banged-up phone speaker. "Where are you?" Syd asked.

"Not far. I'll send my location."

Syd, by this point, was wondering what the fuck Mitch was doing so close to his place, and a less impulsive man would have known better than to wander unarmed to the exact location Mitch now sat, but Syd was not that man. Mitch's past offenses notwithstanding, Syd had believed him when he'd said he'd been beaten—after all, the news of Mitch's antics, his address, and his license plate number were now public knowledge among stock buyers, some of whom Syd had assumed might try to take matters into their extralegal hands.

"Syd," Mitch wheezed when he arrived, and Syd noticed that he was indeed in dire shape—left eye bulbously swollen, nose misshapen. Or that he had hired a really talented makeup artist, a possibility that could not be fully discounted. "Sit with me, Syd." He spoke like someone with a bad head cold.

Syd squatted warily on Mitch's left. "What were you..." But then he noticed the handle of the gun protruding from his jacket pocket, and whatever part of him had been unconscious these past couple months woke up.

"I needed you." Mitch's hand looked swollen and bruised, but he nonetheless draped his right arm genially around Syd's shoulder. Syd kept a watchful eye on his left. "I missed you."

"I missed you too," Syd mumbled. He wanted to believe Mitch missed him like he'd believed him about the beating, but he didn't think he could believe him about anything ever again.

"We had some *good* times," Mitch went on, speaking at a higher register than was typical for him. "Didn't we?"

"Yeah."

"Remember when you punched me in the face?" He cackled roughly. "Oh, boy."

"Yeah."

"Thanks for not breaking my nose." He tried to sniff, but the twin streams of blood on his upper lip barely responded. "I think it's broken now."

Syd nodded in stoic agreement. Mitch's face, in its twisted incarnation, hurt to look at. He badly needed an ambulance, was Syd's general sense.

"Remember when we talked about drugs?"

"Which time?"

"All of them."

Syd couldn't help but feel that Mitch wasn't exactly picking the most representative examples of their relationship's essence.

"Remember when I taught you how to tie a tie?"

A familiar heat in Syd's chest. "Yep."

"Except I had to look it up first." He laughed weakly. "I never told you, but I watched a video on it. Remember when I taught you how to eat lobster? I had to look that one up too. Remember when—"

"Mitch," Syd interjected softly.

"Yeah?"

"Is there anything else...you wanted to say to me?" Perhaps an apology could win Mitch back his trust. He doubted it—he hadn't forgotten the gun—but it would be nice to hear, if nothing else.

In lieu of an answer, Mitch slumped forward and remained in that position for several minutes, and if not for his labored breathing, Syd would have assumed the worst. He eyed the gun again, unsure whether Mitch even knew of its presence. Maybe he'd forgotten all about it. Or maybe he just wanted to lower Syd's guard before he fired. Well, Syd just wouldn't let his guard down then.

"Did you ever care about me as *more* than a manager?" Mitch asked, lifting his head slightly.

"You mean as a dad?" He patted Mitch's back as lightly as he could manage. "You're not exactly old enough to be my dad."

"No, as like a...never mind." Mitch coughed a few times—the coughs of someone in a truly bad way. "I think I'm concussed. Can't even remember what I'm doing here."

Another few minutes of silence. The cars on the distant streets created satisfying *whoosh*ing sounds as they drove through puddles of rain. Syd had always found the noise bothersome when it was accompanied by water splashing the pavement at his feet, but here, in the safety of the alley, it brought an odd comfort.

"Tell Sydney," Mitch began.

Syd nearly corrected him but then decided it was in his best interests not to. "What do you want me to tell Sydney?" he asked.

Mitch coughed again. "Tell Sydney...I loved him."

"Loved?" The sound of the streets' rushing water combined with that of Syd's head's rushing blood, drowning out everything else. "Anything more you'd like to tell Sydney? For *me* to tell Sydney, I mean."

A string of drool dangled for a few precarious seconds before landing unceremoniously in Mitch's lap, and with its anticlimactic descent, Syd felt his last spark of hope for their dead relationship fizzle out.

"Did you call an ambulance?"

"*You* did," Syd lied. "Remember?"

"Oh. Yeah."

More rushing water. More rushing blood. The gun in Mitch's pocket. More drool.

"Should I propose?" Mitch asked.

"Propose?"

"Marriage. To what's-her-face."

"Hayley?"

"Yeah, Hayley. Should I, do you think?"

"I dunno. Do you love her?"

No immediate answer—Syd wondered for a moment whether Mitch would terminate this conversation like he had the others. He seemed to be suffering from short-term memory loss. His brain was probably floating in an inflamed, hemorrhagic sea right about now. Or perhaps his faculties remained intact and he simply hadn't pacified Syd enough to feel comfortable shooting him. "I don't know. I think so." Mitch lifted his good hand, and Syd flinched, but he was only wiping his nose.

"I just feel like I need to wrap all this shit up," he continued. "You know? Just quit the games and bury the hatchets."

"Which hatchets?"

"All of them." Mitch snorted phlemily. In spite of his condition, he appeared happy. Unsettlingly so. "Lots of people are pretty mad at me."

Syd eyed the gun again. "What are you going to do?"

"First, I'm going to propose to Hannah. To Hayley, I mean."

Syd reached a prudent hand into Mitch's loose jacket pocket. Fucking this up could mean his life. "Yeah? How are you gonna do that?"

"Surprise her. Cook her a meal when she gets home from work tonight."

"Tonight?" If he did this right, Mitch wouldn't ever know what came next. His final thoughts could be the good ones.

"When *I* get home, I mean. After the ambulance and the hospital and all that."

And if they weren't—if Mitch were merely *acting*, in service of some twisted evil he psychopathically believed was a greater good... well then, to hell with him anyway. "And then what?" Syd drew the gun out.

"Then I gotta make amends with all the people I scammed." He coughed again. Syd let the sound mask the click of the safety's release.

"Anyone else you want to make amends with?"

Another pause. Syd held the barrel to the back of Mitch's head, a few centimeters away, trying to keep his shoulder stable, his hand trembling. Syd was crying. He'd apparently been crying for quite some time. Mitch wouldn't feel a thing. Syd was going to do it.

"That one woman at the coffee shop. God, what was her name?"

Syd fired. Mitch fell backward onto the wet cement, a stream of red pulsing from his skull, creating a pink river whose trickle joined the satisfying *whoosh* of the peaceful, rainy night.

"Are you proud of what you did to him?" I ask Syd now, in the murder wing, both of us watching each other through the glass.

"I'd do it again." His voice doesn't betray any facetiousness, but then again, he's been well-trained.

I stand up. "Well." I tap my papers on the counter a few times with the hand not holding the phone. "I think that's everything. Thank you for agreeing to all these interviews. You've given me a lot to work with." He stands up in turn. It's creepy the way he keeps mirroring me. "Oh, actually—one more thing."

"Yeah?"

I flip through my notes. "I didn't get what happened when Mitch came to visit you in the hospital."

"Because he *didn't* come visit me."

"I'm sure he did. He texted Hayley saying he was headed there. I tracked down the woman working the ICU desk, and she confirmed she'd seen him."

"Well, *I* never saw him." His mouth twitches as if deciding which position to assume. "I kind of hoped I would, but..."

"He was there," I insist, "and I think it's important I write about it. It's a pivotal moment in your story."

Shrugs. "I must've been asleep."

I jot down that the scene will have to go un-dramatized if the book is to remain true and accurate.

"But you write fiction, right?" he asks, his voice wavering. "It's your job to make up stories? Make 'em believable?"

"Actually, with the type of fiction I write, I usually try *not* to make them believable. To keep the artifice intact."

"Whatever. Tell me about Mitch visiting me."

"But I don't—"

"Then make it up. Make me believe it." He's desperately maintaining eye contact despite every effort on my part to break it.

"Okay." I shift uneasily in my seat and flip to the place where the story cuts off—a gunless Mitch in a hospital waiting room. I take a breath.

"When Mitch entered your ward, you were asleep."

"Obviously."

I continue: "The place smelled unnaturally sterile—that brand of sterility that's so overbearing it's gotta be covering something else up. In the bed opposite you, someone who looked to have been in a grisly accident and only tangentially resembled a human being—limbs twisted in all sorts of directions—gurgled at semi-regular intervals. On your right, a machine tracked your heartbeats. An oxygen tank's tube had been wrapped behind your ears and across your nose. You were propped up on three or four pillows, drooling, looking mildly jaundiced—"

Syd waves a dismissive hand. "I get the picture."

"Mitch watched your chest heave and then heave again, waiting anxiously during each pause between breaths—like he wanted to make sure you were able to make another, and another—and the one emotion he felt, more than anything else, was relief. He'd almost feared you hadn't made it. He didn't believe you were okay until he saw you.

"And 'okay' is a bit of an overstatement, I suppose, but you were *alive*. That's all that mattered to him, really."

Syd winces.

"Sorry. Anyway, he placed a chair at your left, leaned forward, and kissed your forehead—"

Shortly: "He wouldn't do that."

"Okay. Then he, uh...he was still clutching some of the magazines he'd been reading in the waiting room—*Cosmopolitan* and embarrassing fluff like that. Stuff that, if someone had witnessed him reading it, he would have defensively claimed only to be skimming out of sheer boredom. But there were no witnesses here, so he opened *Cosmopolitan* to a random page displaying an ad for women's perfume. A blonde model in a skimpy white dress sat curvaceously on a polished mahogany floor. He held the picture up to your closed eyes. 'How about this Syd?'"

"Wish I could have seen it." Syd looks down at the counter.

"Then he read the ad slogan aloud: 'Feel beautiful.' Gave a few ironic chuckles. 'Do *you* feel beautiful, Syd?' He flicked your oxygen cord. You, as I'm sure you can imagine, didn't respond, but he pretended you did. 'Yeah,' he said. 'Me too.'

"A few minutes passed in silence. The mangled guy gurgled. The beeping of the beats on your heart rate monitor regularly and palliatively interrupted the room's otherwise asphyxiating silence. Mitch imagined how the beeps might be factoring into your sleeping thoughts. He pictured you dreaming about going on some road trip with him, and he—knowing him—had run out of gas, and now the car's dashboard read 'empty' and was beeping with the same exact pace and timbre as the monitor in the hospital room, and the sleeping you's imagined dream began—as much as dreams can be said to have beginnings—with Mitch shaking you awake in the passenger seat and you opening your eyes to the interior of a stalled car on a dark, winding road in the middle of some Vermont forest and Mitch asking whether you know where the nearest gas station is. Then, in his imagining, a kind of argument about why dream-Mitch hadn't just filled up his tank at the last station commenced, and the real-life-Mitch in the hospital room began lamenting the fact that every interaction between him and you, both real and imagined, always descended into argument. He wished, achingly, for just one conversation that ended on good terms."

"Okay, stop."

"But this one would, is what I'm saying." I find it difficult to terminate a story once I'm on a roll. "Mitch knew that too—that this conversation *would* end on good terms because it wouldn't really begin, and so it wouldn't really end. In a sense, it's *still* going on."

"I said stop."

"He was relieved to see you asleep and peaceful rather than upright and confrontational because he didn't know what he'd even say to you if you had the means of replying. He certainly wouldn't be showing you perfume ads.

"And while he was perfectly willing to stay all evening and watch you sleep, he didn't want to converse. Not out of lack of love—quite the opposite," conscious of the fact that I at least owe Syd the courtesy of ending this in a manner that brings him some form of closure. "He knew he'd fucked up, and he felt guilty. He couldn't stand to further tear what had already been torn. But this visit, in its silence, felt like a sort of partial, metaphorical sewing-up. A restoration of *one* side of a relationship he now knew he valued more than he'd thought. He sat and watched you breathe for as long as he could bear. Upon your first stirrings, he headed out."

Syd is knitting his fingers together so tightly that there are little white impressions on the backs of his hands. He seems to be making an active effort not to blink. "All right, then," he says.

"All right," I repeat. "I think that's it." I've developed an acute fear that every minute I spend as a murder-wing tourist is being shaved off the end of my lifespan—a superstitious karmic thing. "Thanks again for everything. I know this must have been difficult to talk about."

"Wait," he says, just as I move to hang up the phone.

I bring it back to my ear.

"Are you a hybristophile?"

I laugh. "Not exactly. I do find you interesting though."

Syd furrows his thick brows so that for a second, they form a united front. "So you are?"

"I'm a journalist."

"They're not mutually exclusive."

A fan whirs somewhere in the distance. The tape, I fear, will soon run out of memory.

"It's just that...hybristophiles are everywhere. I get lots of fan mail, you know."

"Are you sure that doesn't have more to do with you being a famous actor? You got fan mail before, I would think."

"Not like this. Let me show you something." Then he sets the phone on its back on the counter, walks over to his uncomfortable-looking twin bed, and heaves a massive pile of letters out from under it. He carries them the way you might carry a newborn baby, but they're plentiful enough to obscure his line of sight, and he drops a few as he totters back, which hopefully wouldn't happen in the baby-carrying scenario. When he plops the pile down, it spreads into a scattered mess that covers the entire counter. Some letters haven't been opened, others have been opened but remain inside their envelopes, and others have been removed from their envelopes and presumably read. He looks at me like *See what I mean?*

"Can you read me one?" I ask, my karmic fears temporarily silenced.

He rips one open at random to reveal a Hallmark card whose cover features a cartoon golden retriever pouting in a doghouse and reads, *Get well soon.*

"No 'Get out of jail soon' cards available?"

Syd gives me a stern and meaningful glare.

"Too soon?"

He doesn't answer. Opens the card and clears his throat. *"Dear Sydney,*

"I saw you in Sgt. Nebula and thought you were totally hot. Then I found out you'd shot a man and thought you were even hotter. I bet he deserved it. Keep your head up. Actors are everywhere, but murderers are special. I'll wait for you, as long as it takes.

"Love,

"Natalie, age 17

"*P.S. The dog made me think of you. You're kind of in the doghouse right now, if you know what I mean.*

"*P.P.S. Try to behave yourself so that there's still time for us to have kids together once you're released. My biological clock is ticking.* She dotted all her i's with hearts." He spreads the card flat against the glass. The prewritten Hallmark message on the inside, crowded between lines of blinding, sparkly pink ink, reads, *Sickness is temporary. Soon, you'll be right as rain!* Unless you're terminal, I add, mentally. Maybe they make an alternate version that reads, *Sickness is permanent, but that doesn't mean you can't have fun!*

He shuts the card and purses his lips. "There you have it." Gathers the pile into a more carriable clump.

"Any others of note?"

"Nope. They're all basically like that. Except..." His roaming gaze comes to an abrupt halt.

"What?"

"Nothing, it's just..." Lifts an unopened envelope. "The card I wanted to send my dad. The one Glen never mailed. Not sure how it got here."

"Do you remember what it says?"

"Not really."

"Wanna read it?"

He pauses, passing it delicately back and forth between his hands, and then tears it open in one swift motion. Pulls out a folded, white piece of cardstock featuring two bald, pencil-drawn stick figures— one short and one tall, the short one sporting a red hunting hat— holding hands. "*Dear Stanley,*

"*Is it okay if*—" He clears his throat, his eyes beginning to water. "*Is it*—" he tries again. "Just—here." He holds the splayed card up to the window. His handwriting is cramped and uneven and messy. The words span both sides of the fold and run at a slight downward slant.

Dear Stanley,

Is it okay if I call you Stanley? I asked this guy Glen, who's been looking after me, and he said it's fine. Calling you Dad just feels weird.

I kind of hate you, if I'm being honest. Don't take this the wrong way. It's nothing personal. I kind of hate Glen too, and if I get a third dad someday, I'll probably hate him too. But I want to talk to you. We've never had a real conversation or anything. I sort of remember one time when I was really young and watching Winnie the Pooh *and all, and you stormed into the living room and said, "What's this shit?" and I cried, and you apologized. That's about all I remember, though.*

I'm mad at you for leaving, but I'm mad at myself too. I sometimes wonder whether I did something to scare you off. If I did, that was lousy of me, and I'm sorry. I didn't mean it and don't remember it. And if I didn't, well, I hope you tell me I didn't when you respond to this letter. You don't have to say the true reason, but I'd feel a lot better if I knew it wasn't my fault. That's one of two ways you could make it up to me.

The other is by coming back. I won't hold a goddam grudge—we can start right where we left off. I also won't expect you to dote on me or send me to private school or anything phony like that. I'd actually prefer if you were strict but fair—not a huge pussy like Glen but still able to have fun every now and then. I've always imagined my dad as sort of a dork. Someone who knows better than me but occasionally does something stupid that reminds me he's still just a regular guy after all. It's up to you which stupid things to do, I swear to god it is. I just want you to make me feel Wanted. Everybody wants to feel Wanted, you know?

I picture my dad as scrawny and bald. Not like totally bald but with hair that's receding a bit on the sides. It's always a good sign when someone has hair that's receding a bit. And a young face. When people have young faces it's usually because they live wild lives. But if you're totally bald and wrinkly or have Elvis hair and a beer belly, don't let that discourage you. I'll love you either way.

I don't love you yet, though. I can't love someone I've never really known. But if you come back, I'll do my best to understand. Even though I'm upset, it's not like I'd kill you or even punch you the way I sometimes punch kids at my school. I could never hurt my own father. It might take a while before we're rustling each other's hair or playing catch or doing the sorts of things I picture dads doing with their kids, but until then, I'm happy to just sit with you in silence.

Your son,
Sydney

"Is this all true?" my agent Norma asks, setting the printed manuscript of *Meat Puppets* onto her desk with a filmic *smack*, looking tired and run-through and about one or two nonsenses away from completely cutting me loose.

"Pretty much."

"When you say 'pretty much'…"

"I got everything I could and filled in the gaps."

She lifts a hand to her hair, which is pinned back with one of those gravity-resistant spear-pins I've never seen anyone else under fifty use. "Right. Because I guess I'm just not clear on the timeline here. Mitch died last August. You conducted all your interviews with Syd after that point. When did you interview Mitch?"

"I didn't," I admit. "Never got the chance. But I *did* talk with Ned and Hayley and Benji and—"

"So everything about Mitch's internal state is made-up?"

"I extrapolated based on the information I *got*. Which is a lot, I'll have you know."

"What about his childhood memories? The Catholic school stuff?"

"Squeezed what I could out of Hayley and supplemented it with experiential knowledge. That's what all biographers do."

But she's shaking her head. "Biography is not *fiction*, Hannah. There are *rules* that must be followed. Journalistic standards that must be adhered to. Fact-checking that must be done."

"It's mostly true, though."

"'Mostly true' won't fly. *Especially* when the key relationship here seems to be the one between Syd and Mitch. You can't accurately characterize a relationship between two people when you only have one side of the story. Not without looking extremely dishonest. Hell, even the biographies that end up on *shelves* have biases. Since the beginning of time, biographers have canonized the subjects they like and demonized the ones they don't. They manipulate the negative space to create whatever narrative they *want* to believe."

"So you're saying I wouldn't be all that out of the ordinary, then," I said.

"You'd be even worse than that, is what I'm saying. You're leaning so heavily on the Syd interviews that this isn't even *your* narrative—

it's his." She flips to the murder scene. "Answer me this, Hannah: how biased do you think a killer is against the man he killed?"

I remain silent, mainly because I can't come up with anything that won't prove her point.

"This is more...are you taking notes on this?"

I write, *Norma: Are you taking notes on this?* in my notepad.

"Are you?"

Are you? "I guess I'm not done writing it. Not sure I ever will be."

"You're always taking notes on everything. It's exhausting."

"I care about accuracy."

"Right. Well, I'm telling you that *this*—" She signals to the stack of manuscript pages. "—is more fiction than biography. And the only way we'll ever sell it is if it's marketed as such. This shouldn't be a problem, though—people are always writing nonfiction and calling it fiction. If we publish it as fiction, you'll be covered."

And in my cowardly refusal to catch a lawsuit, I acquiesce. The research that concludes this book has instilled me with a painful awareness of The Law and all it entails, and I both fear and respect it. Sure, I've never murdered anyone or run any black-market gambling businesses, but I don't want to toe the legal line, even with Syd and Hayley—the only people held criminally liable for any of this "novel"'s shenanigans—receiving what to anyone else must seem unconscionably generous sentences.

Syd pled guilty to second degree murder. He initially wanted to plead self-defense, but the lawyer he'd spent a good portion of his acting money on advised him against it. New York wasn't a legal concealed-carry state, but proving Mitch had intentions of murdering Syd would have been an uphill battle, especially with Mitch's autopsy report showing bodily injuries so severe that even attempting to kill Syd in those last moments would have been nearly impossible. So Syd received thirty years in prison with the potential for early release if he behaves himself. But behaving himself has never been Syd's forte.

If there's one person who can be said to have benefitted legally (albeit not personally) from Mitch's death, it's his would-have-been-widow Hayley. Hayley, who the court couldn't prove was anything more than a tangential *accessory* to a felony gambling scheme (the stock website designers had been hired by Mitch, and Mitch had run the early stages of the operation out of *his* house, and Lindsay testified in Hayley's favor, for some reason), and whom I've been advised to reassure you was *not*, in fact, anything more than that (this book is "fiction," after all), was fined what she and Mitch owed, plus an additional $5000, and given 200 hours of court-ordered community service. She's been making a dent in the latter requirement by teaching a free, after-school pottery class, and despite the painful and embarrassing irony of now being a financial advisor in tremendous monetary debt, even *she* admits to scoring the legal jackpot with her sentencing. Dead men tell no tales,[30] which means they also make excellent scapegoats.

I thought I'd let Hayley have the last word of this little book. It's only fair after everything she's been through. So that's where I'll return to—my one and only interview with Hayley, in my atypically clean house. You've already heard a lot of her story, but now, after about three hours of rigorous listening and notetaking and recording on my part, both of us alternately pouring piles of Flavor Blasted [sic] Goldfish onto our respective plates and apparently crunching them so loudly that when I later review the interview tapes, it'll be like taking one of those hearing tests where common English words are buried in a sea of white noise, I ask her whether there's anything she'd like to add. I tell her it'll go right at the end of the book, unfiltered-like. This is where readers can get to know the real Hayley Duker.

"But they won't *want* to get to know the real me, will they?" she says. "They'll only care about me insofar as they can link me back to Mitch. I mean, that's the only reason *you* contacted me, right?"

"Maybe, but in the little time we've been acquainted, I've come to appreciate you as an individual. You're just as fascinating as him, I think."

"How so?"

I swallow the bite I've been crunching. "I get the sense that in

---

30   Live ones don't either, apparently, because soon after Mitch's attempt to reverse the deal with Ned, the bastard *did* send journalists to Ned's house to ask about Syd's attack, but Ned slammed the door in their faces—successfully this time, what with them being unable to stop it on account of their hands being full of cameras and microphones and notepads. He didn't do this for moral high-ground reasons, he maintains, but out of a stubborn refusal to give Mitch the thing he most desired. Well, now Syd is locked up, and Mitch is dead, so Ned might be the one person for whom this ending is a true win-win. Minus the brutal beating—lose-win-win, I guess.

your soul, there's a constant push and pull between the 'you' you believe you should be and the 'you' you really are, deep down. And I think you've found a way to have it both ways—to have fun and take risks and live dangerously while still putting on the guise of someone who hates fun and risks and danger—because appearing to *enjoy* something is worse, in your mind, than engaging in it." I shove a few more Goldfish into my mouth. "But come on, Hayley. You *do* enjoy it—*did* enjoy it. Didn't you?"

She doesn't reply for a few seconds. Nibbles idly on a single fish. I've noticed that she eats each cracker in two bites while I often eat several crackers in one. I wonder what this says about our respective characters.

"I think readers' number one question is going to be 'Why didn't she leave him?'" Hayley predicts. "And I've wondered the same thing hundreds of times—believe me. I've just never even been able to explain it to myself, so how the hell am I supposed to explain it to others?" Pause. "But I don't think love always has a neat explanation. The truth is that I never wanted to do any of that stock stuff. I just wanted him to love me." Her face shows none of the telltale signs of lying/ acting. "Did he love me?"

"I—"

"Sorry. Stupid question, I know."

"No, I just—" I clear my throat. "I just can't provide a satisfying answer. I'm not telepathic. As a writer, I like to pretend I am, but I'm not. It's all an illusion."

"When people read this..." She gestures broadly with her noncheese-dusted hand. "...*thing* you're writing, will *they* think he loved me?"

"I don't know that either. Can't read their minds."

"Right." She fiddles with the spout of the Goldfish carton. "You know, there have been times when I've thought about buying another gun and heading straight to that jailhouse and popping Morris in the head."

"Yeah?"

"Oh, yeah. But when I get right down to it, I don't think I ever could. And I don't think Mitch ever could have either. That's where we're different from Morris.

"And I'm worried people are going to read this and just assume I'm another one of Mitch's 'victims'.... 'Victims of Mitch Anonymous.' You know they have a support group for people who dated him?"

I tell her I attended a session.

She snorts bitterly. "They asked *me* to attend one, believe it or not. A few of them came up to me after his funeral—which, don't even get me started on the optics of *that*."

"So you're *not* a victim, then?"

"No, I am not." Points sharply to my spiral notebook, in which I'm doodling a series of complex geometric designs. A few cheese flecks from her fingertip leave little grease spots on the page. "Get that in writing, word for word. I. Am. Not. A. Victim. A lot of people get [Mitch] wrong. He's not some master manipulator. And if he was [sic], I wouldn't have fallen for it. The stock thing was a mistake, but our relationship wasn't. Get that in writing too."

I scribble down her answer even though I'm tape-recording the whole interview. Most interviewees don't really understand the journalistic process, so concessions must sometimes be made for the sake of putting their minds at ease.

"You know, maybe you should get together with Lindsay again," I suggest. "She's lost a partner too—not in quite so graphic a manner, sure, but in *some* sense. It might be helpful to talk things over with someone else who understands."

Hayley's already done that, but not with Lindsay. The week after Mitch died, she made a trip to his parents' house. She'd only met them once before the funeral—Thanksgiving of 2022, shortly after Mitch had begun "managing" Syd. But that was the last time Mr. and Mrs. Larkin had seen or heard from their son—from their perspective, he'd all but vanished off the map. Then they received the call that he'd been murdered, and everything changed.[31]

---

31   I got what follows from Hayley, and Hayley got it from Mitch's parents, so the accuracy is debatable. But according to Hayley, Mitch's mom drove out to the beach that day, after she got the call. She laid a towel down on the sand, just far enough from the shore to be out of wave-splatter range. The towel had a yellow smiley face on it and was faded after many washes. The weather was spitefully perfect. She didn't cry, sitting there on the beach. She sifted through the sand in search of relatively large pebbles and threw them into the water one by one and watched them

Mitch's mother is short with dyed-red hair she avers used to be that color naturally, but besides the hair, she doesn't resemble him much. His dad, however, is his spitting image—tallish, thin, poorly dressed, and even possesses his mannerisms—his awkward gait, his sporadic, intermittent eye contact. When Hayley swung by their place, bearing a traditional Midwestern casserole, they cordially invited her in, and Mitch's mother prepared coffee for the three of them. Hayley took a morose seat across the kitchen table from Mitch's father. She had to keep looking away while she talked to him lest his similarities to Mitch become too uncanny.

"I'm just happy he found someone," his dad told her with a sniffle.

"What do you mean?"

"He always *was* a bit different." A full-sized crucifix, like the sort you might find in a cathedral, hung above their fireplace. Atop their living room couch was a random spread of magazines and a few assorted remote controls. "Can't imagine where he got it."

The coffees' surfaces rippled and threatened to spill over as Mrs. Larkin carried the mugs to the table—one in each hand and one sandwiched precariously between the two.

"How many mugs have you broken doing that?" Hayley asked as Mrs. Larkin set the trio of coffees down with a relieved sigh. Hayley's featured a cursive Bible verse inscribed in lavender over a pale blue backdrop: *We fix our eyes not on what is seen, but on what is unseen, since what is seen is temporary, but what is unseen is eternal. -2 Corinthians 4:18*

"Too many," Mrs. Larkin replied, chortling in that hearty way that people chortle when something unfortunate but completely out of their control has happened.

"Ever thought about making multiple trips?"

"I've told her that," Mr. Larkin cut in. To Mrs. Larkin: "Have I not told you that?"

---

sink with barely a splash and observed how the water's surface kept mending itself and pressing on, not slowing down or breaking pace even momentarily, a monster far greater than what it was absorbing. She thought about all the other pebbles sitting on the ocean's floor, gradually corroding over millions of years, and how the vast majority of those ones won't be thought of once by any human being for the rest of time and how lucky *these* ones were—to be thought of, as individuals, even for just an instant.

"I always think I should make multiple trips after I break one, but then the time comes when I need to carry three mugs at once, and I think, well, I'll be less clumsy this time," Mrs. Larkin explained.

"Such is life," Mr. Larkin quipped mystically. He wiped a tear with his pale, liver-spotted hand.

Hayley blew on her drink. An image of Mitch sipping and then expelling expired coffee behind Nelson's Bookstore, which bookstore Hayley was later forced to sell to pay legal fees, entered her mind unprompted. She never got to say a proper goodbye to that store, she tells me. It all happened so fast. From an outsider's perspective, it looks like she got the long end of the legal stick, but can you imagine losing the most important person in your life and being court-ordered to pawn off the few things that remind you of him? I tell her I can't.

"Were we bad parents?" Mrs. Larkin asked.

Hayley nearly inhaled her coffee.

"Were we wrong for the way we brought up Mitch?"

"We did the best we could," Mr. Larkin said with that overconfident Mitchian air. "He didn't die because of us—he died because some *thug* decided it was a good idea to shoot him in cold blood. That would have happened either way."

"I regret not spending more time with him as an adult, though," Mrs. Larkin said, grabbing a napkin from the center of the table and dabbing her eyes.

"He never wanted to."

"But *we* could have made more of an effort."

"How were we supposed to predict that some random asshole would..."

Hayley, choking on coffee until just a second ago, carefully asked, "Do you guys know anything about the guy who did it?"

They shook their heads in ignorant unison. Mr. Larkin sniffled and grabbed a napkin of his own. Hayley feared she'd soon be grabbing one too.

"He wasn't 'some random asshole.' Mitch knew him. Quite well, actually. Or thought he did," Hayley said.

The Larkins exchanged inscrutable facial expressions—some secret married code. "Well then we clearly did *something* wrong, if he was hanging out with—"

"Look, a lot of stuff is going to come out within the next few months," Hayley explained. She took another sip of coffee, which tasted damn good when she could swallow it properly. Choking always made things taste worse. "About me, about Mitch, about Syd—the guy who did it. That's kind of why I came here. I don't know what this trial is going to look like."

"Well I would hope it looks like that *fuckwad* getting locked away for *life*."

Mrs. Larkin eyed him with pointed religious conviction, and he did a quick, apologetic sign of the cross.

"It's more complicated than that," Hayley went on. "Just...whatever happens, you knew Mitch, right? And I knew him too. So even if they try to characterize him a certain way and make out that we didn't know who he *really* was, behind the scenes, nobody can ever take away the Mitch we knew. You know that, right?"

Mrs. Larkin wailed, and Mr. Larkin patted her on the back with a baby-burping force.

Hayley grabbed a napkin. "We can talk about something else if you want," she muttered, mainly for her own sake. For the past week—the past two years, honestly—she hadn't felt like she even *existed* independent of Mitch. And now, without him, she feels like nothing more than some gutted carcass from which people scoop out what little more they can get of *him*. She gives me a weighty look. Hell, neither of his parents bothered to ask her how *she* was holding up, or how *her* financial advising job was going (they were under the impression that Mitch too was a financial advisor), or whether *she* was processing her emotions in a healthy way that was conducive to long-term happiness. All anyone ever wanted to discuss was Mitch.

She can't fault a grieving couple, of course. She used to imagine bearing and then raising strawberry blond kids of her own with Mitch and, when they got old enough, telling them the epic saga of the human stock trade. When she and Mitch were in the thick of it, this vision of the future was all that kept her going—the idea that whatever happened would be either a triumph or a lesson she could pass down to the next generation, the way her mother had passed down the story of being in college and pulling an all-nighter studying for an exam and eating so many jelly beans that before she knew it, she'd eaten two whole bags, and needing to leave the exam early to puke up a clump of gelatin so large it would have formed an intestinal blockage. Or the way my dad told me about riding his bike into a ditch as an adolescent and getting all scraped up and spraining several limbs and how he should have just *thought* about what might happen if he rode his bike into a ditch—nothing good, obviously—before he'd done it. We're all the sums of the stories others have told us. And we choose to believe those stories because they feel meaningful and real. They become part of our identities.

Now this one is part of mine. And if it's become as real for you as it has for me, then I can rest assured that I've fulfilled my journalistic responsibility to the truth.

Because this *is* the bare, unconcealed, unacted truth. It may be "fiction," but it's the truest thing I've ever written. You can trust me.

Acknowledgements

Here I've been told I can use at least a few people's real names. So I'd like to thank my publisher Apocalypse Confidential; my editor Jacob Stovall; my readers Matthew Sutija, Eli Stock, James Thorley, Jennifer Smart, and David Smart; my interview subjects Nell Sullivan, Benji Manheim, Hayley Duker, Freddy R., Greg B., Scott F., Raya L., Ryan K., Ned Wesham, Lindsay Stewart, Annabel Olsen, and most importantly Syd Morris, whom I've promised an advance copy of this "novel." Heaven knows he has time to read it.

Oh, God, who else? Editor Nathan Jefferson and the folks at the *Los Angeles Review of Books*, who have been extremely gracious in promoting my work; Adam Smart, who at one point came up with the exact word I needed and told me, "Now you have to put me in the acknowledgements"; my first grade teacher Mrs. Miske, who served as my first ever beta reader for my first ever "novel"; and the nice older gentleman at the hairdresser in 2006 who told me he'd look for my name on the shelves in twenty years.

About the Author

Hannah Smart's short stories and essays have appeared in the *Los Angeles Review of Books*, *West Branch*, *The Boston Globe*, *SmokeLong Quarterly*, *Berkeley Fiction Review*, and *Cleaver*, among other outlets. Her work has been shortlisted in *The Masters Review* Chapbook Open, nominated for two Pushcart Prizes and one *Best of the Net* anthology, and discussed in *The New Yorker*. She is the founder and editor in chief of experimental journal *The Militant Grammarian*. *Meat Puppets* is her first novel.